I0637651

TIMELESS: BOOK I

Timeless: A Novel Trilogy: Book I
©2003, 2008, 2013, 2025 M.R.M. Parrott
Appendix
©2003, 2008, 2013, 2025 M.R.M. Parrott
Notes on the Text and Cover Art
©2025 M.R.M. Parrott

Designed by M.R.M. Parrott
Paperback & eBook Cover Art: *Prism (Lower Chakra)* (2002,
Columbia SC, Digital, Triptych 2003, 2025)
©2003, 2008, 2013, 2025 M.R.M. Parrott

mrmparrott.com

Published by rimric press
First Edition, Paperback, Columbia SC, October 2003
Second Edition, eBook, Chicago IL, July 2008
Third Edition, eBook, Columbia SC, October 2013
Current Edition, Paperback & eBook, Charleston SC, August 2025

ISBN 0-9746106-0-7 | 978-0-9746106-0-3

*The following novel is a work of fiction and does not depict any
actual person, product, service, establishment, organization,
locale, or event*

rimric press is the imprint of rimric corporation
rimric is a trademark of rimric corporation

rimric.com

All Rights Reserved

TIMELESS
A NOVEL TRILOGY
BOOK I

M.R.M. PARROTT

rimric press

CONTENTS

∗

Timeless: A Novel Trilogy

CASSANDRA
Once I betrayed him I could never be believed.

CHORUS LEADER
We believe you. Your visions seem so true.

- Aeschylus, *Agamemnon* (*The Oresteia*)
Translation by Robert Fagles

PART ONE

1

The minor chords of the *'Libera me'* were haunting, Milona Devon thought, and the rush of emotions produced tears in her eyes. The Fauré *Requiem* filled the intimate hall with soft notes emanating from a polished mahogany stage, flowing across the upholstered seating and upward to the reflective paneled ceiling and walls. Milona enjoyed hearing such music performed by the student choir and orchestra, as part of their practicum series, because to her it seemed much more delicate. Professional musicians would certainly outperform the students, she thought, but this performance of the *Requiem* had an innocence professionals might not capture as well.

Her father also sang with the choir, a guest tenor among other guest soloists and musicians, whose passionate voice she had not heard for quite some time. It has been too long, she thought, as she looked up to the rounded shapes of the silver and gold acoustic panels. She noted the soft, warm light of the recital hall, and as she turned to each side, she could see the expectant faces of the audience as they looked on the singers. While she watched her father and the others sing, he emoted the words and the choir returned the phrases in dialogue. The voices of the choir began to overlap and then build, finally blending into a single poignant echo, singing *'Tremens factus sum ego'*, and almost piercing the hall, she thought.

She lifted her gaze again toward the ceiling and then gently returned to her father's face. So much she had missed him, she felt, recalling details of her childhood, spent looking up to his integrity and passion. She remembered the days, playing near the canals or working hard in school, the nights of family singing, visits to the theatre and the concert stage, or her father's lectures. Her mother was always there with them, a quiet, guiding force behind them, keeping them grounded in many ways, she thought.

Slowly looking across the young female singers on the front row, Milona passed from one to the next, noting their innocent faces. She almost forgot this performance was only a recording until she eventually passed over faces and came to look on her very own, years younger, standing at the end of the row opposite her father. How long it had been since hearing such music, she again thought. How long it had been since being brought to tears at such stunning, classic beauty. She wiped a tear from her cheek as she watched herself sing. Then she remembered how upset she was on that day of the performance, disappointed for her father, as he became short-tempered when orders arrived for him to report to *Mars 3* within forty-eight hours. They were all hoping his vacation would last a bit longer before he left, before he went again to work for months on the remote station. She recalled being upset that he was leaving again, but at least they had this performance, this innocent evening.

She stopped her recollections, reminding herself it really was only on a whim to watch the performance this morning, to just sit and listen for a moment, yet falling into the sweet, floating and haunting notes from her youth. Until recently she had not been able to bring herself to watch this performance. It was just too painful to deal with, she remembered, as the choir's voices continued through her. Something seemed missing from it, though, she figured, as the singers echoed *'et lux perpetua luceat eis'* through the hall. I look at my own face, she thought, but it doesn't seem as lonely as I was, as lonely as I remember being that night. The bright, blue eyes seem sad, but not as charged with meaning as I recall. Perhaps I'd merely built up these memories in my mind.

I wonder what Jon would say about all of this, she thought. A therapist like him, he would have a field day! I'm sitting here, watching my father and myself performing. Maybe I'm avoiding dealing with my real feelings by watching this, or with our relationship, Jon could say. Well, I fear it's too late now, Jon. Despite your many qualities, I just can't let you further into my life right now. It's too difficult to keep secrets when you think you care about someone, but maybe it's all for the best. We're really just friends, anyway, right? Perhaps, Jon, one day I can sit down and tell you everything, or maybe you will meet somebody else who can give you what you need. Jon doesn't need someone disappearing out of his life every few days, she thought, keeping him in the dark, holding him at arm's length. But, then, I'm not really sure what I...

A beep interrupted her thoughts. She looked around, almost confused due to her nervous thinking to herself and focus on the music, looking around at the other audience members. Then she looked down at her wrist communicator, which was receiving an auto-answer message. Of course, she quickly thought, as the metallic communicator beeped a second time to let her know the call was about to begin.

"Major Devon, Director Zhang will be ready for you in twenty minutes," said Zhang's assistant, Whitaker, on the other end of the call.

"On my way, Lieutenant," she replied.

She found the lieutenant's voice direct but reassuring, and she dropped any thoughts she was having about Jon or her father as she spoke over the relatively loud music.

"Yes, ma'am," Whitaker replied, and then her communicator beeped once more at a higher frequency to signal the end of the call.

She looked up again at the singers, allowing a slight sigh of embarrassment at the interruption to her moment of repose. It really was nice, she thought, as the singers continued on without pause. No one in the room was aware of her conversation or the beeps of her communicator, and it seemed to her to be almost like a dream. Trouble is, she thought, looking around the room and suddenly displaced from the scene itself, I'm not sure if it's a dream-dream or a nightmare-dream.

"Stop program," she said, not quite aloud.

The music and the images, the singers and the audience members, the very hall itself, all stopped abruptly and quickly began fading away. The entire scene of the recital in which Milona sat now evaporated around her as the music halted, still echoing in the now fading room. It is always an amazing effect, she thought, as the scene fully disappeared, leaving her sitting alone now in her quarters aboard the station.

She looked around at the large, ashen coloured room. The auditorium chair had now faded away, revealing the leather reading chair supporting her. Across the room, a blank viewscreen and her lounger and shelves became fully visible, and nearby the two large windows with the blinds drawn, past them the small kitchen, and then the lavatory and closet doors. Her quarters suddenly seemed too quiet to her now that the music had ended, the acoustics of the recital hall faded with the reverberating last notes of the music, only the low-level hum of *Orbis* now audible. It even seemed too dark to her now, the low light in her quarters barely navigable compared to the previously bright recital hall.

After sitting a few seconds longer to gather her thoughts, she stood up and turned away from the far windows, glancing at the large black-edged and blank viewscreen, but then she paused for a moment. What a strange mood I'm in, she thought, as she again glanced around the room. She noted, almost with a new set of eyes, the woven rug underfoot which she had found in Afghanistan, the antique wooden bookshelves from America scattered with tablets and rare paper books, the plants and European artwork, all cutting against the basic blue-grey walls. She walked over toward the bookshelves, her eye caught by the shining metal piccolo flute lying on one shelf. She picked it up and recalled her mother giving it to her years ago. This was really her instrument, she thought, looking over at the cello leaning against the bookshelves. She only gave it to me because she feared I would forget all about her once I was stationed up here.

Putting the instrument down, though, she began clearing her thoughts, realizing she needed to get going, to meet the director. She turned and began making her way toward the shiny single door, which reflected like a mirror her tall, trim frame, her black dress uniform coat and trousers. Her shoulder-length, dark reddish-brown hair was pulled back tightly into a tail, and the light from the ceiling lamps in the sitting room caught her rank squares, three black-edged brass squares together on each side of her collar, as well as her service ribbons and medals on the front of her coat. She stopped abruptly in front of the door and clasped her hands around behind herself, then let her arms hang as she stood staring at her visage, trying to pull her thoughts back to her sworn duty, though allowing that the music was a welcome distraction. She ribbed herself that she had whittled away enough time with nervous energy, though listening to mine and Father's performance again was really nice. But, it's time to get back to work, she thought.

*

The Reconnaissance Special Force major knew her 10:30 UTC meeting with the Operations Director of Intelligence was now only minutes away. It was to be an informal interview, Lieutenant Whitaker had told

her, before the formal meeting with their United
Nations Command Chiefs and others on the team, all
led by the UN Chancellor and key senators. They were
to decide the final status of this unprecedented new
operation. The major and her commander, Colonel
Ford, had already worked out the technical plans of her
mission, but they knew the real test would come later
that day when the Chancellor is to preside, as the
politicians are brought on board, now that testing and
training were done.

Milona found herself feeling a little on edge, as
she continued to look at her face and uniform. She
recalled having met Director Zhang only once in
passing, at a social function held by *Orbis's* Station
Chief, and she had never met any of the senators, the
Command Chiefs, or the UN Chancellor. She
wondered how formal they would all be with one
another or with her, and how these meetings might
proceed. Stop worrying! she warned herself. All I can
do is present myself professionally and things will be
fine. Reassured again, she thought further, surely I'm
just more nervous about the mission itself than about
these meetings. Then she wondered why Director
Zhang wanted to meet with her separately, but as she
had told herself so many times before, they all knew
this mission was quite an undertaking. She also knew
they needed to trust her, yet still, she found herself
uneasy at being so trusted.

*

Walking again, the stainless steel door leading

out to the corridor opened automatically with hydraulic precision as she approached, the sound echoing into her room. Along with the door and the muted rumble of the station, the only sounds Milona could hear outside her quarters were the thuds of her black dress boots on her sandy grey carpeting. She hardly slowed her pace as she noticed a Recon captain passing from the right, who nodded to her informally. She nodded back and passed through into the corridor and waited as her door closed behind her solidly. She pressed several light buttons on the panel to the right of the doorway to secure it, then turned to her right to continue counter-clockwise around the station to the Intelligence Sector and Director Zhang's office.

As she walked, the cool air felt still in the quiet, curved, white corridor along Reconnaissance Sector, her boots now clapping more notably on a polished tile floor, and she remembered why this massive ring-shaped station was so quiet this morning. Of course, she recalled, it's because everyone is preparing for the dress parade to mark the Chancellor's visit. Normally, these corridors would be full of passing officers, she thought, now finding herself vaguely aware of her own reflection amplified by the stainless panels running along the walls, and she noted a few other officers further down the corridor.

Then she thought about how deeply she had slept the night before, exhausted from continuing last-minute training. Having pulled herself together into a dress uniform so quickly this morning, she seemed to be in a daze, thus forgetting what was happening today, why she was here, and how busy she was going to continue to be. It'll be an interesting day, she now thought, still hearing herself and her father singing the mysterious Fauré choral music in her mind, all of it flowing through her as a poetic background.

2

Quiet the mind, Peter Nexin thought to himself while powering his bicycle along, quiet the mind. He spun the pedals smoothly around and around, evenly applying the force through each pedal stroke to the black anodized wheels of his white, lightweight racing machine. As usual, he wore traditional cycling clothes, sporting a white helmet and black-framed glasses, a plain white jersey, blue shorts and bright, multi-coloured socks and shoes. Peter took in the scents of the countryside as he spun, noting the red-yellow light glancing across the tops of the deep green trees around the edges of the open fields and in the forested areas, the wind coming in from the South outside the city, rolling through the new leaves and sprouts. It was just beginning to warm up for the season, he thought, feeling the thickening Southern weather on his fair skin, and it seemed more full of life to him than it had in weeks. The saturated hues under open skies, the wind blowing through the trees, and the smells of the Earth among the passing cars. The sublimity of it all is what helped to quiet his mind.

He still found it difficult to avoid thinking about things which interrupted this quietude. Thoughts of his courses and students, concerns over whether his theories would be well received by his peers, his position within the department and other nagging worries still crept into his mind. Cycling was always akin to meditation for Peter, though, as he could experience his worries in the context of the trees and the winds, coaxing himself to confront these thoughts within a larger view. Stop worrying, he told himself, just spin the pedals and take in the reality all around you. It's all wormholes in the foam, Peter, that's all it is, he said to himself. Just quiet the mind, he repeated, there really are no worries, only scenes in an unfolding drama.

"Wanna take the flats back?" Jack Crowley shouted.

Peter's best friend was only one or two wheel-lengths behind, spinning just as smoothly and surely in Peter's draught on a similarly equipped blue bicycle with bright silver wheels. Jack wore a red helmet and bright orange glasses, with his red and yellow jersey and shorts, along with black shoes and bright yellow socks providing spinning circles of colour as he rode. They had been quiet for miles as they pedaled together, and Jack found himself thinking about his work, but mostly he allowed himself to tune out, as he put it. He was able to think of little more than the sounds of their tires rolling on the pavement, Peter's gearing as it whirred, and the rush of the ground beneath his handlebars.

"Yeah," Peter eventually called out, turning his head. "We should catch a nice tailwind on the way back in, that way," he continued.

Peter just knew Jack was on the same wavelength much of the time, even if he wouldn't articulate it as well as Peter might always like. The late afternoon during the golden hour, the colour of the light, the way things were that time of day, out on the road with a good buddy, chasing each other down, it was all that mattered for either of them along mile after mile of pedaling. The Universe is full of beauty, Peter thought, reeling from the light, smells and wind, while Jack took delight in the mechanical simplicity of two efficient bicycles powered by human bodies at their peaks of physical intensity.

"I'm gettin' ready for that beer, Jack. How about you?" Peter asked.

"Oh yeah," Jack said, tipping to Peter that the previous forty miles in the hills of Eastover were beginning to take their toll, but not enough to cancel the beers. That'd be to miss out on one of the best parts of the ride, Jack would often say.

"Great," Peter returned, now allowing himself to feel he could come off the pace.

After a few more pedal strokes, Peter let off just a bit, and Jack rolled up alongside, wondering why Peter had been pushing as hard as he had, but recalling that he probably had pushed the pace just as much at other times. They continued rolling through the flat fields and outlying sections on their way back toward downtown Columbia. They started chatting about various things, and Peter thought about the mysterious woman who had been sitting in on one of his courses. He found himself thinking of her often, he recalled, as Jack spoke about his day at work.

Eventually, Peter and Jack both grew tired of their own conversation and began to pick up the pace again. Jack took off first, speeding away from Peter with a powerful jump up to speed, looking back with a grin, his brushed aluminum wheels looking very fast to Peter. Only a moment later, Peter snapped to form and chased, eventually catching up to Jack, who offered Peter a chance to return the challenge.

"Nice jump!" Peter yelled, then powered himself off of Jack's front wheel in turn.

*

The two continued their racing, rolling wheel-to-wheel through the last miles of suburbia and inner city blocks, on their way toward the sidewalks of the Vista, then to the outdoor sidewalk tables of a bar-and-grill in the newly renovated area of town near the Statehouse. They arrived, finishing the last of the liquid in their bottles, put their bikes aside and sat down in full gear at one of the open tables. Each sat poised at the restaurant table, feeling slightly out of place as they removed their helmets, even though wearing biking shorts and jerseys was not a large social offense to most people downtown. Passersby took note of the two and their bikes, but Peter and Jack did their best to ignore them all.

"Steeple-chasing to the end," Peter said, "that was pretty cool."

"Yeah," Jack said, wiping his forehead. "So, what was that you were saying about a new student? You mentioned her the other day, too."

"Oh, she's not a student," Peter said, "she's just someone who asked to sit in on one of my classes. I think she's just some curious layperson interested in the subject. Seems to know a lot, said she was a writer."

"Hi guys," said the female server who came by behind Peter, whose short red shorts and tight shirt caught both Jack and Peter's eye, as intended. "Can I get you something?" she asked.

"Yeah, a Harp for me," Jack said.

"Same here," Peter agreed.

"I'll leave a couple of menus here for ya', in case you want to get something," she said, leaning in and then darting off back inside to attend to her other customers.

"I'm not sure how late I can stay," Peter reported, almost unfazed by the young beauty, finding his thoughts winding back to his worries. "In fact, I probably ought to get going pretty soon."

"I think you're uptight," Jack said with a grin.

The edges of Peter's mouth began to curl upward, his green-speckled, light brown eyes rolled around the street scene around them, up toward the sky, down over the renovated multi-level brick buildings, and then back to his friend's face. Jack laughed at Peter's exaggeration, and Peter laughed in return at Jack's suggestion that he was uptight.

"Well," Peter said. "I am thinking about how we just did a pretty hard fifty miles this afternoon, and now we sit here waiting on beer," he explained, not wanting to get drunk, as he knew he had to teach in the morning.

"I think I want to stay out a bit late tonight," Jack said.

"Well, we did some hard miles today, and I have to be up in the morning for my Eighteenth Century class and then the Intro class in the afternoon. I'm also expecting some news tomorrow on one of my papers. I'll just have a couple of beers and call it a night. You can do what you like."

"Alright, Old Man," Jack quipped with a sarcastic tone. "You just can't hang like you used to, and you're taking it out on me. Whatever."

Jack often liked to tease people this way, provoking defensive reactions, but also having fun with himself. Peter laughed under his breath.

"Well," Peter returned. "I think I'm also a little preoccupied with this new work which is swimming around in my head," he said, as he waved his left hand around above his sweaty hair.

"Your new 'sci-fi' work?"

"Well, it's not really Science Fiction, so much," Peter added, "as it is a theoretical study of the possibilities of time travel, a look at how it could be possible to construct a certain type of time machine, all from a metaphysical perspective, or what is now the Philosophy of Physics."

"Oh," Jack mused, expressionless.

In his present mood, Jack was instantly overwhelmed with the subject, but was still somewhat interested in hearing about it in connection to his own work. He felt they could talk about it some other time, but not now, he thought.

"The whole problem," Peter continued, well-aware Jack was tuning out, "is in thinking of *Time* as a 'substance', so if you really just think of *Time* as a recording of events, then..."

"Enough!" Jack interrupted with a smirk. "My head is hurting as it is."

"You guys want something to munch on with your beer?" the server interrupted, putting the pint glasses down as she passed by, checking each table on the now filled row with a glance of her eyes.

"Uh, I'm good, for now," Peter said with a smile in her direction, trying to play the social game a bit better for Jack's benefit.

"So, this 'layperson', as you put it, sounds hot," Jack said, taking a quick sip.

"She is," Peter said with a sip of beer, "not beach girl hot like our waitress, but hot in that... Jaclyn Smith way."

"Jaclyn Smith?"

"*Charlie's Angels*, the original?" Peter snipped as a question, adding a small laugh, taking another sip.

"Oh," Jack offered, sitting back in his chair.

"She is really beautiful. Don't remember her last name, but her first name is Milona. She caught me the other day, after Logic, and asked if she could sit in for Intro Philosophy. Just this beautiful brunette, out of nowhere, man, and she's as smart as a whip, and has this really faint Euro-accent."

Peter lifted his gaze up and away, futilely trying to avoid fixing his mind on Milona further.

"*Ou là là*" Jack said, with a wry smile.

"Yeah," Peter said with a smirk, taking a gulp of the still cold beer.

Jack leaned up and took a sip of his own beer, then Peter took another larger gulp of his, nearly finishing the rest of the pint.

"I really need to go, man, I hope you won't be angry." Peter stood and pulled his wallet out of a back jersey pocket.

"I've got it, Old Man," Jack said with a smile. "I might go on home myself, but you can owe me one."

"No probs. Take it easy tonight," Peter said, hoping he wasn't committing a huge social gaff by leaving so soon.

"I will. Just want to sit here for a while," Jack said, feeling very pleasant, taking in the people and cars passing, enjoying the mathematical randomness of the activity all around them.

"See you tomorrow, I guess," Peter said, walking over to his bike, tossing a leg over the saddle and then pedaling away.

"Yep," Jack said, nodding at Peter as his thoughts increasingly moved toward his work.

*

Seems such a show sometimes, Peter thought to himself as he rode away from Jack, sitting back there in front of a pub with the setting Sun across the Congaree River behind him. Socializing in general, I mean, it's so draining when I've got other things to think about. Maybe I take myself too seriously, but who else is going to get these things done? I know from experience that too much drinking and not enough writing make Peter a frustrated Philosopher.

Her pushed on the pedals, up the grade toward the Statehouse and across its manicured grounds, his legs feeling tight from sitting down after their hard ride. He rolled through the downtown streets, across The Horseshoe on the USC campus, down through the Five Points district, and then into the older tree-shaded Shandon neighborhood nearby. He felt like everyone's eyes were on him, a lone cyclist in an endless stream of overbuilt, gas-guzzling cars. Peter knew it was always difficult to be the one black sheep in a crowd, but somehow he wouldn't have it otherwise.

"Quiet the mind," he said aloud to himself as he pedaled and pedaled up Blossom, turning a right and a left, eventually arriving on Wheat Street, "quiet the mind." He thought to himself, since I have to review for teaching tomorrow, I'll make a quick dinner, something easy to make, pasta maybe. I don't feel like cooking anything elaborate tonight.

He rolled onto his driveway, which led to his roomy yet modest bungalow-style, slate-coloured house with its white trim, then noticing again how neglected his yard and shrubbery began to look. He rolled on into the small open garage in the back, where several other bikes of all types were hanging across a wall, while pulling off his helmet and hopping off the bike. He hung the machine up on a set of wall hooks then locked it to a wall joist, hung his helmet on a wooden hook, and walked over to pull the garage door closed.

3

Milona still had plenty of time to get to the director's office at Intelligence, but felt she had to hurry. She walked away from her Section 4A residences, partial glass panel doors with an etched UN Reconnaissance seal closing behind her. She walked quickly, but thought of things far away from her footsteps, reminiscing over her background, her father, and of course, thinking of her mission. The music still moved underneath her surface, she found, as good music always would, rushing beneath her emotions as if to carry them away. She was grateful, though, because her nerves seemed soothed by the motion, nerves which allowed her to hardly pay attention to the passing staff officers, mainly specialists and corporals, who nodded or saluted her. She only returned the gesture for a passing superior officer, to whom she nodded.

"Ma'am," she said to the passing UN Defense colonel, noticing the four brass squares on her relaxed collar and the many decorations on her chest, each flashing as she passed. The colonel's black hair was pulled back behind her head dressing, falling down the back of her floor-length blue duty uniform.

Walking across the bright common area, its

white walls again set off by stainless panels and a long silver line chest-high on each level, Milona's thoughts were only occasionally interrupted by the display of artworks or technical drawings of various stations, colonies or ships.   This common area mostly had drawings of the many classes of ships used in Sea, Air and Space Groups interspersed with a few loungers and chairs, plants and a large window. She then stepped up to the elevators at the mid-point of the two sectors, between the two residence sections on this level, waited for a second or two, then stepped into the lift nearer to her as a Reconnaissance corporal exited. He saluted her with an older, North American salute style common among some Special Force staff officers. He must be a new arrival here, she thought, turning around inside the lift.   Just got his second charcoal, probably.   Well, congratulations to him if it's true, she wished. This lift was a sand coloured one, rounded with stainless panels around the midsection, with communications access panels and buttons inset. She looked at herself once more as the shining doors closed in front of her.

"Level Six," she said with a slight pause, and the lift moved smoothly up from Level Four.   She figured she would jump on the roller up on Level Six instead of trotting the whole distance. "Let's go, let's go," she whispered under her breath.

'Level Five,' the prompter said, in what Milona had always found to be a soothing international voice. 'Level Six,' the voice said, and then the lift came to a smooth stop.

Upon exiting, she felt distracted, drawn to the inner and outer ring windows on either side of the spacious deck. Heavily reinforced windows continued nearly floor-to-ceiling around the entire station on this level, exposing one to a feeling of Outer Space with breathtaking views all around. Level Six, often called the "Promenade", was a favourite place for many to visit, to enjoy a stroll, or to have a look out at the Earth, Moon and stars, though it was quite difficult for some to stomach at first. At the moment, she certainly found it quiet enough. She did not immediately notice anyone around the ring, and curved her path across, toward the inner windows. She thought to take another pause, despite her rush, and looked out around the curves of the slightly rounded, powder blue coloured, twelve-level exterior of the inside face of the station. She moved her gaze up to the deep black of Space beyond, with its myriad of stars, passing ships, then looked down to study the bright blue Earth below.

She could not help thinking about when she was young. She recalled the rather quiet Dutch life they lived, and she remembered they had been especially happy around that time, singing in the choir. It was seeing Father's performance again as tenor, she thought, singing as passionately as ever, just days before he was killed in that accident on Mars. Because it was a scientific mission controlled by the UN, they wouldn't tell us very much about what happened to those scientists. He was just... gone, she thought. That was all which seemed important. But it's all so clear now, of course. He had been the one to introduce me to the idea that the Military might satisfy my curiosities. Or was it only wanderlust? It was just months later that I was able to pull myself together to enter early enrollment in the ISB with Mother's support, she recalled. Maybe Father would have been proud to know I'd been accepted into such an esteemed Brussels school. Maybe he would be proud of me now, I hope.

All these years, she thought, yet she had barely stopped to reflect on it. All the work and dedication to excel at her studies, obtain a commission in UN Command, with Special Forces and Intelligence cross-training. Surely, I must have known my aspirations to be a part of the United Nations stemmed from my father, but listening to the Fauré performance brought it all back. Of course it was my father's influence which led me to the UN, she thought. He helped set up some of the current Science programmes for the Directorate in the latter part of the last century. He was one of the first to know about confirmations of extrasolar life while he was stationed on Mars and its stations. In a way, she thought, his dedication and integrity became her own.

*

"Ma'am," asked a passing officer slowing her walking pace, her heels on the bright flooring making the only sounds in the wide corridor. "Are you okay?"

Milona looked up from her view out of the windows to notice only the rank on the collar, four black-edged half-squares, three charcoal and one ivory, and then realized it was her friend. Master Sergeant Jennifer Collett was a Security Administration staff officer for the Recon Sector, and with notable pride wore her olive UN Security duty uniform coat and skirt, her black-on-silver Administrator Badge with grid decoration, and she carried a basic, shiny black duty tablet with her. Jennifer had fair skin and green eyes, stood at average height, though only slightly shorter than taller Milona, and, as Milona now noted, although Jennifer kept her sandy blonde hair short enough so that she would not have to pull it back, it seemed shorter still today. Milona was reminded she had not seen her friend in some time.

"Master Sergeant, hello, I'm fine, thank you," Milona said.

Milona was almost thankful of being interrupted from her somewhat brooding thoughts. She continued the rank formality out of habit, again forgetting the corridors were virtually empty this morning. Though respectful of the UNC's military structure, Milona was not one to put too much stock in such ranks among friends. Besides, as she thought, the two of them filled completely different roles on the station. Still, as the superior command officer it was up to her to put a technically junior staffer at ease.

"Jennifer," she added, shaking her head at herself negatively, "I'm sorry, I was far away."

"You looked pretty down, Milona," Jennifer said. "Everything okay?"

Jennifer, however, felt at ease as she touched the small indicator on her device to keep it silent from any incoming messages. As her commander would often note, the master sergeant was a dutiful administrator who ran the station's Reconnaissance Office nearly single-handedly, and could be counted upon to stay on top of her messaging and duty rosters. Yet, not having seen her friend Milona for some time, and because everyone was preparing for the Chancellor's visit, she felt she could afford to be slightly out of touch for a moment or two.

"I'm fine, really," Milona said, "just thinking about my father, actually. I've been so busy lately, but I was going to message you soon," she offered, hoping to compensate for her aloof behaviour.

"Sorry to interrupt, then," Jennifer said. "What are you doing for lunch? It's pretty quiet around here today."

"I hadn't thought about it," Milona said, looking at her communicator nervously. "I've got a meeting, well, now, actually, and another after lunch. I may be out of touch for the rest of the week, too."

"Beep me if you want to chat," Jennifer said. "I don't have plans today. Obviously, everyone, including Will, is busy with the dress parade."

"Yes, my meeting is related to the parade."

Milona hesitated to tell her friend anything further on the matter, and hoped Jennifer wouldn't ask, as the master sergeant had a much lower Intel clearance, even though her job at Recon certainly would give her an R3 there. It might have been apparent anyway, Milona reasoned, since she was wearing her dress uniform and was all the way over here in the Recon sector headed for Intel.

"But I hadn't planned anything, either," she added with a brighter face, "so I'll see what happens after my meeting?"

Milona turned to walk away, then turned back.

"I'm sorry to dash, Jen, but I'm going to be late.

Maybe I will see you for a quick lunch?" Milona then looked hurried as she walked away.

"Ta-ta," Jennifer said with a smile, then looked down and touched her device again to bring it back up.

Before turning on her heel, Jennifer took a second glance at Milona nervously walking away. I wonder why she is so jumpy today, Jennifer thought to herself, turning back to review her tablet as she continued on toward the Reconnaissance Office. She noticed there was a new message in from Will while the device was asleep, and this brought a smile to her face as she walked.

*

Milona knew she would be late now, even though she was pleasantly surprised to bump into Jennifer, not having seen her in over a week. I'll have to be extra careful at lunch, she thought. Maybe I'll just talk about Jon or something, and she'll surely talk about Will. A little girl talk will clear the air between us.

To make up some time, she decided to hurry onto the treadway, a curved travelator running between the four elevator cores on most levels, which could take someone around the station in minutes. She grabbed one of the rails and stood motionless on the roller for a moment, trying not to feel silly by using it. She usually avoided this convenience, but under the circumstances, she felt a bit disoriented, after becoming absorbed in the performance, thinking of her father, and seeing her dear friend, all in the space of a few minutes. Jennifer must have thought I was running away from her, she feared, rolling her eyes.

Eventually, the treadway passed her along and nearby an empty informal lounging area between sectors on the outer side of the deck, and she watched as the thin line along the floor changed from black to red, one of the station's subtle orientation keys. Everyone aboard was so preoccupied this morning, she thought, so who would be caught lounging on the Promenade. Someone had left a viewscreen on, and she could hear a news panel discussion, but she was not looking at the screen, a smaller model in the distance of the lounge area. It sounded to her related to recent UN Senate committee hearings at the Senate Complex in Sydney. One panel member was suggesting UN Command was sitting on a big news item.

"...I think this visit to *Orbis* may be related to these... alien confirmations," the commentator said. "It's hard to believe it could happen in this day and age, but maybe since the UNC has confirmed they received messages of some kind from Outer Space, I can only speculate that the Secretary-General in Brasília is keeping the details quiet until our inexperienced Chancellor can meet with the heavy lifters."

Milona simply listened as she passed by, uninterested in reacting to the sneering discussion, though she found it difficult to tune it out, even as her thoughts were becoming dominated by her mission. The commentator was only half right, she managed to note. Before long, everyone would know the full story.

*

After another minute of thinking to herself, she finally arrived near the elevators in the Intelligence Sector and stepped off the treadway. She quickly walked toward the lifts and over the large red and silver seal on the tiled floor, a traditional UN globe logo with a signal tower insignia in the middle. Like the simplified insignia for other command divisions and branches of government, the signal tower denoted the Intelligence Directorate. She stepped into a lift, directed it to Level Eight, waiting as it rose. After exiting, she passed and acknowledged several superior command officers, and moved toward the main entrance to Intel, walking across another seal on the floor.

She arrived at the large double doors, above which there was a smaller version of the seal. Her silver-blue eyes, fair face, deep brown hair, and black uniform were again reflected back to her in another set of mirror-like doors as they opened onto an outer sitting room. She passed several Intelligence officers on her way through the sitting area and short hallways, and found yet another set of doors awaiting her, which opened as she walked toward Lieutenant Whitaker. Behind her, the doors closed with a dull metallic thud.

4

Peter awoke from a deep sleep to the obtrusive beeping of an alarm clock, which he kept across the room from his bed. He often thought this was a clever way of tricking himself into getting up and out of the bed, rather than snoozing. Feeling a little warm as he looked up at the unadorned, light blue walls, having slept in his blue-checkered pajama pants and a black t-shirt, he looked over at the red letters across the bedroom, reading 7:30. He threw off the sheet and stepped over to shut off the noise, noticing along the way his legs still felt a bit tight from his ride with Jack the afternoon before. He kicked at the air and stretched each one across the wooden floor to help loosen up.

He stepped through the small open area, it's cream walls turning into the deep red of the sitting room and pastel greens of the kitchen and dining room. He made his way around to the kitchen sink and looked out the window into his backyard, feeling a faint sense of being watched, somehow. Time really flies, he thought to himself, reflecting on the changing of the seasons outside. Wormholes in the foam, that's all I need to work on to finish the theory, but it looks like today will be blocked out. Though, my garden needs some work, he smirked to himself, also thinking of his married older sister who now lived in Atlanta. My sister would have me shot if she could see this, green thumb that she is. I've been so focused on my work I've kinda let it go over the last couple of weeks. Of course, anyone else would think all of it looks fine, but anyway, this weekend, he said to himself, maybe I can get out there and do some work on it.

"Don't worry, Paula," he said aloud, "I'll get those vegetables cleaned up and weed those flower beds for you." He found Paula frequently present in his mind, her career-minded sisterly wisdom coming to him often at strange times. I sometimes wonder how I would have fared without her, he thought, especially after Mom... He stopped his thoughts, remarking to himself how grown people can be steered, long after their childhood.

He put on water to boil for his usual morning coffee, also turning on the radio for background music. They were playing Vivaldi, he noted to himself, almost as a trivia answer, and then he went into the second bedroom he used as a library to power up his computer. Let's check the weather, he thought, as he adjusted to the brighter light of the yellow room and pressed the power button on his black machine. The fans and processor started, an internal speaker beeping as his black-edged LCD monitor came to life, scrolling line after line of the system booting itself into runlevel 5. He would often enjoy the quiet mornings to read the news, check personal mail, or write a few sentences with a clear mind. He looked blankly at the screen, then turned and walked back across and into one of his bathrooms, ran cold water, splashing some on his face and over his hair to wake up for his ritual "coffee time".

What was I dreaming? he asked himself, looking up into the mirror, his wet hair looking more brown than blonde in the dim light of his bathroom. Something about a woman who was motioning for me toward her, he thought. His muddy thoughts were of no use to him this morning, he mused, but perhaps they would become clearer that afternoon or evening. Maybe it was her, he again thought, remembering he occasionally had strange dream fragments since Mother passed away years ago. Dad would say... well, Dad would say nothing, he supposed, turning to go back into the kitchen. I guess no one's background is perfect, he thought, pulling his favourite blue coffee cup out, setting up the small black dripper atop it as the music continued. He poured the boiling water over the grounds and watched it bubble through, wondering why this day was already beginning to seem somehow different. It wasn't Mom, he thought, recalling his dream again, and it wasn't Paula. It was someone else entirely occupying his thoughts.

Grabbing a blueberry bagel to go with his coffee, he headed back toward the computer, slowly trying to bring his thoughts to the here and now. He opened a browser and looked at the weather reports, noting it would be clear and cool as he sipped his coffee and ate the bagel. He looked at the news on the Reuters website and glanced at a few posts on a couple of his favourite discussion forums. Nothing was even mildly interesting this morning, he thought, it's just too early for me, I suppose. He shut the machine down and took the now empty cup to the kitchen, rinsing it out and looking out of his window again, and then he pushed himself to his bedroom to get ready for his first class.

*

Peter later came through wearing a blue button-down shirt with dark green trousers and hard-soled black shoes which clapped on the hardwood floor. He was starting the first tugs on a blue and gold checkered tie, a white t-shirt showing behind his open collar. He quickly finished, grabbed his bookbag from the dining table, and hurried past the laundry at the back corner door, locking it. Outside, he took in the still morning air and thin yellow light as he headed past his garden into his small garage. He remembered his commuter bicycle had a tire problem, with not enough time to bother with it. The mountain bike will be fine, he thought, dismissing the road, cyclocross, and other bikes in his collection. He unlocked and pulled his red mountain bike off its hooks, walked it toward the garage door, pulled it open, closed it and hopped on the saddle, throwing his bag across his back, taking off down the driveway toward the campus. He felt he was running just a moment or two short on time, so he took the most direct route straight down Devine along the neighborhoods instead of taking a more scenic way.

With the spinning of pedals, he now found himself feeling rested and wide awake, rolling easily in the cool and clear weather. As he rode, he feared his day would be nothing like the silent morning offered. I think I just need to get through this one, he thought. Tomorrow will be lighter, since I only have the Logic class. He noted the passing cars and other stirrings in the seeming stillness, as he thought about how he had never been a morning person despite its obvious beauty.

Eventually making it to campus, he rolled past several students up the shaded brick path near the Humanities buildings, up the walk to toward other bikes, threw his right leg over the saddle and stood on the left pedal as he rolled up to the rusty bike rack. He locked the bike and trotted toward the beige rock-faced Humanities building along with the other students and professors. He leapt up the stairs to the Second Floor and then down the bland hallway, crisscrossed with people, toward the classroom. As Peter's lanky figure passed the length of the hallway, his shoes clapped against the floor, and when he finally stepped into the assigned classroom, labeled "201" above the door, a lock of his hair fell down to touch his forehead, and he brightened his complex looking eyes to focus on the students before him.

"Sorry to disappoint you all this morning," he said with a laugh.

He noted the stack of essays on the desk and dropped his bookbag with a playful smirk, holding his pose for a moment to induce any possible laughter he could get. The students let out a collective sigh with their laughs. Because the professor was not really late, but was less early than normal, they had all considered just leaving.

"I know you were getting excited about cutting out of here," he added, laughing.

"Since you're all winded," one young student said in her strong Southern accent, "we should all just go home."

"That's funny," Peter quipped, "but we have to at least cover something today, since we took off early last time. The time is always running against us, it seems."

The young woman sat staring at one of her favourite professors without reaction, as she turned a curl of her red hair around and around with her fingers. For a second, she wondered if Professor Nexin had a girlfriend, but her thoughts ran off again just as quickly to what she had planned to do that evening. Peter took a moment or two rummaging around in his bag for the textbook, feeling for a moment the full thrust of boredom in the room. It was always a terrible feeling for just a second or two, he noted, as the blood rushes to the face and the silence pounds against the ears.

"So," Peter blurted, wondering how he was going to entertain those young minds, "we were talking about Leibniz, as I recall, and I was going on and on about this idea of the folding of matter on itself. As I mentioned, the ideas of temporal shifts and Relativity come out of this period..."

He pressed on with his lecture as the minutes passed, and the faces before him became incrementally more interested in the subject at hand as he spoke. He was always careful to pause for dramatic impacts, leaving a few holes in his presentation to spur questions, always encouraging such opportunities for the students, because he felt it would often inspire them, and perhaps lead to deeper discussions, which he so loved. Peter felt he enjoyed teaching about as much as anyone could who taught in the Humanities, but it was the reality of the administration and its budgetary problems which made the job far more draining that it should have been.   Inspiring young minds was something he found easy to do, but keeping himself on the good side of his department chair was not.

*

As he spoke, Milona appeared outside in the hallway from the far stairwell, walking slowly and quietly, dressed in khaki slacks and a checkered pullover, carrying a brown leather jacket in one hand. Too late, she thought to herself, as she approached the classroom, but then, that's what I wanted, I suppose. She stepped close to the edge of the doorway and leaned against the wall with her back, listening to Nexin, then slid down and sat on the floor. She let her head fall into her hands as she thought about what to do next.

"So, Einstein was a great eclectic," she heard Nexin say inside.   "Everyone attributes the ideas of Relativity to him, but he was only drawing on a very rich intellectual background from Berkeley to the German Enlightenment."

Milona thought hard about her objectives, but could not help entertaining the notion that a small attraction to Nexin was growing within her. She found herself more and more fascinated with this man from the past she hardly knew, yet wondered if she knew him too well. What was his family like? she wondered.

Did he have siblings? Was he seeing someone they had not noticed in their visits?   She tried to push the questions down, because she knew what she had to do was far more important, but it didn't make it any easier for her. She listened to the remainder of his class, among the chatter of the other classes, staring blankly at the wall opposite where she sat.

After he finished his lecture, Milona stood up and watched the students, all young inexperienced souls, she thought, pouring out into the hallway, as the other classes ended and other students filed out. She remembered being in school herself as they passed, all immediately talking with each other about non-academic matters. It seemed to her they were forgetting the powerful ideas their professors had just outlined seconds before, yet when she was in school, students were far more engaged and likely to get into fierce debates. These USC students seemed to be simply going through the motions, Milona mused. Peter followed them out, running his fingers through his hair, and Milona dropped her thoughts of cultural comparisons. He saw her standing there before him, obviously waiting on him. What a beautiful vision, he thought, when a woman is standing still.

"I was... wondering where you were," he said.

"Sorry, I finished typing this up late," she offered with a shrug, pulling the essay, bound in clear plastic, out of her jacket pocket, "I didn't want to interrupt, so I stayed out here." She handed Peter the short paper she had written for another one of his classes also due today.

"That's okay," he returned. "You're only sitting

in for your own research, so there's no worry about deadlines."

"Really?"

"You're not a student, you're a woman."

"Don't remind me," she said with a smirk, looking around at the young faces passing by, "I feel like I'm in a time warp whenever I'm around here."

"Sorry."

"Oh, no," she said, correcting for what she thought Peter might have taken to be a social error. "Listen, what are you doing for lunch?"

She asked the question while allowing her eyes to intimate the unspoken query of whether Peter was seeing anyone.

"Haven't thought about it, actually," he returned, glancing at her paper to make sure he recalled her name correctly, and at the same time finding himself curious about her mysterious facial expression. "There's the other class later today, so..."

"Interested?" she added, as if mechanically prodding him with either a soft undertone, a very distant possible sensuality, or mutual understanding.

"Sure," he responded, though with a subtle resistance he tried to understand from himself. "I have to grade the previous papers for the other class later this afternoon, though, he added, so we'll have to keep it down to a roar."

"Around Noon, then?" she asked, looking at her watch, then back to Peter for approval.

"How about eleven-thirty?" he offered.

5

UN Intelligence Operations Director Lieutenant General Laurent Zhang spoke only seconds after the major entered his office. It was furnished, like all administrative spaces on board, with beige walls and flooring, along with the usual tan-paneled, black glass top interactive desk, but Milona also noticed tasteful touches from Director Zhang, such as his black display shelves, many Oriental artifacts and artwork, and the distant sound of Japanese reed music he was playing in the background. When she had briefly met him before, she remembered finding him a striking man, well-built and tall, with dark eyes and greying hair at his temples. He wore his highly decorated red Intelligence dress uniform coat and trousers very elegantly, she noted, as he stood up from his chair. She saluted the lieutenant general, noticing the light flicker across the three separate gold squares on his collars, as he motioned for her to sit down in the black chair near the other side of his desk.

"Major Devon. Welcome. At ease," he offered in a calming tone while sitting back down himself.

Zhang looked back to his desk where he had been passing through a dossier rendered on his desk surface, tapping on the surface to turn the pages.

"Thank you, sir," she said as she sat down.

"So," he began, referring to the file, "Milona Kaatje Devon, thirty-two years old, born in Amsterdam to your French mother, Belina, and well known Dutch father, Doctor Gotthard Devon."

Milona hardened her face for a moment as she blushed, feeling the man could look right through her.

"You attended the International School of Brussels after your father's accidental death, and later the Royal Military Academy there, and even earned a Performance Certificate for cello at the École Normale de Musique after moving to Paris to rejoin your widowed mother."

Milona pulled her eyes away from the director as memories of youth again flooded over her. How cut and dried one's life sounds, she thought, when read back from a dossier!

"You were offered a commission as a second lieutenant by the UNC, tested well for Reconnaissance work, moved up to captain quickly enough, and eventually your assignments led to your Intelligence agent clearances and then to these latest training visits to the past."

The director paused for a moment, allowing the major to catch up to the moment, sensing she probably felt as if she were on trial here.

"Major, the references in your 201 from your previous COs, including a special note from the Science Director, tell me you come highly recommended. You've been an invaluable special agent. I hope General Venda hasn't noticed you missing from Recon lately," he said as they both laughed. "Of course, I was the one who authorized you be given Case Officer clearance under your Sec-Chief Colonel Ford a few weeks ago for *Operation Tempo*, and then advance Unit Chief with Lieutenant Mathis for *Mission Progenitor*."

Milona could not avoid allowing a little smile as she nodded her head. She was not officially aware the Operations Director himself authorized her latest clearances, and it seemed now that all of her nervous worry might have been unfounded.

"As they used to say, Major, 'let me get down to brass tacks'," he added, joking with an older American drawl and closing the viewing image on his desk surface, to which Milona allowed a slight snicker under her breath. "Do you think we've got an accurate theory?" he continued with a slight look away, "I mean, if Peter Nexin did not detail his thoughts to scientists and engineers of the period, then how can we account for the later published theories and personal journals on time travel and subspace theory coming out of MIT, some of which place the breakthrough right back with him at USC?"

"I..."

"But," he interrupted, "if the published accounts do lead to Nexin and he wasn't the... progenitor..."

"Respectfully, Director, I can't tell you at this point, until I can get closer to him," she said, recovering her nerve to speak up.

Zhang looked only slightly perturbed by the interruption from the junior officer before him, but briefly took a second to study her stern pose and quickly wiped his face of any concern. Certainly, her qualifications are exemplary, he thought, and of course, we're far more deeply troubled with the matter at hand than with the major's ambiguity or her future career.

"Well, we can't very well ask the man, can we?" he added, trying to keep the major on her toes.

"No, we cannot, sir. He is far too intelligent for that. If I ask him directly, I might plant the idea directly into his thoughts, triggering, if you will, the very thing we are trying to discover," she deduced.

"What do you mean?" he asked.

"We can't be sure that... We can't know... Well, sir, this mission definitely gives me a strange feeling," she fumbled.

Milona found herself trying to brighten her face in the soft light of Zhang's office. For a moment, she only noticed the faint light falling onto the director's face, realizing her thoughts must have slightly seemed incoherent.

"Need I remind you how dire our situation really is, Major?" he said, dropping his head toward her. "The latest intel coming through *Atlantis* puts this slow, massive and mysterious temporal distortion field within reach of our orbit sometime in the next few days!"

Zhang was likewise under tremendous pressure from the Director-General and the other chiefs to get *Mission Progenitor* right, and on the first try, something they all found patently obvious considering the possibilities, but it was just as difficult to pinpoint. His current difficulty, Zhang found, was in keeping the major from being too intimidated by the mission itself, while at the same time making her understand the seriousness of the realities involved. Milona stiffened her back as she listened.

"We've already lost several *Deep Mystery* scouts in the Def-Recon mission," he continued, "and very shortly we could expect anything ranging from mildly odd electromagnetic disturbances of communications, to dispersions of energies which could destroy the solar power stations right in their orbits. Any number of our other sensitive installations could be vulnerable, not to mention all the larger stations and colonies."

Zhang then hesitated to push the point further with the major, as he could now tell she well understood these possibilities. He leaned toward her and softened his voice slightly. "We don't want to see the chaos that reigned during the depressions, not after so much has been accomplished internationally. But," he continued as he sat back in his chair more calmly, "what really worries us, Major, is there is an even more devastating possibility."

"More devastating, sir?" she said with pause, as she felt Zhang studying her facial expressions.

"As everyone knows from the news, we may have potential new friends out there. Or, we may have enemies. Of course, there are still a handful of small separatist and seditionist regimes and organizations down there who oppose UN world government at every turn, despite taking its funding. They could seize the opportunity given by any disruption to launch attacks."

"I see, sir."

"I hope so. It could even turn out this distortion cloud, or field, or whatever they want to call it, is a part of some extrasolar plan far beyond us. Or the anomaly could just be something of which extrasolar enemies could take advantage as well. We just don't know. But any of these outcomes could easily return us to the plague-stricken desperation not seen since the Dark Ages in Ancient Europe, or the more recent Global Depressions, when the world was ravaged for decades by collapsing governments, vast inequities, plagues and terror. Most family histories, as you well know, most government data, and whole libraries of information were all lost. We have to be very careful with this operation, because we cannot trace every contingency through the historical record."

"Yes, sir," she said, recalling all too clearly that her family history, as with most, was known in very little detail.

"To even consider any of these possibilities is disturbing enough, I think you'll agree, and of course, the Chiefs will go through this all over again later today, but I just wanted to prepare you."

"Of course, sir."

"We do anticipate a 'go' on this, but it's not certain. We cannot predict what the Chancellor or senators will decide, but unless they shoot us down outright, you will only have a two forward days in our time frame to complete your passive probe, ensure executive action is required and carry it out with impunity."

"This is a benefit of keeping temporal experiments separate from our other research and developments," she offered, realizing she was stating the obvious, now wondering if the director was telling her everything.

"Yes, Major," he agreed before adding a pause, "I suggest you get some rest this afternoon, because I'm moving up your mission schedule. If we're a go, you will return to the past by sixteen-hundred UTC today. Therefore, you must find out for sure if this Professor Nexin initiated any form of temporal subspace research through his writings. Do it well, and this is a career-maker, Major."

"Understood, sir," she replied.

Milona fully grasped the implications of her mission all too well, but also felt a slight quiver about the fate of a possible future so automatically presumed to outweigh even one unique individual.

"Carry on then, Major, the clock is ticking," the busy director quipped as he stood, fully aware of the irony of his turn of phrase as he offered a grin. "I will see you when we all greet the Chancellor at twelve-hundred," he added with a pleasant smile.

"Thank you sir," she responded.

Milona's racing thoughts were interrupted by this dismissal, but she smiled back to him as she stood and nodded, then turned to leave. She walked back through the doors into the outer office, passing his lieutenant, who nodded her way as she continued out toward the corridors.

Zhang watched as his brilliant, beautiful, highly trained asset walked across the office, thinking about how Major Devon was so much more than even she thought herself. She has legitimate concerns about this mission, just as we all have, he thought, even if I didn't let her get a word in edgeways. She'll make a fine section chief one day, as soon as she makes lieutenant colonel.

Feeling he had detected a slight hesitation in the major's thoughts, the director thought perhaps it was due to the gravity of the situation, he wondered, but it sure seemed like a deeper problem troubled her. Actually, she reminds me of myself, he mused, and that transition through captain to colonel can be difficult. Zhang was immediately drawn to his past, recalling his early Reconnaissance Counter-Terrorism missions under the Intel Asia Chief, and he reflected for a second. He saw a quick succession of images in his mind, people talking, laser fire, small explosions, but then he thought about how long ago all that had been, and then he quickly brought his thoughts back to *Operation Tempo*.

"Get me a datapad ready with the major's reports," Zhang said through the doors to Lieutenant Whitaker, expecting to look them over while he took lunch, ensuring he would be ready for their meetings.

"I've been reading them over, General," UNS Lieutenant Colonel, Doctor Olen Nadimov responded unexpectedly.

Nadimov was a tall and strongly-built figure with short, dark hair, dressed in a sparsely decorated Intelligence uniform coat and trousers showing his three brass and one ivory rank squares on his collars, yet wore a scientist badge. He had just arrived at the station, had spoken with the lieutenant, and then appeared at Zhang's office with a dark anodized duty tablet as well as a larger polished model in his hands.

"The major's mission could involve too many

questions," Nadimov continued. "I think there must be another way, sir."

"Well, Colonel," the director said, nodding a negative to Lieutenant Whitaker across Nadimov's shoulder and reaching for Nadimov to hand over the tablet. "Nadimov, when I conferred with the SD on your being put in control of the techs in Berlin, I hadn't thought you would be taking such a quick and aggressive lead. What have you got in mind?"

Zhang was visibly irritated by Nadimov's boldness as he took the tablet and looked it over, but he also realized the Science Director's wizards, including this new Section Chief Nadimov, should also be given leeway, given such dire circumstances.

"Of course, General. We've been working on something, sir," Nadimov said, passing the larger polished metal tablet he brought.

Zhang put the tablet on top of the smaller one on his desk and looked it over.

"It's a shield, sir, working at the very quantum level," Nadimov continued. "We've made great strides developing this in the lab. It's just that we just need further authorization to conduct some tests."

"Tests," Zhang returned.

He looked up at the bold scientist standing before him. Director Franklin's new Technical Lead for *Tempo* was moving very fast, he thought, remembering that Nadimov was a talented physicist and now a section chief and lieutenant colonel who, after all, had participated in UNS's recent discoveries from the start. Still, he wasn't making friends easily, Zhang mused.

"Sir," Nadimov continued, "I also do not

believe this temporal mission can work without mangling the timeline. If we can destroy the distortion field before it gets here, we'll have a definitive solution."

"Let's get the Science Director and discuss this in more detail over lunch," Zhang offered.

6

Looking down at her communicator as she walked back toward Reconnaissance, Milona could not contain her excitement or her relief. She almost ran right into a passing Intelligence officer, tuning out her surroundings for a moment as she emerged from the doorway of Intelligence toward the lifts.

"Sorry Captain!" she offered, still walking.

"No problem, ma'am," he said as she flew by.

"Call Jen," she said, smiling and turning back. Her wrist unit beeped faintly as it alerted the master sergeant's communications sign number she had preset.

Milona felt as if a weight had been lifted, and she couldn't wait to tell someone. Of course, she thought, she couldn't tell Jen much, but she could tell her quite a bit without giving the whole thing away. Milona noticed many more people about, and figured they were all scurrying for lunch today, and she passed many more staffers, command officers, the occasional division officer, most wearing their dress uniforms.

"Yes Major," Jennifer answered.

The master sergeant had just given several orders to her assistants, then she plopped herself down at her desk, crossing her legs as she looked at her communicator. She could see it was Milona calling as it rang out a small horn noise.

"Jennifer, how about that lunch?"

"Great," she responded, surprised to hear from Milona, "where are you? Headed this way?"

"Yeah, nearby."

"I'll be able to break away in a few minutes."

"That's fine."

Milona continued on, walking with a notable spring in her step, and after a few minutes, when she arrived at the Reconnaissance Office on Level Eight and passed through the double doors and into the foyer, she found Jennifer walking from right to left giving further instructions to the assistants, not even fully realizing her friend was standing near her. Milona just now noticed Jennifer's badge below her decorations, and wondered why she had not noticed it before.

Of course, Milona knew very well that officers who donned these solid silver or gold badges, which were decorated with symbolic UN emblems or insignia and colours for various special services, were all to be afforded extra deference, irrespective of their actual rank grade. Jennifer's badge clearly indicated she had command authority practically equivalent to a full colonel. Such an important *Orbis* office, Milona thought, and now found herself feeling silly about how she had been treating Jennifer lately. She looked around for a second and found the office otherwise quiet, with little more than the station's infernal hum under the occasional office chatter to fill her ears.

"Is this a bad time?" Milona offered.

Several of the five Security Administration

junior staff officers nearby knew Major Devon and were surprised they had been working away and had not noticed her.

"No, ma'am," the corporal nearest to Milona offered, as they almost stood.

"Carry on everyone," she casually offered back, following Jennifer into her office, as all the assistants returned to their activities. "I'm sorry to rattle everyone," she added toward Jennifer.

"No, it's okay," Jennifer said. "It's been a busy day. RG advancers and other Recon DO's have been coming in all day. Let me lock this down..." she paused, pressing several keystrokes on the surface of her desk, "...and then we can get out of here."

Her desk's systems went into secured sleep mode, as well as her several tablets scattered across both the surface and a nearby bureau. Jennifer smiled at Milona as they turned and walked out of her office and into the main foyer toward the doors.

"Good work," Jennifer said to everyone. "Take your lunch when you can, and beep me with any problems."

"Yes, ma'am," they each responded.

The doors opened and the two passed into the corridor. They walked several steps toward the elevators before either of them spoke.

"Is the Level Five Mess okay?" Milona asked.

"That would be great."

"I'm really impressed," Milona said as they stepped onto the lift. "Level Five," she added, as they inched over between several other Recon command officers who nodded to both Milona and Jennifer.

"Captains, Lieutenant," Jennifer said as Milona nodded to them all, as if to say 'at ease'. "Impressed with what," she asked, taking the cue as the well-known lift voice spoke.

"You run that office like a battle commander," Milona said. "You're really good. You always have been. I'm sorry if I've never mentioned it."

"Thank you, but not hardly like a true battle commander."

The lift arrived at Level Five and the two of them stepped off, heading down the bright corridor and into a large and colourful Mess Hall, which opened up to a high ceiling and out toward its giant windows across the outer ring. The Earth's dark side was now visible through the windows, with the Sun in the distance. They found the hall nearly full of officers in their dress uniforms, and the space was reverberating with all of their conversations.

"I'm starved," Jennifer said, as they looked at the menu list for the day.

"What is Will doing for lunch?"

"Oh, he's eating on the run," she said smiling, "near the Defense Hangar, I think he told me."

"How about this table, here, near the windows," Milona said, and they both sat to wait on a server.

"Administrator," someone said, nodding to Jennifer, and only then "Major," he added to Milona. The Security Administration specialist looked a bit overworked to Jennifer in his service uniform shirt and pants. It was a busy day for everyone, she thought.

"Hello Specialist," Jennifer said, "I'll have hot tea. Milona?" she said, motioning to her.

"I think water will be great for me, I'm parched," Milona said, thrown off by the change of protocol.

"Yes, ma'am," he said, stepping away.

Milona couldn't wait, her face brightening while at the same time she reasoned about what she could or should tell.

"Well, guess what?" she asked.

"What?"

"My meeting went very well," she said.

"That's great!"

"I was worried about nothing, it seems. I've been working on a, well, a special assignment, and in the end, the operation commander told me I was doing invaluable work."

"Well, he would," Jennifer said flatly, feeling that Milona was being a little arrogant in a way.

"How do you mean? I didn't say 'He'."

"Look, you can cut the act with me," Jennifer said, lowering her voice slightly. "You're forgetting where I work. I see things. I approved your latest assignment status report. I know you're involved with *Tempo*. Exactly what you're doing on your missions I don't know, but you're answering to Colonel Ford, and today you must have been meeting with OD Zhang, right? He's given to compliments I've noticed, and you are an outstanding command officer. You deserve it."

Milona was flatly stunned, as if the wind had been knocked out of her, as if there had been a big party of all her peers already going on and she was invited to it late.

"But you only have R3 clearance," Milona

fished, "How do you..."

"I was moved up to R2 weeks ago," Jennifer said with a tinge in her voice to sting Milona, "I'd had full 3s for months before, since Lieutenant Colonel Banks was reassigned to *Mars 5*," she added, sitting back a bit, then looking around with a smile. "I'm even up for sergeant-major this month. In fact, before the colonel left, he'd indicated they were considering jumping me right into a command officer grade in Security Admin or Recon Warrant, major perhaps, because, as Colonel Banks said, meaning SA General Vorley, 'She couldn't afford the time to bring anyone else up to speed.' They'd made me an Admin as an interim promotion."

"Oh, Jen, I'm so sorry," Milona said slowly and with a lowered voice, as the specialist brought their drinks. "I had no idea," she added, leaning in toward her friend.

"Ma'am, anything on the menu sound good?" he asked Milona, nervous to interrupt.

"Yes, the lentil and potato soup with tossed salad," she recited, recalling it from her glance at the menu board.

Milona tried to cover the shame in her assumptions. She watched as Jennifer looked once more around at the menu on the far wall. How bright and professional her friend had become, she thought. To be an administrator as a master sergeant was itself a huge reward, and to think of being fast-tracked from staff to command was quite a rarity. I've been so focused on my own situation that I've not only neglected my friends, but caught myself looking down my nose at them!

"Ma'am?" he asked Jennifer.

"Well, I'll have the same, thank you," Jennifer said, smiling at the young man.

As the server walked away, Milona tried to think of something to say, feeling around for a start.

"What does Will think of all of this?"

"Will is up for captain soon, which is also good, but he thinks he might very well be stationed at Treasury for a few months."

"Still in Security Response?" Milona asked.

"Yes. The General of Response has a shortage of medical technicians in Hong Kong, and Will's had strong comments from his CO."

"I really don't know what to say," Milona lamented, feeling a few feet shorter.

✳

Milona stepped onto the lift now in the Defense Sector, along with several other officers. She still felt distracted by her lunch with Jennifer, a lunch in which she had made a fool of herself. Her visit, though, had dragged on long at the end, and she found herself once again rushing to get from the Reconnaissance Office to the Defense Sector, taking the roller and missing out on enough time alone to regroup emotionally.

The drop through levels eight to three seemed interminable, despite the lift being full of other officers, all heading to the largest hangar on *Orbis*, the Reception Hangar, where the UN Chancellor was to arrive within minutes. Milona fell silent, her emotions all turned around from an eventful day which wasn't even half over. She tried to remember Director Zhang's words, and thought about how she would make a better effort with Jennifer when this was all over. She thought again about her father, and how she should put up with anything in order to see this through. She knew she was a lucky soul to have such an assignment, and she hoped he would be proud of her.

Officers poured out of the lifts on Level Three and headed toward a very large opening into the upper part of a two-deck Reception Hangar. The Chancellor's entourage would be arriving directly from the Planalto in Brasília aboard the *Diplomat*, a heavily armed, customized forty-metre three-deck silvery escort-class ship, which carried engine outriggers on either side of a wide body craft with a snub nose and cockpit. It was highly modified with panels for hidden guns and sensors, controlled by the Chancellery Guard. A twin ship, the more blueish-silver *Statesman*, was for the Vice Chancellor and had arrived separately. There were other light blue escorts for the Secretariat, Senate, Treasury, and Court, though less fortified, but the visit today was limited to the Chancellery escort.

The Defense Logistics and RG people must be having a hectic day, indeed, Milona thought as she trotted with others down a steel staircase leading to the deck level of the massive, cold, and bright hangar. There were now rows and columns of Intelligence officers dressed in red, Reconnaissance in black, Defense in blue, and Security in olive, all making their formations at attention for the parade.

"*Diplomat* and Chancellery expected in zero

five," the adjutant said.

Milona joined her section chief, Colonel John Ford, a solid, if weathered, operative, and her entry officer and prober, First Lieutenant Geoffery Mathis, a muscular younger man with blonde hair. Both officers knew of Milona's meeting with the director, and reasoned she would probably have taken a later lunch. The three marched into a line with seven others assigned to their line, then fell in with the other Reconnaissance lines on the right column facing the shield. The two columns of officers were arranged by the four divisions facing each other in these rows of ten, with a wide corridor between them for the Chancellor to pass. Beyond them all, toward the hangar's airlock field were several extra rows of Defense Logistics, Security Patrol and Reconnaissance Guard staff officers, some in battle fatigues and flightsuits, others in various coloured service jumpsuits with coded sleeves, who maintained craft and hangar gear, the RG officers being part of the station's detail.

"Parade Rest," the adjutant said.

Only a moment later, it seemed, the polished silver-grey, sleek *Diplomat* could be seen arriving outside the hangar with three detail corvettes, a heavy whine of engines filling the hangar. Along with one of the corvettes, *Sting Ray*, also modified from the usual ninety-metre design in silver with red, black, blue, and olive graphics, the *Diplomat* entered through the airlock shield slowly and smoothly. The two ships landed past the landing crew and toward the dress columns, their landing claws extending, with the tail of the larger craft appearing not far from the shield at the hangar opening.   Beyond them were the other two corvettes, each black, and large numbers of silver-blue Defense ships outside forming a perimeter.

Milona had never seen the *Diplomat* up so close, noting as she gazed to her right her luminous silvery colour, solid polished landing gear, and the metallic "UN1" designation underneath the matching UN globe on the nose. She'd never seen either of the special corvettes up close, either, its large outrigger engines winding down.

Everyone watched as the boarding ramp extended from underneath the nose of the *Diplomat,* while four special Reconnaissance Chancellery Guard officers in black ran across from the corvette with disrupter rifles, posting themselves on either side in front of the craft. The Chancellor soon appeared, along with a detail of more CG officers, followed by key senators representing the World Affairs and Command Committees, the Chancellor's advisors with a number of gifts for *Orbis* commanders, and several journalists from the civilian press corps.

Madam Chancellor Nishiko Kitamori was tall and wore a simple, fitted grey suit coat and trousers. She had her black hair pulled back tightly, and having walked surely down the ramp, took in the large hangar full of people.   The four Command Chiefs then approached from the far end of their formations, saluted the Chancellor, and then all of them shook hands informally. Milona was frustrated at not being able to make out what they were saying from her distance away. The senators and others were welcomed, and the Chancellor was then given offer to inspect the military, which she did so at length, nodding to the various commanders within the four UN Command divisions.

The Chancellor had been elected with her running mate, Vice Chancellor Kyle Jasthi, on a strong vote from the Asian nations, along with visible support from her Japanese Grandfather, former Secretary-General Hashizen of the Pacific-Asian Federation. The Chancellor was the fourth woman to hold the six-year office, but she had no military experience. This visit to *Orbis* was largely seen as symbolic on that count, and noted by many in the press as hastily scheduled, given the rumours of hidden news. Milona, as well as many others she knew, thought this symbolism was no doubt itself a cover for the highly classified meeting with the UN Command Chiefs and Intel directors who were already aboard. *Operation Tempo* was unknown to the press, nor was it known that Major Devon and the others on her team were involved in temporal missions, because the temporal capabilities of the UNC were also unknown. This trip was obviously of high importance to everyone for many reasons, Milona noted.

As the Chancellor walked, holding her hands behind her back and with a highly respectful countenance toward the officers, Milona's thoughts wandered. She could suddenly hear the ticking of an ancient clock in her mind. Milona pictured Peter Nexin's bicycle, of all things, and she recalled a time a few days before when she had stood outside a classroom building on a windy afternoon and studied the bike, looking it over with an equally cold stare, clearing her mind as best she could to go inside and sit in one of Nexin's classes. To Milona, that was a precious and stolen moment, in a way, when the impending worry of what might happen in all of this seemed so far away, when her fascination with the simplicity of technology in Nexin's world overcame her awareness of the gravity of her mission and the complexity of the present crisis. Eventually, the Chancellor reached the end of the line and nodded back toward the chiefs her approval, about which there was little question in anyone's mind anyway.

"Parade At Ease," the adjutant said.

The formations of officers opened up informally, as the Chancellor's CG detail and her supporters crowded nearer to her. Many officers wanted to get pictures or offer their compliments and handshakes. To meet any UN Chancellor in person was a treat, and many officers were fans of Nishiko Kitamori personally, finding her beautiful, strong, and yet personable. Milona thought, as she watched the scene from afar, that compared to the last Chancellor, who had been a former general in Defense, Kitamori seemed relatively stiff when near UN Command.

7

"But, Lenny," Peter said to the perplexed young student, "you didn't conclude your paper that way. You seemed to set up a certain argument for Cartesian Dualism in the beginning, and followed that line through the middle, but then at the end dropped it and sounded like you were arguing for Realism, so that's why I couldn't give you an 'A'."

"But, Professor Nexin, this will kill my average," Lenny pleaded, with obvious concern only for his grades.

"Relax," Peter urged, "this is just one 'B plus' in the mix. Don't take this as a negative. Take this as a hint at how you'll make an 'A' on the next paper, and for the course."

"Okay," Lenny lamented.

"Okay?" Peter checked, to be sure.

"Okay."

"Your average is still in the 'A' range, so stop worrying so much."

"Okay," Lenny said again as he turned to exit. "I'll see you in class this afternoon?"

"Until then," Peter said.

Peter felt the need to guard access by students to

his personal feelings, and as Lenny made his way down the hallway, he shook off his worry about this young man, one who seemed too young for the college experience. Peter reminded himself, every semester there is at least one in each course who totally obsesses over their grades. A person's whole professional life, he thought, seems dependent on undergraduate grades these days. No one cares about talent or intellect, just these abstract records, and there is just so much competition for every little slot in life.

Peter felt he should move his thoughts elsewhere, and thought maybe he would check his email one more time before heading out to lunch. He sat down in the wooden chair at his grey metal desk in the off-white office he shared with two other adjunct professors. He pressed "F12" on the beige keyboard before him, a key he used as a preset to run the email software, and the program opened slowly. Nothing there, he noticed, and then decided to shut down the sluggish beige machine, hitting a function key, then an arrow key to select the shutdown command, then "Enter", and again to confirm. He leaned back in the chair as the machine shutdown and reflected for a moment, trying to think on nothing at all, as he stared blankly at the ceiling. Peter was attempting to create a dividing point in his mind between student concerns and the institution on the one side, and his lunch date with Miss Devon and the weather outside on the other. Now there's something to get excited about, he thought, not the vagaries of what passes for Higher Education in America.

Peter stood and took off, out of the office and

down the hall, out the doorway and onto the open campus. He took an indirect route through the lush gardens near the Horseshoe, feeling awkward about meeting this mysterious Milona, but he wasn't about to turn such a gift from the heavens down, he smirked. Anytime a beautiful woman invites you someplace, you just say 'yes', he noted to himself with a smile. He turned a corner around a brick fence and the smile fell away from his face for a second, as he noticed a man sitting in a plain brown car at the end of the horseshoe. Peter, it's just some businessman, he thought, just stop it with this nagging feeling!

He then continued down the brick pathway toward the wrought-iron gate, turning his thoughts back to the beautiful weather, the sky a clear blue, and a crisp, cool breeze was blowing through the trees. He made it across the street and onto the historic grounds of the Statehouse, eventually spotting Milona not far away, down the walk near some azaleas. He continued toward her as she noticed Peter and made her way toward him.

"This is a strange place to meet," Peter said, loud enough so that Milona could hear, as she approached him.

He watched her walk up, now wearing her brown leather jacket, which set off nicely against her khaki pants and brown ankle boots, he thought. Of course, it is a bit cool, he noted, rarely needing a jacket, but she looks like some kind of a spy, a mysterious figure indeed, he mused.

"What's strange about it?" she asked, exuding positive energy about the surroundings. "It's a beautiful

Southern day, you are here, what else could a girl possibly ask for?"

Milona certainly had a mischievous look about her, he thought.

"The Statehouse?" he quipped. "I've never thought of the Statehouse as a place to meet someone. No, wait. I take that back. I met someone here for lunch once, I just remembered."

"Let's go someplace else, then, if you have a bad memory," Milona offered.

"No, no, I didn't say it was a bad memory. I'm just being silly, that's all. I guess I'm just feeling a little strange about meeting you."

"Let's walk over that way," she said, noticing activity in the distance which might indicate a good place to eat.

"It really is nice today," Peter finally offered.

They turned to walk around the grounds, talking as they strolled, slowly winding toward one of the delicatessens at the South side of the complex. They talked about the foliage, the State's history, the students in his classes, and other fleeting subjects as they walked along. Both of them felt surprised at how easy their conversation had flowed now that they could speak freely. Peter found himself more comfortable thinking of Milona as a new friend rather than as a student or teacher, and Milona found herself lost in another stolen moment with Peter, far away from the worries and troubles of her mission.

✳

"You said a while ago you felt strange meeting me," Milona said as they waited for a crossing to clear of passing cars. "Why?"

Milona found herself almost skipping next to Peter's strides, finding the whole situation such a breath of fresh air she could hardly contain herself.

"Well, you're a very mysterious person," he said while looking slightly away, unsure about how she would take him. "I mean, with that jacket, that outfit, and your light accent, you almost look like... some kind of a Russian spy or something..."

Milona snickered aloud.

"...Sent to assassinate me for some unknown reason. I know it's silly," he finished as they crossed the street toward the sandwich shop, which looked crowded to Peter, noting the many people sitting outside eating and talking.

"Are you serious?" she asked, laughing. "A Russian spy? That's pretty funny, and by the way, my 'light' accent is Dutch, not Russian."

"It could be a cover. Sorry."

"Anyway, why would you be so important? What are you into? Any subversive interests?"

Milona knew he couldn't possibly be on to her real secret, but Nexin was more likely just a little bit rattled by having someone suddenly interested in him out of nowhere. She figured she ought to be a little more playful to disarm him, but she also felt playful.

"Well," he murmured, "What if I were some big important person. But, maybe it was that I wasn't so much aware of it, see, and you were sent to 'take care of it', as they say?" Peter made a gun with his finger.

"Who's they?" Milona innocently asked, looking up to the restaurant's sign above the windows and tables outside, and around at the other buildings.

"I don't know," he said, reaching toward the brass handle of the door, embarrassed now at his folly.

"You're adorable," she teased. "Russian spy."

They stepped into the restaurant, waited briefly in a short line, making small talk about the surroundings, and then up to the counter to order.

"May I help you?" said the young woman behind the counter.

"Yes," Peter said, turning to Milona, "what would you like?"

"What are you going to have?" she asked, being polite, but also seeking guidance.

"The smoked turkey sandwich," Peter said.

Milona remembered she had been avoiding meat since starting these missions, not that she was sure why, but she wasn't about to change now. She was at a loss as to what to order, anyway, in a situation of past social expectations without a clear idea of how to proceed.

"I think the veggie sandwich sounds good," she said, relieved to have made a decision. She hoped her selection wouldn't give her any ancient germs or viruses, but then she remembered the medical injection given to her would certainly keep her safe.

Milona relaxed as Peter ordered for them, asking her if sweet tea would be fine, to which she nodded, and she tried to regain her playful attitude from before. She pulled a small leather pouch out of her inside jacket pocket, and put a US ten-dollar bill on the counter.

"Let me take care of this," Peter said, pulling his wallet out of his back pocket.

"But, I invited you!"

"It's okay," he said, sensing that she seemed a little off balance about the situation. "I want to," he added. "Besides, ten isn't enough."

After ordering, they sat and waited for their lunches to be prepared, and resumed talking about the bustling deli and surrounding area. Shortly, they were presented with clear containers and white cups of tea, and they took them and walked back outside. They each took sips of their drinks as they headed back to the Statehouse grounds.

"Okay, maybe you are important," she offered, enjoying the tea as they walked up the sidewalk away from the deli, unable to let the reference go.

Peter steered them toward shaded benches back on the statehouse grounds.

"Maybe you are," she continued, "going to be just that kind of important, one day, not that any of us could see it now, of course. You never know, there's always time. You're what, about thirty, a promising young philosopher? Who knows?"

Peter's thoughts ran wild. Perhaps I have been silly. I'm no more important right now than that concrete over there. Someone to be walked on. Maybe when my book comes out, but right now, well, thinking I'm being watched by Russians to see what I'm really like is pathological, or certainly pathetic.

Milona then leaned inward and kissed Peter gently on his cheek as they walked, something she found surprisingly exciting and easy, noting she was nearly as tall as Peter with her boots. She put her drink into her right hand and pulled on his arm to stop walking, turning toward him. She put her hand on his face and smiled. Peter's incredulous countenance and interrupted thoughts let Milona know that he was as taken aback by her kissing him as by what she said about him. They found themselves floating for a moment in a mental space they both found vague, each feeling nothing other than what was plain to their eyes, yet their thoughts intimated endless possibilities between them. Peter held his drink against his body with his right arm, and then returned her gesture with a gentle brush of her cheek. A rush came over them as their thoughts fell as silent as rolling rivers.

They eventually found a suitable bench nearby, and said little as they sat down to eat. Milona was surprised at how hungry she was, gobbling up her sandwich with hardly a thought of her earlier concerns. The vegetables, she noted, tasted about the same, but simpler somehow. They would not have been grown with the advanced compounds common in her time, she thought. How odd it seemed, she mused, to be eating with this person from the distant past, from a different culture and place, compared to lunch with Jennifer on the station, she teased herself, taking the last sip of her tea as Peter seemed to be finishing his lunch.

"Let's go for a walk," she posed, jumping up to toss her food and drink container into a trash can.

"I can't say no to that," he quipped.

She lifted Peter's hand and led him away from the bench. He tossed his containers into the can, and smiled at his new friend as they sprung away from their quick picnic spot. Peter felt a refreshing confidence about this new woman who seemed suddenly to be in his life, but he was also mindful of his emotional state. He knew he was given to falling fairly easily, so he tried to remain slightly distant to be prepared for any possible letdown. He tried, anyway.

"How was your lunch?" he asked, hoping that her seeming reticence was gone.

"Oh, it was really good," Milona said, "it had red onions, peppers, mushrooms and sprouts all dressed in oil. Very tasty."

"Great," he said, tickled by Milona's delight.

"What are your plans tonight?" she asked.

"Don't know," he responded, still dazed by sudden friendship. "I thought I might go out to my old haunt, a bar right over there in the Vista, actually, you can almost see it over there," he added, almost hoping she would take him up on the suggestion.

"Yes, maybe I'll see you out," Milona said, as Peter smiled, "but what do you have to do now?"

"Well, sadly, I've got to run by the department before the afternoon class," he recalled. "So, I guess I have to go, actually, pretty soon."

"I'll see you in class," she returned.

They both stopped walking again and turned toward each other. Milona made a distinct effort to check her emotions, trying to allow herself to reel just enough in the moment to crowd out her fears of what she had to do, but she also kept a mindful eye on a need to escape those pressures.

"We can go for a longer walk some other time,

of course, maybe tonight," she added, looking into Peter's eyes.

"That sounds... good to me," Peter said, lingering as he looked back into hers.

8

"Colonel?" the three journalists each called out.

Major Devon, along with RSF Colonel John Ford and Lieutenant Geoffery Mathis, all in black dress Reconnaissance uniforms, marched down the Level Three corridor away from the Reception Hanger on their way toward the secured corridors on Level Ten in the Defense Sector. They were met by the press corps members near the lifts.

"Colonel, can you tell us why you're meeting with the Chancellor and senators today?" the nearer journalist asked Ford, holding a civilian-style work pad device to record any comments while the others made notes on their tablets.

"No, sir," Ford said. "We apologize, but as you know we are not at liberty to discuss anything, or even whether there's anything to discuss."

Ford was becoming accustomed to the spotlight, his more recent missions and commands taking him farther into public view than ever before.

The three were joined by two Reconnaissance CG officers at the lift doors and all five stepped inside as the journalists looked angered at being brought all this way to still be told nothing. It was apparent to each that this trip was far more than a simple military inspection and hand-shaking ceremony, but they were at a disadvantage, surrounded on an orbiting space station by so much military hardware, accompanied only by the disciplined silence of the UNC on their own turf. The doors closed as a Security Administration staffer from Master Sergeant Collett's office approached the journalists with orders to escort them away on a complimentary tour of *Orbis*.

"Ladies and Gentlemen of the press," the corporal said, holding out a hand to guide them to an adjacent lift, "did you know that *Orbis* was originally launched to replace the aging International Space Station and to control the growing satellite and power grid systems?"

Ford continued to lead Devon and Mathis and even the RG officers down a corridor in the secured area on Level Ten, reaching a tall set of metal doors which slid open, leading them into a large circular Meeting Hall sometimes used as a situation room, and which was nearly identical to halls in the other three sectors. For the Chancellor's visit, she used a secret secure lift from the Reception Hangar directly up to the Meeting Hall, with the others taking various other routes to the hall. The three entered to find the Chancellor and Vice Chancellor with their advisors, all four Command Chiefs, Director Zhang and the Science Director, the Region Chief for all the stations and the *Orbis* Station Chief, the Secretary-General from the Secretariat, and the key senators. All stood and mingled near their black and titanium chairs around a matching ring-shaped table.

"Welcome, Colonel, Major, Lieutenant," Chancellor Kitamori said, turning away from an advisor toward the Colonel and his team.

Kitamori spoke with a soft humanist voice, Milona noted, sounding much like the seasoned health services administrator she had been in civilian life.

"Again, we very much appreciate your being here. I know it could not be easy to keep all of this to yourselves," she added.

The three of them acknowledged her understanding without speaking, merely nodding with a smile to her and the others as everyone around the room found chairs to occupy.

"Those of you who are here," she continued, looking around the room as everyone quickly sat down and settled, "I believe have been a part of these discussions for weeks. We are, of course, in the final moments, and so today, I would like to give everyone here an opportunity to speak. Let us begin with an update from UNC. Director-General?"

"Madam Chancellor," said Director-General Nikolai Lorentz, Chair of UNC and General of the Intelligence Directorate, a respected officer in a highly decorated red dress uniform, "I don't think the other Command Chiefs will disagree, I'd like to let the Operations Director update us at this point." He looked around for objections, receiving only nods. "General Zhang, please."

"Madam Chancellor," Zhang replied as he referred to the table surface for his notes rendered from the office by Lieutenant Whitaker. "As you are all aware, our preparations for *Operation Tempo* have included numerous scout missions, visits to the past using *Calendar* as training and research for *Mission Progenitor*. Section Chief RSF Colonel Ford, Unit Chief RSF Major Devon, and Case Officer RSF First Lieutenant Mathis, have in fact made dozens of visits to various time frames in order to ensure the integrity of the timeline should we choose to execute.

"Classification prevents me from divulging too many details of our plans even in this meeting, but over the several days since we last met, we have thoroughly studied every angle of the proposed mission, from the mechanical and temporal effects of temporal travel, to any localized effects on the subject's own immediate surroundings, to the propagated timeline stretching out years and decades, all the way to the present. From an operational standpoint, we can be quite sure about the technical parameters," Zhang said with emphasis, looking around to Science Director Franklin, "but it should be noted that due to the length and effects of the prior world-wide depressions experienced, there is still unfortunately some measure of uncertainty in executing *Progenitor*. This uncertainty cannot be eliminated before we begin to experience disruptions from the approaching field, but we should not let it deter us. It is my recommendation that we proceed to execution."

Milona felt a chill run up her spine.

Zhang ended with a nod to the Director-General.

"General Zhang, thank you," Lorentz said. "Madam Chancellor, I'd like to call on our Science Director for her update."

"Of course," said the Chancellor.

"Doctor Franklin, please," he said.

"Madam Chancellor," the distinguished UN scientist replied, appearing worried. The grey-haired doctor and major general wore her red dress uniform coat and skirt and blue-on-silver badge, and looked particularly nervous to Director Zhang, "I would have liked to be able to report that the scientific team in Berlin, who have been working on this challenge around the clock, had pioneered a method by which we could confront our problem directly without resort to the temporal distortions and risks therein. However, I regret that I cannot do so at this time. Some of the most respected scientists at the disposal of the UN have not yet been successful in isolating the elements of this field so that we might counteract its potential effects."

"Doctor Franklin," Lorentz asked, "are you telling us that your team will not have results in the next twenty-four hours?"

"I am sure we all feel disappointed," she offered, "but at this time the *Tempo Programme* simply is not likely to yield an experimental result with enough accuracy in time to be deployed."

"So," the Chancellor asked, "the operational side of *Tempo* seems to be the only option, Director Franklin?"

"I'm afraid so, Madam Chancellor, at this time."

The Science Director had offered her assessment at what she felt was great professional embarrassment and with noticeable personal disappointment, as silence fell over the room for a few moments. Everyone then lingered on what the Chancellor might have to say.

"Senators?" Kitamori then asked after a moment of reflection, deciding to open the floor to informal talk.

"Madam, I think this is all very risky," India's Senator Prikosh said, a soft spoken woman leaning forward in her white and camel robes. "What if this does not work? How can we go back to our respective national representatives, our peoples, and tell them their senators kept such a huge secret from them?"

"I agree, Madam," Australian Senator McCallum said, a brash man in a grey coat and trousers. "How do we really know these temporal visits will yield the result we need, without a catastrophic military or technical blunder?"

The operatives all suppressed the urge to speak up to the senator's aspersion, as they looked at each other for support.

"Madam, what choice do we have?" France's Senator Levy asked, a polite gentleman in an off-white coat and trousers, who also served as Vice Chair of the Senate. "Do we simply sit here and wait for this field, or cloud, or whatever it is, to hit us like some kind of cosmic tidal wave and hope we can surf it out? Or do we take a chance on this mission, because it sounds as if Operations Director Zhang has worked out every reasonable contingency."

"It's murder!" the white-robed Iran Senator Hassan bolted, putting a fist forward. "No matter how we look at it from our point of view, we will be murdering an innocent civilian to save ourselves."

"What it is, Senator," General of Defense Whitney interjected, "is the only way out at this point."

The General and Vice Chair of UNC pushed

herself back from the table and crossed her legs as she spoke, the light flashing across her many decorations, her five gold squares, and her gold UN Command Chief Badge on her blue dress uniform.

"Out of what?" Senator Hassan asked. "Do we know for sure this disruption field will have any ill effects on our systems or our populations?"

"Yes, Senator, we do!" the Science Director noted, showing a bit of strain at the conversation, "At the very least, this field will interrupt electrical circuits and microwave transmissions, leading to a world-wide loss of power for a minimum of hours to days, at least until it is restored."

"Of course, Madam," Director Zhang added, "for any doubters here, Science Director Franklin's assessments, as well as other forecasts, actually go much further than mere power outages. There would be explosions happening all around us, destructive distortions of temporality and physical space, and even if we only experience simple power failures, there are still the rogue nationals and terrorist groups down there who will take any opportunity they can to subvert the UN's authority."

"Madam Chancellor, I don't see any other option," General of Reconnaissance Vadas said, a weathered-looking man in his black dress uniform. "Not at this time," he added. "Our team is ready."

"Director-General?" the Chancellor asked Lorentz, then looked to all others, "Generals?"

"Madam, we have to consider the safety of billions of people in our care," the General of Security charged, leaning forward in her olive dress uniform.

"Even if the timeline is dramatically altered, if it averts this field, then it has to be worth the risks to everyone alive right now," she pleaded.

"I have to agree with my colleagues, Madam," the Director-General said, "we've been over this again and again in the last week or two, but given the hard work our people have put into this, I have to trust them. To do nothing is foolish. To wait too long on a technical solution is unwise."

"If I may speak, Madam Chancellor?" Colonel Ford said, surprising Milona and Geoffery as everyone turned to the command officer.

"Yes, of course, Colonel."

"With all due respect to the senator's opinions," Ford continued with a nod, "I want to say that I trust Major Devon and Lieutenant Mathis with my life. I've worked with the major only for a short time, but both she and the lieutenant have integrity on par with the finest officers in service. They tell me they are ready and willing to carry out their orders, and I have complete faith in their ability to do so."

"I second that," RSF General Venda said.

"I agree, too," Director Zhang added. "The operatives are more than ready for this mission. But let me stress this about the major in particular, with no offense to you, Lieutenant Mathis. If we do not execute at this time, then no one else here can help us, because Major Devon's detailed contact with the target cannot easily be replaced without severe consequences to the timeline, or at least, complications with our Temporal Alliance, not to mention ourselves."

Milona and Geoffery both blushed at the

unexpected show of support and focus from the colonel and generals.

"Major Devon?" the Chancellor asked, Milona suddenly jolting with nervous energy. "We're talking about you as if you were not in the room. Do you have anything to say about this?"

"Yes, Madam Chancellor, thank you," she said, slowly rising emotionally to the occasion despite her clear surprise. "First of all, I would like to thank all of you for your confidence, and even for your doubts. Training for this mission has been a privilege, but even your reservations have given me deeper understanding of what we all do. This is not an easy position for any of us to be in, but should you choose to execute this mission, Madam, my promise to all of you is to do my level best in every way."

"I don't think any of us seriously doubt that, Major," the Chancellor said, "but as you are obviously aware, we are all struggling with a very awkward decision which has unprecedented ramifications."

"Yes, Madam Chancellor," Devon said.

Milona realized she may have failed to make her point, but it probably did not matter. Minds were already made up, she mused, and her personal opinion was of little value toward affecting them.

"Well," the Chancellor said to the room, "I'd like to have an informal vote on this. All in favour?"

Slowly hands raised around the hall, from Milona, Mathis and Ford, to the directors, the four Command Chiefs, and even a strong majority of the senators and generals. Kitamori looked around as more hands went up to note only Senators McCallum and

Hassan were not holding their hands up, but those two would not have agreed to a cup of coffee, she thought.

"Time is wasting," Kitamori said. "Director Zhang, your XT call for *Mission Progenitor* is a go."

Milona breathed a sigh of relief, and she thought she could feel it in the room as well.

"We're still in silent mode, everyone," the Chancellor continued, "absolutely no one is to speak a word about this! I'll ask the Command Chiefs that if anything changes the picture here whatsoever, I want to know immediately. And Senators, if I am notified of any changes of operational value, I will let you all know immediately. We are in this together, everyone," Kitamori concluded.

*

Ford, Devon, and Mathis, along with nearly all the others in the room, had pushed away from the ring-shaped table with a heavy feeling, relieved to be in a go situation, but certainly aware of the contingencies. Devon looked at Zhang, who nodded back at her with a smile of approval, and then he nodded as well to Ford and Mathis before moving toward the Chancellor. She then watched the Chancellor and the politicians slip away from the table and toward their exit, all seeming to talk of unrelated issues, and followed by the chiefs and directors.

"Chancellor Kitamori really impressed me," Milona said, turning to Geoffery, who shook his head in agreement saying nothing.

"She's much tougher than she seemed before,"

John whispered.

Milona watched from afar as the Chancellor stopped to shake hands with the chiefs and directors. She thought they would make their way back down to the *Diplomat* to return to the surface, but not before collecting their wayward press corps, who had been sent on a phony tour loop around The Promenade.

"I'm glad we're still in business," Geoffery said.

"There was never any doubt," John added, "most of these things are just formalities, Lieutenant."

Yes, Milona thought to herself, minds had already been made up.

9

Stepping through a small hangar and into a silver, two-seat shuttle, Milona now wore her black service jumpsuit with her hair swinging around her shoulders. She tossed a fairly heavy shoulder bag into the space behind her seat, and the hatch came down after she sat inside.

"As you were," she said.

Milona found the pilot a cheery young woman with long black hair pulled back from her blue service jumpsuit, noting her single charcoal and ivory half-squares.

"Major," the young officer acknowledged, as she turned from the cockpit viewscreens. "Welcome aboard fifty-eight. I'm Specialist Maria Garcia-Gomez. We'll be underway in just a moment."

"Thank you, Specialist."

Milona took a quick breath as she settled in, and felt fairly well rested from a short nap in her quarters. After calming herself following the previous meeting with the Chancellor and others, she was happy to be able to lie down quietly, if only for a few minutes.

"I've looked at your flight plan, Major. Andrew Jackson Station?"

"Yes, Specialist. I've got to post there for a couple of days to update some of their Recon procedures. There is still so much work to do in North America."

"Sounds fun, ma'am," she said. "I see you're on a priority run. The trip should take about ten minutes, given where *Orbis* is currently. This is only a standard coupe-class craft, after all."

"Carry on, Specialist."

The pilot pushed a button on the viewscreen, which then displayed flight plan and clearance information for the craft. She pushed several other control buttons and Milona then felt the small shuttle gently lift off the deck, a slow lift forward through the airlock shield at the Reconnaissance Sector shuttle hangar, and then out into Space beyond *Orbis*.

"The weather looks wet for you down there, Major," Garcia-Gomez said after a time, looking at a secondary screen which displayed conditions and weather animations at the destination's area. "Thunderstorms are rolling through the area, but should be gone by afternoon."

"Oh, it's just as well," Milona said, "I'll be inside most of the time."

Milona tapped a light button on the screen in front of her, scrolled through several channels, and settled on a world news summary which was replaying the Chancellor's visit.

"That was quite an event," the pilot said, unable to avoid noticing the transmission.

"She seemed so stiff," Milona said, "compared to General Bretian."

Milona was careful not to mention anything about her later meeting, hoping the specialist had not seen any pictures of her in connection to it.

"Was she as stiff behind the scenes, Major?" the pilot asked innocently enough, but it was also to Milona's horror.

"No, Specialist, she wasn't," she replied. Milona was a bit set off, but then she relaxed, recalling the journalists must have been able to transmit what they captured in the corridor.

Milona looked back to her viewscreen and continued watching news reports. She had never been so visible before, she thought, but maybe it wasn't so bad to be recognized by a UNC shuttle pilot.

The shuttle sped far away from the station and toward the surface, curving around slightly underneath the planet, passing the large power matrices above Antarctica, as the two adjusted their sense of direction to suit. The pilot took her small craft through the atmosphere and into the cloud cover over the South Atlantic.

Milona had long lost her interest in the news and simply looked out the window. Then she could see a Joint Command Sea Group below on the blue ocean surface. Becoming clear, the silver command ship and carrier with their joint graphics looked dark grey as they hovered with corvettes, destroyers, a carrier, all silver with red, black, blue or olive panels, and submarines were peeking up from under the waves. A *Nording* training exercise, she thought, recalling her own training missions with the *Putin Sea Group* in the Pacific when she was a second lieutenant no so long ago. A few miles farther in toward shore and she could see three massive brown cargo ships flying slowly north through the darkening weather.   The shuttle continued across the grassy lowlands and eventually the specialist smoothly put the craft down on a landing platform in the forests of a former US Army Base.

"Here we are, ma'am."

"Thank you Specialist," Milona said graciously, "it was a smooth ride down, and I appreciate the conversation."

"You're welcome, ma'am. I hope your post goes well, ma'am."

Milona smiled at the pilot as she tapped the hatch release button on her screen, opening the hatch on her right. She jumped out, grabbing her shoulder bag as she got out into the rain. The hatch closed as she trotted away from the shuttle and down the staircase off the landing platform. The site was a large power station which sat in the middle of a forest that greeted her, its intense microwave beam illuminated for safety in the weather as it reached up into the clouds, the metallic buildings and other equipment gleaming in the remaining mid-day light streaming between the passing storms. The shuttle lifted off behind her, its drive thrusters whining, as Milona ran across the breezeway toward the double doors of the facility.

"Major Devon," Major Fred Waters greeted with a wide grin, the Intelligence Counter-Intelligence Station Chief for the remote location, "it's always nice to see your pretty face."

Milona noted his brown civilian coat and trousers, as he stood at average height with a deep tan and blonde hair.

"Yours too, Waters," she said with a sarcastic tone. "It's been two days," she added, as they walked down the corridor of the power transmission station.

"Two agonizing days," he swooned.

"Enough," she said, smiling.

They approached a large grey metal door on their right, and both waved their right palms across a panel on the right of the door.

"I assume Mathis is already here," she asked as the heavy door slid open to the right.

"Of course," he said, as they passed through into a featureless room.

The metal door slid closed behind them as the small room lowered itself down slowly, revealing itself as a lift. The far wall then opened up to a secured area of the station as the lift lowered them down the eight-foot shaft.

The two walked into the control room of *Calendar*, a highly classified installation within the remote power station, concealed among the microwave beam receiver systems which stored and converted minimal amounts of power from the orbital matrices in the atmosphere as a cover. The location was considered ideal by the Director-General, within the boundaries of the old US Army base, Fort Jackson, allowing them to insert covertly into the past.

"Geof!" Milona said with excitement in order to play with Waters, "good to see you!"

Milona patted Geoffery's shoulder as she spoke, feeling it had been weeks rather than hours since she had seen her principle special agent, his flaxen hair and overbuilt physique a natural draw. He seemed especially attractive in the blue suit and tie ensemble for his businessman cover. Of course, she thought, it had only been two days since they had finished their last mission, and the parade and meeting was only hours before, but so much was happening so fast, it always felt for them as though weeks had gone by when seeing someone again.

"Glad you made it here okay, Major," he said. "It was coming down pretty hard out there a few minutes ago."

"How sweet," Major Waters said, sarcastically.

Waters was only joking, but felt a bit like a third wheel, and even though she was also playing, it was Milona's intention for him to feel that way. Waters shook off any concern, though, exchanging a nod from the Senior Control Officer indicating they were ready.

"Mitchell says we're ready," Mathis said, "but, I'll wait for you to change? Ladies first?" he added, wondering if she wanted to go through the chambers first.

"Of course! Excuse me, gentlemen," she said with a bat of her blue eyes.

Waters gave a wry look to them both as he moved on into the control room, Mathis following behind snickering under his breath. Mathis felt the working relationship between all of them was quite enjoyable sometimes, even as a junior officer.

*

After a few moments, with her clothing changed

to a more suitable outfit for her cover story, brown leather ankle boots under a pair of khaki slacks, a checkered pullover shirt with a brown leather jacket, a smaller dark brown shoulder bag, and with her hair falling onto her shoulders, Milona stepped across the hall from a locker room and into the control room, greeted by all the men's eyes as she entered.

"At ease," she said with sarcasm, clearing her throat with a grin.

"We're ready for you, Major," said RSF Sergeant-Major Mitchell.

Calendar Senior Control Officer, who always looked particularly striking to Milona with his greying temples and leather-like skin, turned away from the other engineers to speak, the light catching his full grey hair, his four-charcoal rank squares and blue-on-silver badge with the cube decoration catching the light. All of the Special Force engineers wore black service jumpsuits, while another officer, a Security Medical lieutenant in an olive jumpsuit, approached Milona.

"Ma'am, I've got to check your inoculation," the first lieutenant said, holding a small polished device in her hand which could detect or perform injection.

"Of course."

The physician put the tip of the device against Milona's neck, noting previous injection marks had healed, as Milona nodded back her approval, trying not to think about the injection, focusing randomly this time on the physician's badge, which looked scratched across the red cross and white globe when she had leaned in close enough. A faint rush of chemicals passed through Milona's dermis and into her bloodstream, a mix containing a number of preventive measures designed for short-term protection.

Milona found herself nervous after the doctor injected her, but it was not due to the inoculation, which was something she had become accustomed to receiving. She had been on many time missions already, she recalled, even some missions which seemed more like vacations than military objectives. During one not long ago, she recalled, she had even visited herself as a young girl singing in a choir with her father. Perhaps that is why she watched it again this morning, she mused. Somehow, she still felt tense about this mission, though. It was usually a painless trip through *Time,* which she had done again and again, of course, but this time it was charged with added significance. But why? she wondered. Why was she doing this to herself?

"Sergeant-Major," she asked, "since my return has been moved up, we are still set for morning in the past?"

Milona was looking at her wristwatch, one she found in an old Parisian shop and often wore when off duty, which now showed five minutes before four o'clock, still set since returning from a previous insertion.

"Yes, ma'am," he said, "it will be approximately zero-eight-hundred at your entry point."

She turned the dial on the watch as she nodded, moving the hands one way, then the other, forward to match her target time, then looked around the cold metal surroundings of the chambers and control room. The men and women in their roles all watched her in return as she stepped into the initialization chamber. She felt a tingle from the light field between the two chambers, and then turned back toward the technicians.

"Launch window confirmed," the sergeant-major said. "Synchronizing with microwave shutdown and air traffic. Begin counter-clockwise sequence, on my mark. Five, four, three, two, one. Initialize."

Milona made eye contact with Mathis, Waters and Mitchell as the resolution chamber immediately disappeared behind her. She fought the instinct to be startled at the loud and hard clap. The warp-driven pods used the latest cesium-pulsar systems, and generated intense energy fields around the chambers, creating a bubble of space-time accelerating many multiples faster than light. This instantly created a localized effect of temporal displacement, adjusted by the field intensities and engine calibrations. The gap between the two chambers was surrounded by a field which promoted a space-time bridge to form between the two chambers.

"Have a good trip, Major," Mitchell said to soothe her nervous countenance.

"Thank you Sergeant-Major," Milona said, grasping the strap of her shoulder bag.

The resolution chamber reappeared instantly with an equally loud crashing sound, and Milona turned to look into it. In the blink of an eye, she saw herself appear opposite herself, inside the chamber just inches away. Her clothing, hair and the look on her face were identical to the way she looked during initialization. Just as quickly, she looked again upon herself, but now from the resolution chamber, seeing herself back in the initialization chamber, only for a split second before fading away.

"We've got a passenger, Staff Sergeant," Mitchell added for the controllers on the other side, using a secure digital signal to speak with the Army controllers in the past, a frequency which would now transmit freely through the generated wormhole.

Milona could also see the sergeant-major and other staff in the control room, and before it all seemed to fade away, another man in an Intelligence uniform she did not recognize then appeared next to Waters and Mathis. She stepped through into the opposite control room, through which she could see the US Army's control staff in the past. She moved away from the chambers as the view into her present, the control room was fading into a view of the past, the plain chambers.

Standing next to Waters, now as Mathis was readied to follow, was Section Chief Nadimov in a red dress uniform. Having acknowledged Waters when he walked up, they now watched as Milona faded away through the chambers. While Waters was always relieved for another successful tunnel, Nadimov stared at Milona blankly and whispered Mitchell's sentiment to himself.

"Do have a nice trip, Major."

10

They stepped up the two steel stairs from the small control room and onto plain grass around its small concrete-walled building. They always tried to be pleasant rather than preoccupied to the Army staff and technicians in the past, even though it did seem they were expected this morning. Milona was happy to see a clear blue sky overhead and feel cool air on her skin as Geof came up the stairs behind her, and the both of them returned the salutes from the Army captain and his crew.

"Good Morning, Captain," Milona said.

"Major, Lieutenant," Captain Oglesby greeted, his chocolate skin showing slight perspiration underneath his olive service dress uniform in the warm sunlight, "Welcome again. How long do you plan to stay for this trip?"

"Probably not more than a day, sir," Mathis responded. "We will need the car and hotel room today, and we are scheduled to leave late tonight or tomorrow morning, sir."

"Very well," Oglesby said. "My team will make sure you have everything you need."

Devon and Mathis returned their salutes and

turned toward the fence as the chambers in the control room were synchronized back with the present, issuing a single loud clap. A new corporal to the team winced at the sound as they passed.

"You get used to it," another Army specialist said who stood next to him, as the remaining white noise from the warp dilations faded behind them in a faint whisper.

The captain led them toward the security fence out of habit. Few people, he thought, wanted to stay near the chambers due to the noises, and the spartan installation had no amenities as a welcome beyond staff necessities. The captain's personnel, also wearing their olive service dress uniforms, saluted the major and lieutenant from the future as they turned and walked away from *Visitor* toward the tall steel-panel fence.

The secretive unit of Army Intelligence officer operatives managed their chamber installation and secured the area surrounding the facility, code-named *Visitor* by the commanding general of the Army base. Kept classified by all involved, the facility sat near the middle of the large, forested training base, and in a perfect location they found, in order to maintain secrecy and cover stories, even though they had not chosen the location themselves.

Oglesby and his staff considered themselves the front line to the future, part of the highly classified Temporal Alliance Program, an Army Intelligence and Joint Special Operations Command initiative, along with direct involvement from the Central Intelligence Agency and other agencies. They were charged to interface with and provide cover for any visitors and to protect US interests. To Oglesby's officers, greeting their visitors from the future was a great honour and a privilege they took very seriously. They stood watch over all functions of their secret facility and awaited the white noise and claps which would usually precede their visitors arrivals.

The group continued across the grass toward the fence, approaching the two sergeants who were guarding the entrance at attention. The three passed through the now opening metal gate and on toward the parking area and a concrete path.

"Agent Gibbs," Milona said, now seeing and greeting the slightly rounded, fair skinned, red-haired man who wore a dark suit and tie.

Awaiting them as they were led by Oglesby, Special Agent Gibbs was a CIA bridge asset assigned to work directly with the people from the future, whom they all affectionately referred to as "Morlocks", a reference to H.G. Wells the agents found amusing. Gibbs had been helping the CIA glean any possible information from their counterparts regarding their visits, any possible targets, or even their military plans, but he found the operation difficult. Like many who served in the program from the several competing agencies, it was Gibbs' understanding that he alone was in charge of the local operations in his time frame, that he was here to brief Major Devon and Lieutenant Mathis, not the other way around.

The Director-General of UN Intelligence allowed such inaccuracies, Milona recalled him saying, because he felt it better to utilize assets instead of working against them. As was often noted in UN meetings, it would be far more accurate to think of the major and lieutenant as in charge and briefing the agents and the other personnel. The men and women in the past were certainly not told much of anything, Zhang often reminded them, and in many time frames they were completely unaware of any temporal activity going on. Milona recalled Colonel Ford once sharing with her that the only reason there was an alliance program in this frame was because they were stumbled upon during an early mission.

"Devon, Mathis," Gibbs said, as the three passed through the large iron gate toward him at the fence line.

They remembered not to try to shake hands with Agent Gibbs, as he did not seem to like it. He led them down the concrete path away from the fence, near a number of parked vehicles, toward an old white-painted wooden single room building used for their briefings. Milona and Geof looked at each other with an understated grin between them as they walked behind the shorter man.

Oglesby followed, and then ushered them up the wooden stairs and toward the door as he stood watch outside, motioning with a wave of his hand a standby signal to the several Delta operatives who monitored them, though well out of sight. Gibbs, Devon, and Mathis stepped up and inside, then closed the door behind them.

"What do you have planned today," Gibbs asked as they all sat down at a natural wood table in the middle of the room.

"We have a light day, Special Agent Gibbs,"

Milona replied, "I've got a couple of classes in Philosophy at the University and Lieutenant Mathis will be meeting with the legal firms downtown. Same as the other day, really."

"You weren't expected until later," Gibbs asked, "any special reason why you're early?"

"No, sir," Geof said, as he and Milona looked to each other. "Our CO moved our arrival time to take advantage of a weather pattern at the *Calendar* site," he added flatly.

"I see," Gibbs said, as he paused for a moment.

He could not think of any other questions for them, given that he had no other leads, and that he was under orders not to interrogate the Morlocks in the first place. He was merely sent there to keep a running dialogue with these visitors, but he found it difficult sometimes to hide his frustration with their lack of information. Gibbs always found himself suspicious of the Morlocks, but nothing looked out of the ordinary today, not compared to the dozens of trips they had made under his supervision, as he saw it, so he drew a blank and let them proceed. Perhaps it's nothing, he thought, as he had found himself suspicious of many people and situations.

"We should be going," Milona said, nodding at Geof, and the two stood up and turned for the door.

"Do call me if anything changes," Gibbs asked.

"Of course," she said with confidence.

*

Milona took a second to gather her wits upon

sitting down in the driver's seat of a red convertible car provided by the Army, tossing her bag into the back seat as Geof sat down in the passenger seat. That driver training, she thought, always comes in handy in this frame. He sat quietly beside her, fighting the urge to laugh out loud as he thought about the special agent and his feigned briefing.

"Hold it back," she said in a motherly tone, firing up the engine. "We're not off the base yet."

She looked over and allowed a smile as she popped the clutch and launched the sporty vehicle forward down the drive away from the white building. Gibbs and Captain Oglesby watched them from behind as Geof allowed himself to laugh.

It was such a beautiful morning, Milona thought, recalling that for her, it was only half an hour ago when she was running across a wet landing platform in a heavy afternoon rain. The Sun was now rising behind them in a crisp blue sky, and she found the temperature very soothing.

"It's not a bad assignment," she added, talking as if she were thinking out loud.

"What do you mean?" he asked, still struggling to pull his mind off the agent as they drove.

"Oh. Well, look around," she said, realizing she had spoken aloud.

She guided the car as they rolled through the large forest-like base, down hilly blacktop roads near the center and toward its main gate. He understood what she had meant and did not respond. He had frequently noted how simple the past seemed, even though it was so polluted and vastly unequal, socially and economically. Although, in some ways, it's really not all that different from our own time, he thought, at least not in these remote areas of North America. I could easily live here, because after all, people are still people, he mused.

Milona turned on the radio, looking to Geof for approval. She found it was still set to a local popular station she had found on her last trip, and was pleased the captain's staff had not changed anything. She thought about how she had been finding some of the more mechanical sounding music in the past to be similar to popular music of her day. Other music she found very different, such as the songs with a chanting tone and aggressive instrumentation. Geof instead found he liked much of the more aggressive music, if only because it was so different, but he had little patience for it after a few minutes. They listened to several songs without comment as they drove on, enjoying the morning air from the open car.

As they rolled through the main gate and away from Fort Jackson, through the neighborhoods of the South Carolina capital city, Milona began to wonder to herself how she could possibly complete her mission. Senator Hassan's words during their meeting rang in her ears again and again, as she thought about what needed to be done. Murder had never been a part of her missions up to now, most were mere observations, making recordings, doing simple research. There were a few manipulations of social situations, perhaps, but never murder. Of course, she thought, her RSF training was very thorough, including many types of warfare, covert operations and counter-assassination, and her orders were very clear. But, emotionally and morally, she continued to ask herself down deep how they were going to do it. How could we destroy an innocent person? They eventually arrived near the University's Humanities buildings on campus, and she drew the car to a curb to change places.

"I'll see you at around one," she said in the common lingo, looking at her watch face, thinking it should give her more than enough time.

"Until then, Miss Devon," he quipped.

"See you, Geof."

She smiled and watched as he jumped over into the driver's seat and took off. She then headed down the sidewalk toward the classroom building where Professor Nexin's Eighteenth Century class was to meet, but then realized she was going to be late. She had not thought much about the time of day, but her cover story as an unemployed writer working on a first book had benefited from a certain tardiness on her part, so she decided not to worry about it.

As she approached the building, she noticed Peter's red bike outside, locked to a rusty rack, one they had observed him riding once before. Here is this bike again, she noted, stopping to stare at it for just a moment, studying the lines of its red frame, its polished spoke wheels and components. It seemed such a simple machine to her, so rugged and uncomplicated. She snickered as she thought about how this bike was becoming an icon for her mission, about how she had thought of this very bike while watching the Chancellor visit the station only hours before. I wonder why, she mused, but then it was obvious to her. I've had bikes myself, still do.   Especially during my school days, when I was at the École, I rode everyday.   That was also a red bike, not so different from this one, in fact.

Perhaps, that's it, she thought.   With so many advances, it's easy to forget that some things don't change.   Some simple ideas cannot be improved upon. Even the people here in the past seem to miss that sometimes.   We all do, I guess.   Maybe when I get back, when all this is over, I can go to visit Mother in Paris for a while.   I'll pull that bike out again and go for a ride through the streets of the city!   As she continued staring at the bike, she slowly pulled her thoughts back to her mission, then looked up at the classroom building and again started walking.

PART TWO

11

"Oh no, Milona," Olen Nadimov said, gently putting his wine glass down on the table.

Olen sat proudly in his red dress uniform across a dinner table from Milona on the outer deck of an observation ship, which hovered over the coastline of the Mediterranean. Kanimora's celebrated recent *String Quartet No. 12* played in the background, and a clear, glassy model ship with rounded shapes and people moving inside floated above the table with two playpads laying before them. Olen looked from the model to Milona, her revealing dark green cocktail dress, as he he thought, set off the pulled-up curls of her hair and her bright smile.

"I'm not sure I can let you have it," he continued, "You didn't win, because..."

"Why," Milona said, grinning after taking an elegant sip of her wine.

"Because... You cheated."

"Oh, I cheated, then?" she said, crossing her legs so that he could better see them, highlighted with sheer tights, batting her eyebrows at the same time as she leaned back slightly with a smile.

"You cheated when you said you'd been to the

ship two times to retrieve the cargo. The transport logs show you were there only once."

"So, you caught me fudging numbers. It's a game, Doctor," she said, gently brushing the toe of her shoe against his leg.

"I dunno," he continued, "I think it establishes a pattern of deception."

"A pattern? It was one little thing," she pleaded as she leaned inward for emphasis.

Olen could not avoid taking delight at her curves, the gentle, fair skin of Milona's neck, shoulders and cleavage. He reached out and touched her hand, turning his fingers under hers on the table cloth. She smiled with satisfaction that her clear signals had not been missed.

"Enough of this particular game, though," he said directly, dropping his head.

Milona returned his look without indication, doing and saying nothing as she sat motionless. He could feel the lack of air circulation on his skin as he sat, his mind racing with nothing other than the string music and distant movement to indicate any passage of time. He began to feel stupid as he sat there staring at her, wondering why he had put so much faith into her scripted responses.

"Save program," he said, disappointed in himself as he continued to stare at Milona's welcoming avatar gaze.

He looked around at the model, at the view across the deck, at the whole fantastic scene he had created. This basic program was a popular one, role-playing holo-games which could be modified as one liked.   Before *Tempo* became all-consuming for everyone involved, Olen had spent some of his free time making modifications to the logistics game, but as quickly lost interest in his "Crystal Ship", despite having added Major Devon to it rather recently.

"Stop program," he added.

The music and dining deck, the observation ship, the Mediterranean and the lights of Monaco all faded away.   Milona faded away too, as Olen sat holding a blank look on his face matching hers.   I'll never get a satisfactory response from her, he thought to himself, standing as the chair underneath him faded away.   I'm not even sure if this major's personality is anything like that!

"Open blinds," he said, turning slightly.

He walked over toward the balcony doors of a high-rise apartment as the blinds opened the room, letting in the bright mid-afternoon light and crisp air of Berlin.   Glass doors slid open as he approached and he walked out onto the balcony, leaned on the rail, and overlooked the massive city toward the Southwest.   He had taken some time away from the Science Centre to regroup, and now fell into a near trance as he found himself studying the skyline of the city, the colours of many commercial and military ships passing by, the people and cars moving along the streets below, the sounds and scents of trams, music and restaurants.

Although he thought he was probably coming off as aggressive earlier, he felt deeply honoured to be aboard that incredible space station *Orbis* for lunch with the Science and Operations Directors and to see the Chancellor's visit among the other red-uniformed

Intel officers. Where I come from, he thought, such an opportunity doesn't come along so easily. I wish Director Zhang had more faith in me, but then, I'm really a true outsider, I suppose. "A stranger in a strange land," he mumbled to himself, as he looked across the wide cityscape of Berlin.

What a society! He swooned, taking in the endless vista as he looked back and forth across the sprawling historic city. Such vast technological prowess across the globe and well into the Solar System, sustainable democratic systems blended with cultural traditions, a distributed five-branch government with minimal poverty or terrorism, it seems. In my day, most of us lived in constant fear, the ones who were lucky enough to live. The disease and corruption, the wars and arrogance, somehow it didn't seem so scary until I saw all of this. It makes sense to me, now, and I think I want to stay here. I could be happy here in Berlin with UN Science, or the Intelligence Command Centre in Moscow would be nice too, or really anywhere. Anyway, I cannot... Olen fought the sudden emotion as tears formed in his steely eyes. I cannot go back! he thought.

"I cannot go back," he said aloud.

*

Olen studied himself in the mirror, noting his jet-black hair, flush, deep skin and bright silver eyes, staring into himself as he splashed his face with water from the running tap. He had turned on some Jazz music from a local Berlin trio in the background, and every few seconds he could feel a small rush of breeze come through the apartment from the still open balcony. He ran his hands through his short hair, and then looked at the reflection of his dress uniform coat. He unbuttoned it from the collar as he looked on it with a still uneasy pride. His rank display was three brass squares and one ivory square, all with thin black edging which fit snugly together, while his small number of ribbons for his rank sat below, and just above his blue-on-silver Scientist-Engineer Badge which featured the atomic cube insignia. The detailed UN emblem-etched buttons then revealed a plain white form-fitting shirt underneath. He took another moment or two to stare at himself in the mirror. After weeks in Berlin, he was still filled with the utter amazement of even being there, overwhelmed with everything he found so new. He turned away and lay the coat over onto a dressing rack, and then out of nowhere, it seemed, the problem struck him again. Damn it! he thought to himself.

"Run program, 'Shield Five'," he said, looking back at himself in the mirror, thinking it was a wonder he could stop thinking about this problem at all.

The Jazz music fell silent, and the sitting room down a short hallway was immediately filled with a brightly coded spherical simulation of an amorphous field approaching a model of the blue Earth. The field was coloured with red particles with a flat grid of yellow particles imaged between the planet and approaching field. He turned to his right and walked the few steps into the room to watch these red particles pass through the yellow field, touching, and then dispersing the model Earth.

"Pause program," he said, walking right through the particles across the bright room and toward the balcony. He picked up his larger polished duty tablet, pressed a few strokes across its surface and then looked up again at the dispersed particles.

"Replay program," he said.

The red particles reset and expanded to resemble a cloud, then again progressed toward the grid, and again passed right through it, touching the model Earth again, and then dispersing the model planet. The doctor tapped a few buttons again on his tablet surface.

"Replay program."

The program proceeded exactly as it had the first time, as he again walked through the simulation, back and forth across the room.

"Replay program!" he said again, and he watched as the simulation had again failed.

Olen's frustration with these simulations was compounded by the fact that this was the very latest version directly from the lab. He had set up full access to the laboratory data so he could remain updated with any changes while away or make changes himself. It was evident to him they simply were not given enough time to work out a fully functional solution.

"There's got to be a way around this!" he lamented, tossing his tablet across the room and onto a camel lounger. He was then relieved the tablet did not break apart on a harder surface.

"Stop program!" he said quietly under his rage, shaking his head as he paced back and forth around the apartment.

As the model faded away from the room, he grabbed his dress coat again and turned, going back into the main room.

"Why you, Milona?" he said aloud.

Why was the major in the middle of this? Why had *she* been making these trips to the past? Why her? He continued to fume and wonder as he pulled on his duty coat and buttoned it.

"Why do you get to live aboard *Orbis* and lead a team studying the precious Professor Nexin?" he continued aloud.

*

Assured his emotions were as straight as his clothing, he then walked out into the sitting room, grabbed the tablet from the lounger and looked to see if he had broken it. He turned and headed down the hall toward the door, then pushed a button on the doorframe to open it, as he did not like the auto-open feature on such main entry doors. He walked through, waited for the door to shut behind him, and then pushed in his code to lock it. He headed down the floor's warmly coloured corridor toward the lifts, walking with purpose and thinking of little else than the great problem, and then arrived at the building core, stepped into an open lift which had been called when he locked his door. He pressed for the ground level and stood silent as the doors quietly shut in front of him.

I have to ensure she does not mess things up for me, he ruminated, as the lift sped down, through forty-three of the ninety levels in his private residence building. He then stepped out of the lift at ground level and walked through the peach-coloured lobby, passing several people crisscrossing the large space, and out through double glass doors and onto a busy Berlin streetscape. The sounds of the city, the beeps and rushes of machinery, the conversations of passersby, all suddenly filled his ears.

"Good afternoon, Doctor Nadimov, sir," the doorman said, his deep brown uniform contrasting against a green metal and glass exterior of this residential tower in a clear afternoon light.

"Thank you, Thomas," he returned. "It's such a beautiful day."

"Yes it is, sir."

"I should be back late tonight."

"Thank you, sir. Have a nice afternoon, then."

Olen quickly walked down the busy sidewalk continually alerted, as he was out of habit of hearing them, by every passing car and metro tram. Various hydro-fusion drives made distinct whining noises as they sped past. He found he was slowly becoming accustomed to these sounds in the largest cities, and it helped if he tried to focus on the various fashions of passing pedestrians or cyclists, so he noted the details of long robes, revealing dresses, work-worn trousers and shirts, various types of business suits, and UN uniforms like his own.

He arrived at the express tram stop and stepped down three solid steps into a waiting area which was full of people, and then he noticed a tram coming down the channel. As it approached, he could make out the direction sign, reading "Tiergarten", which indicated his timing happened to be just right. The long white tram sped down the channel and glided to a stop above its guide rails, brake thrusters filling the air with their own noise. Boarding along with the others, people counters clicked furiously as boarders passed by door scanners. He looked around and between people, many of whom seemed to read or play on tablets and other devices, and eventually he found an open seat near the rear of the brightly lit car. I'd sat down just in time, he thought, feeling the gravity fields pull on his body as the long tram sped up to a cruise, gliding down the channel now at nearly two city blocks per second.

It's more than just my career, he thought to himself, now relaxing from having made such a quick transition from his apartment to the tram. He looked down at his tablet, an advanced scientific model from the laboratory of many they had on hand, and reflexively pressed a virtual button to check for any messages on its screen he may not have heard. It could mean my life, he continually mused, remarking at his own fascination with the now familiar device. The major's mission is jeopardizing my own past, and I've got to find a way to keep her from affecting me. If I can do that, he thought, looking back up and out of the tram windows onto fast-passing city blocks, maybe I'll be able to live here in peace.

12

Lieutenant Geoffery Mathis brought the red car to a stop at the end of a cul-de-sac near the complex of Humanities and Business Administration buildings to pick Major Devon up at their agreed upon time, finding her waiting there with a cold and distant look on her face. Milona plopped herself down into the passenger seat beside him, tossing her jacket onto her bag in back, and felt out of touch with reality, she thought, after her lunch with Peter. She tried to gather herself as he drove them on toward Peter's home.

"How is your day going?" Geof asked with a sense of futility.

The lieutenant knew he should not pry into his major's feelings, but on the other hand he also felt a sense of responsibility to look out for her because they were working on something obviously very difficult, emotionally.

"Fine," she said curtly, but then she wanted to retract it. "I'm sorry, Geof," she added after a second of pause, "I just don't know... I don't know if I can..."

"Of course you can, Major," he interjected. "No one said it would be easy, though," he added.

Geof's words always made sense, as both her

lieutenant and friend, but she still felt detached as they continued on, quietly driving toward the city's Shandon neighborhood.   When they eventually approached Peter's home, Mathis drew the sporty car near the opposite curb and down the street from the house. He turned the engine off, looking toward Nexin's house as Milona gazed blankly out through the windscreen, asking herself how best to go about taking care of the situation, if were to come to it.

"Nexin's disappearance or death cannot not draw attention to itself, other than the obvious effect on the timeline we are hoping," he recited.

He was merely thinking out loud, hopefully to keep his major on target.   Recruited separately by Colonel Ford, Geof had been Milona's right arm during these visits, working tirelessly during their advance missions.   They naturally developed an informal bond and way of working together.

"We could plant a bomb in his car, or in his home," he continued, "using extant technology of this time. But that doesn't seem right."

"Too much to cover," she said, slowly coming around, though still staring blankly, "and the local Police would be at a loss to reason why someone would blow up a Philosophy teacher's home," she added, then turning toward Mathis. "They will be able to find no seedy connections between Peter Nexin and any known criminals, and even some angry student with a failing grade could not possibly have a suitable motive for such an incident, political or otherwise."

"But," Geof theorized, resettling himself in the seat and raising his hand as he spoke, "we could arrange it to look like an accident, living alone in a modest house..."

"His relationship with the college could be strained, though, or so he has intimated in classes," she added, nodding her head.

"Yes," he continued, "his career may not be so bright from his perspective. Of course, he doesn't have the benefit of our hindsight on that count. Perhaps the best thing is simply to shoot him, leaving a suicidal appearance. Gun deaths are very common in this time."

"Yes," she thought out loud. "This would fit into the time period, it would look plausible given his situation, and it would avoid too many investigative trails. There's our plan."

They still had only a small amount of time to finalize their simple plan and find a weapon, but for now the plan seemed as cruel to them as it was simplistic enough, and it could be difficult to carry out. It would mean getting even more involved in Peter's life, Milona thought, as she rolled her eyes and head, overwhelmed. I'll have to establish closer personal access, to ensure the plan would work. If so, would I pull the trigger? Could I actually do it?

"What kind of assignment is this?" she asked rhetorically. "Why do we have to come here, to this time, and erase this good man? Why is it so important to us? We don't even know if he is directly connected through the timeline to this temporal, quantum disruption field," she continued, turning and pointing her finger, "or if the field will even do any damage at all when it does arrive!"

Geof endured her concerns without comment, letting her continue just a moment longer. He had his own doubts, not unlike Milona's or anyone else's, but he felt that he should keep them to himself, both because she was his superior, but also to help support her mission and diffuse her frustrations.

"Maybe this is all a joke," she continued. "Maybe we're in some vast simulation and don't even know it!"

Geof finally had enough, and felt the time was right. He reached over, and pinched Milona on the forearm, hard enough to sting, but he fully knew this was no real test of a simulation. He simply thought that in this moment it would make her feel better, if only for the time being.

"Excuse me, Lieutenant!" she winced, then paused, finally realizing her folly, then she snickered in approval. "Sorry, Geof," finally laughing aloud.

Geof laughed too, and both continued their laughter, each of them laughing harder at the other's laughs, each enjoying a short break from the strain of the awkward situation. After a few minutes, the two tired and regained themselves, and then Geof started the car up again, pulled them away from the curb and drove away from the professor's neighborhood.

The lieutenant found himself thinking this mission was already more emotionally draining and potentially costly than it had first seemed. Even as he had sat there, up in that command station, listening to the Chancellor and senators debate the issue, the risks with *Tempo* were just beginning to emerge for him. He worried that Milona was getting too involved with

Nexin, perhaps she was identifying too much with him romantically, perhaps even falling in love with him, and if things went wrong with their mission that way, the mess left behind could be incredible.

*

Halfway down the street on the next block, Agent Gibbs watched as they approached. He had done some legwork on the professor during their many visits, so he knew whose house the Morlocks were studying, but he could not figure out why. He threw himself down to lay over on his side across the seat to avoid being seen sitting in the plain brown car. When he felt the red convertible had passed far enough away behind him, he sat up, grabbing the steering wheel for leverage.

"I knew it!" he said out loud, slapping the steering wheel as he spoke. "I had a hunch they were up to more than simple research," he added. "Devon has been studying at the school to get close to this professor, and Mathis could have been simply establishing cover and support."

"Bulldog?" said Special Agent Tanner, a CIA case officer on the other end of Gibbs' earpiece radio, "what are you talking about? We don't know what they're planning."

"Need to get the Astros on standby," Gibbs said.

"Bulldog?"

"Cornea, it's just a hunch," he offered, "I'm going to station back at the playground," he added.

Though not disobeying any orders, Gibbs also knew he was not encouraged to follow all of his hunches. Their visitors might be involved in something far more complex than it might seem from the outside, he was told. But that is just what bothered him, he thought, because this time what they were up to just looked fishy.

"If I'm wrong, then there will be no harm done," Gibbs said, and then he waited for the response, understanding the pause as Tanner conferred with their superiors.

"Go ahead, Bulldog," Tanner said, as Gibbs smiled, "but you will be extra careful, you understand."

Gibbs started up his car while he listened and turned around in the street, then tearing down the road on a direct heading toward them and University, smiled to himself.

"We don't want any contingencies with our visitors that aren't fully warranted," Tanner recited.

However, his hunches were beginning to pay off, Gibbs thought as he drove, but he was perplexed about one thing. He couldn't figure out what was so important about this professor. What could they learn from this Philosophy guy they couldn't find in any library, or off the 'net? Why did Devon have to interact with him at all? Gibbs continued down the streets of Shandon, turning everything over again and again in his mind. There is definitely some key... something, I need to find out, he thought. But from what I can tell, it's just not there, yet.

*

Geof continued driving the tree-lined streets of Shandon, crossing through Five Points and into the

University's main campus.   They were silent again during their ride, each of them feeling drained.   Geof thought he would drop the major off, rather than park at the Pendleton Street parking garage they used, since he had plans, including spending much of the afternoon at the offices of the legal firms he was researching. Being mainly on call for his major, they usually parked in this particular building so each could use the car if needed, as the law firms and classrooms were only blocks away from each other.   Reaching the garage, he rolled through the Bull Street entrance, half-way down the length of the garage, then crossed between two of the columns to the next row.

"I think I'll leave you here," he offered, "I just decided, I want to go to a coffee shop nearby, and I've got to go to an office away from downtown."

"That sounds refreshing," she said.

"Yes," he said, "I think I need an energy boost."

"Of course," she said, "I could use one myself. I think that nap time we planned this afternoon sounds unavoidable."

"Use the 'cell', as they call it, if you need me."

Geof motioned to the phone in his coat pocket issued by Army Intelligence. They rarely used the phones, assuming the devices would be monitored, but occasionally they would make use of them, carefully coding their language accordingly.

"I will," she said.

Geof drove away smoothly, and he was looking forward to a visit to the local coffee shop as usual. Milona simply stood in place, again getting a kick out of watching Geof drive a car. How strange it is to be here, she thought, seeming to feel so comfortable with antiquated technologies, wearing the clothes, learning the lingo, arranging a murder. It's all so elaborate, she thought, now starting to wish she were getting a coffee, too, as she swooned. As a result, she found herself a little disoriented, and decided not to walk to the classroom building just yet. She lingered over to the edge of the garage, looking out at the buildings, trees and passersby, feeling the light breeze and listening the building's generators hum. She gave herself just a moment again to think of nothing in particular, if she could possibly manage it.

Unable to avoid thinking, however, Milona found herself feeling increasingly ambivalent about her duties, almost wishing she could stay here in the past and forget about everything back in the present. Back home, she thought, wondering if her small, sparsely decorated quarters on a space station could really be a "home". I suppose I could live in Paris, with Mother, but I'd probably have to leave UN Command to do it. 'You're just like your father,' Mother would always say, 'more concerned with your duty than with being happy.' "Well, I am happy, Mother," she said aloud, "aren't I?" she added, trying to convince herself.

She then walked around a corner to the terrace on Level Three, trying to relax her thoughts, but found it was hopeless, and after a few minutes, she realized she needed to get moving for Nexin's other class. She then turned and walked back toward the corner of the garage, glancing at a large "3" pressed into the concrete, then down the two flights of stairs to the ground level and through the doorway leading to the street corner. Bright daylight blinded her momentarily, but her eyes adjusted as she made her way down the walk behind the Barnwell and Sloan buildings toward the camel-coloured Welsh Humanities buildings. She could feel the faint breeze again, coursing through the lush green leaves, greeting her as she walked. Something doesn't feel right, she thought, but I don't have time to worry about it, and maybe I'm just tired and in need of some sleep. I'm sure it's nothing, but it just feels like I'm being watched.

13

The long tram glided to a stop at Tiergarten after the short ride from Alexanderplatz, the braking thrusters again making noises as Olen and other passengers rose from their seats. The gravity fields helped them move almost normally as they filed out of the car, people counters clicking again, and then Olen's tablet issued a faint, muffled beep, as he carried it under his arm. Olen glanced at it as it displayed a message from the city's Transit Authority, a reminder of an upcoming local political forum and an appreciation for using the tram. He continued with the others out of the express, stepping up out of the channel waiting area to the nearby sidewalk, to cross over toward the Science Centre's Plaza.

He walked across the wide open space, always noting the tall, cubic design of its fountain, as he approached the large, white panel and glass front of the UN Science Centre. The structure housed key leaders and laboratories of the many scientific programmes, their Intelligence Science and Defense Development teams, and was situated near the historic Reichstag. Olen walked with purpose again, amused by the pigeons, the heavy foot and bike traffic crisscrossing the Plaza, and still felt amazed by his luck at being able to see the Chancellor on her visit to *Orbis*. For the last few moments of his tram ride, he had been able to ignore his concern over *Operation Tempo*, although he was beginning to return to his worries about the field research being done by his team.

Making it to the main entrance of the building, Olen took delight as he often did at the angular design of its six visible levels from this viewpoint, its ring-shaped glass and steel observation level above the restaurant, which rotated very slowly over a barely visible gap, supported only by a beveled magnetic field between it and the restaurant level atop the main building. The Science Centre was a regular tourist destination as well, especially due to this magnetic rotation feature, and this afternoon Olen found the usual line of visitors from seemingly every nationality. The member nations were represented by a ring of national flags on the top of the Observation Deck, all leaning outward and rotating with the deck, as it gently turned around and around.

He imagined the visitors now filing inside would go up to that top level, wait to take the stairs through to the floating ring, perhaps enjoy a strong coffee near the windows, taking in the view of Berlin's historical district, and then move on to their other points of interest. He recalled spending a day very much like that when he first arrived, but the crisis at hand prevented him from enjoying much of that kind of free time of late. Continuing in through one of the doors, Olen looked up to the huge, historic UN emblem and its atomic Science insignia repeated on his badge.

He was cleared and waved on by several UN Security Patrol officers at the doorways. They looked ready for anything to Olen, sporting their duty uniform coats and trousers, sidearms and utility belts, plain silver badges with rifle insignia. As he continued through a large, painted steel and glass, sculpture-dominated lobby, toward the elevators at the bare concrete core section of the building, he felt a part of something very important.

With several other officers, he stepped into an open lift, directed it down, and they stood silent after all of them nodded to each other. When they reached Lower Level Two, the steel-lined doors opened onto a concrete corridor leading to secured labs. He nodded toward the others again, and continued down the hall, its left wall accented by a collection of science-oriented artworks, and he passed several scientists and other personnel along the way. "Colonel," "Mister Chief," or "Doctor," each greeted as they passed, depending upon the professional interactions the passing officers had with Olen, who was well-known in this part of the building. Nearly all of his time was spent there, especially in the last few days.

Olen reached the end of the corridor, its large glass panel allowing a wash of light with a view of the River Spree behind the building. He approached another metal double door painted grey to match the bare concrete, across which it read "201" in red. The scanners read his programmed signal from the tablet and opened the doors automatically, bypassing the keypad controls to the right. He then walked into the main office of laboratory, noting immediately the other scientists at work in the modeling lab, all discussing the problems with their own versions of the model. Olen already knew what they were talking about, having followed all the messages since he left the lab late the night before, and he focused for a moment on the faint dance music playing from someone's desk as a small grin came over him.

In the middle of the modeling lab, a very large, dark grey room which limited extraneous sound and light, there was a four-metre-tall model, rendered from the same data he had reviewed and updated at home. It now showed the detailed particle field approaching a dispersion matrix in larger detail. The field passed right through the matrix again, but appeared to have been partially disrupted before reassembling on the other side. Olen realized they had been making some promising changes as he commuted, and felt a tingle of hope in the project.

"We'll have to tweak the polarization of the matrix," Doctor Michelle Lambert then said as Olen crossed the modeling lab.

Lambert was a talented, widely published, and respected Belgian physicist, and was Director Franklin's managing scientist in the Particle Laboratory. She was rather thin and stood at medium height, and today wore her straightened, long sandy-brown hair pulled back, showing the soft, caramel-like brown skin of her neck. She had on a blue blouse and a black skirt under the open white waistcoat common to the civilian scientists. Michelle's blue-on-silver badge just left of her lapel, along with Olen's, caught the faint light as she turned and moved around in the bright display of the model.

"Good work, everybody," Olen cheered as everyone turned to greet him.

Lambert and the three assistant scientists, all dressed in plain clothes, had been so involved they hardly noticed their section chief arrived until he spoke.

"Welcome back," Michelle said with a smile, "did you enjoy meeting the Chancellor up on *Orbis*?"

"Very much so, it was quite the treat," he said, noting across the faces of Michelle and the others a definite look of envy. "I've been following the progress," he continued, "and it looks like you've gotten the field to at least register that there was something in its path."

"Yes," she returned, "We've been working on this all day. We just can't get the field to disperse for more than a few milliseconds. Somehow, it keeps rebuilding itself."

"Keep trying," he urged, "Keep trying."

"Wait!" she said to the assistants. Michelle had subliminally picked up on Doctor Nadimov's use of the word "register", which led her to a thought about the harmonic registers, which led to the question of the frequencies being used, thoughts they had all tossed around before. "What if we boost the array strength two or three-fold, but at the same time, shift the harmonic stack, and on top of that, double or triple the emissions from alternate angles?"

"We... would have to reconfigure the nodes," said one assistant, James Perkins, overwhelmed by the task, but quickly seeing Doctor Lambert's point.

"Get busy," she urged.

*

Olen smiled at this renewed brainstorm and turned away from the modeling lab, walked along the concrete wall of the office, past a few desks divided by red, metal separators, and up a short, honeycomb metal staircase onto a mezzanine row of four glass and red-metal-lined offices against another concrete wall. The first and largest office in the row had been issued to him for temporary use during this project, but a project that was so important it hardly seemed worth Science Director Franklin's time to worry about giving so much control to a relative outsider. If things worked out, she had told him, she was sure the office, perhaps even a better one, would be his on a more permanent basis, and otherwise, it wouldn't matter, anyway. Franklin knew this possibility could keep Doctor Nadimov and the others strongly motivated.

"Play news," he said toward the far wall.

The screen lit up with his favourite network feed, which in this update was covering pundit suggestions about the visit of the Chancellor and senators to *Orbis*. The afternoon light of Berlin streamed through vertical blinds, and Olen pushed a small button to open them a bit more before he sat down on a small lounger to think to himself. Shift the harmonics? Olen questioned to himself. He tuned out the news and scratched his chin briefly as he fidgeted on the lounger. Yes, I suppose that could work, and the energies pulling field elements back together just might be overcome by the alternating directions of disruption. It's brilliant! Olen was very proud of Michelle and her team. Yet, if things stop looking so good for us here, he thought, then I might have to consider the major's temporal mission as the only way out of this jam. However, if she is successful before we become operational, the changes to the timeline could be devastating for me. I've got to come up with a way to set her plans back, somehow. I think I know what is necessary, if I can...

"Olen," Michelle interrupted.

The two doctors were on a first name basis almost since Olen first arrived. He had ensured the two of them got on well, because he had effectively displaced her as the laboratory lead, taking the corner office she seemed to await. However, Doctor Lambert found she had been happy enough these last few weeks without the added pressures of interfacing with UN Intelligence. She knew her chance would come, and then she would be ready.

"We think we've succeeded in dispersing the field!" she added, nodding her head with excitement as she spoke, her ponytail bouncing.

"What?" he asked, surprised. "How? That's great news, Michelle," he added, standing back up, startled they could reconfigure the systems so quickly. "Show me," he said excitedly as he walked toward her, the both of them rushing down the stairs.

"We have you to thank as much as anyone," she said modestly, looking back on him as they rushed into the modeling lab, "We could have spent at least several more hours on this, but you put a bug in my ear which led to this solution. Sometimes, all it takes is a fresh look, which you must have gotten by getting out of here for a while."

"You are very welcome," he said with surprise, lingering with an innocent smile in her direction, then he looked around to everyone, adding, "Okay."

"Replay program," Michelle said, bouncing slightly on her heels with excitement at their progress.

The particle field appeared as a cloud, moved toward the dispersion matrix, and then as the field appeared to begin passing through the matrix again, it started to disrupt, resulting now in a chain-reaction that dissipated its energy throughout the nodal network of the matrix.

"Unbelievable!" Olen yelled, instantly relieved and loosening up everyone else, who all followed him and began to yell and whistle, all running around to hug each other and carry on. "But what about the integrity of the nodes? It looks like you've just burned them out completely," he added.

"If it disperses the field, nobody will care," James quipped, standing near Reg and Sonia, the other assistants.

"True. But are our existing nodes configured to do what you programmed here?" he said toward Michelle. "Just trying to cover everything," he added.

"No," Michelle responded, "but they can be retooled, probably in an hour's time with help. Of course, we still have to get them fully deployed out beyond the immediate Solar System in time, too."

Olen paused for just a second as he prepared them for another commotion.

"But... we did it!" he exclaimed with a jump.

"We did it!" they all screamed in unison.

"Wait, though," he again cautioned. "What if the depth of the real field out there is too large for our matrix, so that various nodes burn out before the entire field passes?"

They all immediately fell silent together, and each began considering possible failures. The more outspoken of the assistants was James Perkins, a tall young man with a strong Scottish accent, dark reddish skin and black hair, dressed in canvas trousers with a white shirt. He had technical officer clearance with UNI and was also an Assistant Scientist in the lab, not just a lab assistant. He held up his work pad, a larger polished metal tablet, and keyed in a few changes.

"Replay program," he said, hoping Doctors Lambert and Nadimov would not scold him for being so brash.

This time the field was a deeper cloud with more intensity, then approached the matrix of nodes, yet the cloud still became fully dispersed through the same chain reactions within the field itself.

"We did it," James shouted, reverting back to elation, and everyone chimed in likewise. Quite relieved, but unsure as to what he had accomplished, he reasoned it out. "Apparently, the trick is in just getting the reactions started," he added. "When that happens, our nodes themselves don't seem to have as much to do with the outcome as they did before."

"So, you programmed them to shut down?" Michelle asked James.

"Yes."

"Then we can power the real units down sooner

and save their capacity for a second pulse if it's needed," Michelle said, nodding and pursing her lips toward Olen.

"Excellent!" James said, suitably impressed with his own work.

"Very impressive," Olen said, impressed with the others and the quick turn of events, looking at this young scientist. He then tapped one of the faintly glowing light buttons on the edge of the doorway, waiting for a faint beep. "Call Director Franklin's office," he said over the chatter of the dancing scientists, followed by a beep from the system as it rang the Science Director's assistant up on Upper Level Four. "You've all done very well," he said quietly, as he awaited the response from the director or her assistant, still with worry in the back of his mind about what he could possibly do regarding Major Devon.

14

Listening to the young students, one Peter was fond of encouraging academically that semester posed her question, and he offered an honest concentration on the discussion. Like many, she frequently sat very quietly through classes, and perhaps, he sometimes questioned, it was her beautiful cocoa skin, cool-looking glasses, or the way she often carried herself, but it did not matter. In every class, there was at least one shy, intelligent male or female student for whom he paid extra attention to coax out of their shell, and in this class, it was Keisha.

Besides, he rarely had such chances to engage in debate, as people in general do not seem to like to have conversations these days, he often noted. They want to be able to speak their mind and have it unconditionally accepted, no matter how irrational, but they deny others the same courtesy by tuning them out. Americans don't think, Peter would say, they grunt. Consequently, he absorbed as much as possible from any discussion.

"But if we can travel through time," Keisha said, straightening her back in the plastic and metal student desk, "doesn't it have to do with the speed of light?"

"Perhaps," Peter replied enigmatically, smiling at her and the others with approval, but also concentrating on the problem as he stood from leaning on the desk to pace over to the edge of the room closer to her for emphasis. "Perhaps it is possible that light speed, which seems incredibly fast to our minds, so fast that we can't really even get a feel for it, maybe that super-speed is just a slow trot to some of the more hidden forces and effects in the Universe?" He then moved to the board to begin to sketch an idea.

During the course of the class, Milona shook off her worry of something not feeling right. She had hurried into the building just as the class was starting, found a seat and settled in. Now she found herself enthralled by the current discussion and watched as Peter interacted with his students masterfully, deep down hoping he would notice her as well. Peter and Milona then caught each other's eyes, looking at each other briefly. Peter allowed a small smile to pass across his face, but he continued, trying to send no signals to the students. He tried to stay focused on the discussion with only a few minutes to go in the class time.

"So," Peter continued, "let's say we instantly took off from where we are standing, say in a ship or whatever, and shot off to the Moon, or to Jupiter, or the edge of the Milky Way, and then came back in less than a blink of the eye. Perhaps then, would we not only appear to ourselves to have gone nowhere, but would we have also travelled backward in time within the same split-second?"

The students, he often thought, seemed positively awestruck by this proposition as he continued to keep up the pressure. Each of them sitting still, either looking at the professor or slightly away, all wrapping their mind around the problem, or so he chose to believe. Peter knew this kind of topic was slightly above the heads of those coming into an introductory course, but he also felt that once in a while, he had to give them something to reach toward, in that way, something very hard to figure out. He wanted to push them with something difficult or strange when he could, rather than simply settle for them memorizing historical materials or attaining low standards.

"Of course, the problems of how this is going to happen, and how the human body can withstand such forces, must be challenged, but scientists can figure those problems out," he said.

Milona implicitly agreed with Peter's ideas as she listened on with the concentration of a pupil, but she was also finding herself overcome with feelings for Peter. She had fought it, she thought, surely she had fought it, but now found herself falling so completely in love with him, right then and there as he spoke, as he gestured, and as he paced around the front of the room proposing what must seem like crazy ideas to these young people. Peter is engaging in a mating ritual and doesn't even know it, she thought.

"But," he added, "why do the official accounts of this temporal shift assume that '*Time* slows down'? How is it that *Time* slows down due to the incredible speed of travel?"

Peter looked at Milona while she was just then finally looking around the room instead of at him. He hoped her eyes could catch his, because despite his ability to focus on the discussion, he found himself falling for her, unable to avoid it.

"What are you talking about?" Lenny quipped, jarring the professor, Keisha, and others, who allowed themselves to snicker to relieve tension.

A prodigy who was now a Physics major, Lenny found it patently ridiculous to question the official Science of Eisenstein's theories. Peter knew that such thinking overlooked the fact that those they studied had all questioned these standard models. Brilliance, Peter often said, was not in memorizing, but in coming up with something new that fit the evidence.

Milona pursed her lips for a moment, thinking she might be a witness to a certain intellectual power in Peter she had not quite seen before. Encouraging her even more toward falling for him was his sheer willingness to question the seemingly obvious doctrines of the day. That Peter was pushing these young students to ask questions in ways they probably would never hear of otherwise, so rare that did teachers ever do this, that it was magnetic. Her next thought, she lamented, was also a disturbing feeling that she now had more of the evidence than she ever needed to complete her true mission. Her excitement twisted instantly into sadness.

"Why," Peter answered, while attempting to impress Milona, "does the idea that going fast necessarily involve the dilation of *Time*?"

"Because," Lenny said, "that's what the

experiments you talked about showed, right? *Time* ran slower when the clock on the plane was brought back."

"Yes, the airborne clock showed a shorter timespan, if you will, by fractions of a second," Peter said slowly, "I'll give you that." Several students smiled and laughed, anticipating a clever wiggle out of this. "But all which has ever been observed, or proven, is that the apparent time measured had been shorter, not that *Time* itself was dilated." The room again fell silent as brains computed this, and Peter felt they were pausing on his suggestion correctly. "The 'Concorde Experiment', which we talked about the other day, seems to definitely show that one clock slowed down due ostensibly to the speed of travel, as do our numerous satellites in Space every day, but does that really mean that *Time* itself flowed slower inside the airplane?" Peter then paused for a moment, allowing the students to reason, "Or, could it just be, that the very real forces of Magnetism which made up the surrounding air, the seat and dinner tray table, and so on, that they physically slowed the clock down?"

"But the clock was atomic," Keisha chimed, "not physical."

"Yeah, that was an atomic clock, not a wristwatch," Lenny added, several other students laughing, Milona finding him cute to watch as he struggled with Peter's logic.

"Atomic clocks," Peter asked, "are not part of the Universe? Atoms don't respond to forces?"

He smiled with a satisfaction of having achieved his goals for the class as silence again fell on the room. The students were all focused on the problem, and Keisha was coming out of her shell quite nicely.

"True," Lenny stubbornly admitted.

"See, an atomic clock is still very much a part of the physical system in which it sits, just as much as any wristwatch," Peter explained. "In fact, I could argue it may even be easier to affect it through Electromagnetic forces, since its elements are not as bound with other physical systems, like the wristwatch could be. But that part aside, the question is why did the clock run slower? It's not because *Time*, this mystical 'dimension' no one has ever shown exists, was itself slower by the hand of Man, in some equally mystical way which has not been shown. Isn't it likely the clock simply found more resistance to ticking, if you will, given the forces acting upon the atoms as they were hurled across the Atlantic on a Concorde at supersonic speeds."

The room was again silent, but Peter could also sense that ticking clock in every classroom just before class time is about to run out. "Next time you're in a car, stick your hand out the window and think about it." He paused for a moment longer to let this last sink in. "See you next time."

*

Blending with the students leaving after class, Milona was finding herself more impressed with Peter than she had ever anticipated. She lingered for a moment or two as if she were a student, thinking perhaps she could ask Peter a question about the class discussion. What interested her was how Peter might envision time travel, and she wondered about his view on how a time machine could be constructed, given his view of the famous clock experiment. Really, though, the truth was she knew she only wanted to be around him, to continue whatever was happening, to avoid returning to reality. She waited for the young people to leave, most of whom she felt were happy enough to be getting out of class regardless of how interesting a particular topic had been. Then she found herself standing with a few of them near the desk, each also waiting their turn to ask various questions of the challenging professor.

"Hello, there," Peter said to Milona, as Keisha, Lenny and a couple of the other students lingered as well after the other students had moved on.

Peter wanted to at least acknowledge Milona's presence, especially after their lunch, but he did not wish to give off the impression to the students that she was a student getting special treatment, even though she was not a student at all. It just looked in poor taste, to him.

"I was just wondering," Milona asked, "how do you think a time machine could actually work, given the kind of forces you're talking about. I mean, wouldn't it have to be done using a wormhole, and not a flying machine travelling really fast?"

Milona felt, given her training, she might actually know more about these things than Peter, but she simply wanted to engage him.

"Yeah," Lenny said, looking to the professor then Milona, "how would you create the temporal dilation in a wormhole?"

"Well, I don't think a flying machine would work," Peter said. "I think creating a wormhole is the way to go about it. If the clock in a plane found it harder to tick, as I've put it, when under great speed, imagine how the human heart would manage to pump blood anywhere near light speed. We talked about this in the other class last semester, you'll remember, Lenny."

"Yes."

"I mean, is it really *Time* that's slowing down in this situation, or is it that a physical system is grinding slower? So, I imagine setting up some kind of a module with some capability to generate a space-time bubble, or a warp field, as they would say on TV. This way, the device creates the field, which itself creates the wormhole, which then makes the dilation relative to two mouths of the tunnel. If you keep the ends of the tunnel together, then in theory it would create a local temporal wormhole. Thorne and others have said that much."

Milona was surprised, since this was basically how she understood *Calendar* to work, but she also knew that science fiction writers and raw researchers of the day had proposed a dozens of different theories on how it could work, so it did not even bother her to be talking about it. Still, she did not know of anyone proposing this particular scenario at this time with the right connections, though.

"So, you're saying time travel could be done by a type of spaceship that doesn't really go anywhere?" Lenny asked.

"Yep," Peter answered.

"Wow," Lenny said. "That's pretty cool."

"Very interesting," Milona chimed.

*

Milona managed to slip away from Peter's classroom discussion with her last remaining social energies, telling him in passing she was exhausted, and perhaps would see him later. She made her way out of the building and into the afternoon light, continuing down the sidewalks with little more than a couple of blocks remaining. She walked very heavily on her feet, awaiting the womb of a hotel room, where she could sleep for a week, if need be.

She looked at her watch, remembering his words. 'Isn't it likely the clock simply found more resistance to ticking given the forces acting upon the atoms,' she recalled. Wasn't that what he said? 'It's murder, no matter how we look at it...' 'No one said it would be easy...' 'You're forgetting where I work...' 'You're concerned more with your duty than with being happy...' Milona's mind was becoming mushy, and in the rush of images from her complex day with the sounds of choral music underneath it all, she found it all too much to sort out while struggling down an ancient street, putting one foot in front of the other, ignoring passersby and traffic.

She finally felt the weight of events fully on her shoulders, and began to think of nothing more than taking that afternoon nap she and Mathis had so conveniently planned into their day. Almost like someone standing on a bright beach, or engulfed within a howling blizzard, or awash in perspiration during a heavy workout on a hot day, she felt utterly overwhelmed and quite ready to collapse. Indeed, it was like all of those feelings at once, she mused, as she walked down Main Street toward the hotel, only steps away. Everything had become a whiteout of images and emotions into which she felt totally immersed without any hope.

15

Olen rushed out of the lift now on Level Five of the Science Centre, turned to his right and headed down toward the secured entrance to the hangar. Like most of the UN's soft worksites, resources were restricted to UN personnel. Olen was waved on by two Security Patrol sergeants. The hangar doorway was not set to detect devices, but the security team was already alerted to the section chief's hurried departure. He stepped into the small hangar, open on both ends at the front and back of the building for traffic routing. He trotted up to a spacious blue four-passenger sedan-class shuttle, the pilot of which had accepted the dispatch and awaited the passenger. The drives were running at low speed as the shuttle sat idle.

Lifting the door, he thanked the pilot and hopped into the front passenger seat as the engines ran up to a higher pitched whine. The experience of the pilot was noticeable to him as she gently lifted the craft off of the hangar deck and then out the rear of the Science Centre, over the river and across the skyline of Berlin. Olen looked out the window, as the view became more dramatic upon leaving the Tiergarten area, this shuttle as one of many rising and crossing over the historic city in the afternoon light.

Director Franklin, who, it turned out was still aboard *Orbis,* had conferenced in Director Zhang during her scientists' news using the main viewscreen in the laboratory. After their short conversation, the directors had agreed the doctor should request the first available shuttle to the station. Olen was understandably pleased, as his team had solved the basic problems, and he was to get up to the directors as soon as possible, proceed to the Intelligence Sector Meeting Hall and make a presentation to the Command Chiefs, updating everyone on these new developments.

Feeling he had only a few quiet moments to think providing no one beeped him, Olen tried to enjoy the ride. However, his thoughts moved away from the stunning view out the windows, and on to his problem with Major Devon. Perhaps I can try establishing an operative on the major's team, or recruit from her team, he thought. Too time consuming. Or maybe a shuttle pilot can be employed, or one of the *Calendar* control officers, somehow keeping them unaware, yet under direct orders, he countered. Too easy to report and trace. But then, what if I dismiss all of that. These shuttles always pass through or near the orbital arrays controlling power, communications and defense as they approach or depart *Orbis*. Perhaps this may be of help.

"Master Sergeant," he said, turning away from the view above the North Sea, as the shuttle began to turn upward, "do you happen to have any knowledge of the orbital systems?"

He had asked her politely enough, he thought, looking up through the upper windscreen, hoping to sound merely curious.

"Sergeant, sir," Sergeant Werner responded.

"Of course," Olen said, shaking his head apologetically. "Sometimes, with only a glance to a collar, it's difficult to tell three charcoals with one ivory from two and one," he added, feeling embarrassed.

"Colonel, are you curious about any system in particular? I used to work on the COM nodes, but I know about most of the systems."

"Lieutenant Colonel," he said, trying to make a joke as he smiled.

"Of course," she said, pleased that the colonel was so easygoing and kind to her. "Any systems in particular, sir?"

"I was curious about something. From where are the satellites controlled, Sergeant?"

"Well, as far as public information goes," she said, wondering why he did not simply call up the information on his work pad, or from the screen in front of him, "in the power matrices there is a node satellite, one within each array, secured to each central matrix to interface with the ground stations. Communications network nodes are free-floating, as are some of the other systems. The defense systems are highly classified, of course. Most of the orbital arrays are controlled from *Orbis*, which was part of its original purpose for being built. Sometimes, the power grids are operated from the surface as systems are backed up, but that's beside the point."

"Yes," he said, turning the possibilities over and

over in his thoughts as the shuttle lifted through the atmosphere and rounded a course toward a line of sight approach with the station. "It would be difficult to take control of any of it, I assume."

"Impossible, sir. All the systems have redundant backups, decentralization of controls, layered security protocols, encryptions, and there's *Centurion*, Defense Development's periphery screen network. This is in place among other functions to monitor the orbital systems controlled from the station or not. *Centurion* will scramble ships to intercept any objects out of line with specs, or help defend systems during an extrasolar attack, if there were one. All of this is on the public internet site for the station, sir."

"I see," he said, wondering to himself if perhaps it would be possible to put a single node out of order. He constructed a scene in his mind: A shuttle would strike the errant satellite after leaving the station, and it would be damaged, forced to an emergency landing. Let's say the pilot would not be able to figure out why the satellite was so far off course, why it wasn't destroyed by this *Centurion* system, or why he wasn't notified about it.

'Maybe the periphery screen is out Major,' the pilot would offer.

'It's happening,' the major would say.

'What's happening?' the pilot would ask. 'There's just a glitch in the outer grid, I think.'

The major would realize she had completely underestimated Nadimov, Olen thought. She would decide not to mention anything to the pilot, since he might be working for me, and she would simply wax cynical about it.

'The decline of civilization.'

'Yes, ma'am,' the pilot would laugh. 'Unfortunately, that satellite damaged our navigational systems. I'll have to put it down short, ma'am.'

'Carry on, then,' the major would order.

She would run to the nearby tram station, but she would be intercepted by someone she would take to be one of Nadimov's operatives. She would kick him out of the way and jump on the tram, making it to the power station anyway...

Interesting fiction, Olen thought. There could be little chance I would find someone, say a Defense specialist or anyone of the kind, who would have access to the *Centurion* systems. The operations of these orbital grids, how the satellites are monitored, and so on, it's all too complicated to put something together on such short notice, especially with my clearances. But even if I could, and if the timeline were also altered in such a way as to take the major out of the equation, anything I set up now would disappear in that timeline, since she would never have been a foe in such a scenario. But, all of this is ridiculous, anyway, Olen corrected, laughing at himself.

"Sir, we're coming in to *Orbis*," Werner said, "so if you want to talk about it further, you can call me. This shuttle's call sign is 'UN-SHL-91'."

"Thank you, Sergeant," he said.

Olen was startled at himself after letting his imagination run away. The strain of the day was getting to him, he mused. What folly, imagining I could possibly gain control of key systems! "Ninety-one, you say? I might call on you for my next ride," he added.

"Yes, sir," she said, bringing the craft into a smaller hanger at Level Three in the Intelligence Sector. "I will be on duty until twenty-four hundred UTC, Colonel. Have a good visit on the station, sir."

Jumping out of the craft, he nodded to the sergeant, and straightened his coat with one hand as he walked across the hangar. Yes, it's all too complex, he thought, stepping into the corridor and to the right toward the lifts, better to stick to what I can control, rather than what I cannot. The reflective doors of a lift opened, he hurried inside then leaned face-in against the far side of the rounded vessel. The doors shut behind him, and he thought for a moment, realizing he could take a treadway over to the main lifts.

He became more and more frustrated worrying about the major, with how and why to interfere with her mission without being discovered, or how to persuade the directors to green light his team's model, or how to stay here without having to go back permanently. All of it swirled within Olen's mind as he stood silent with his face down. What could I possibly affect? he asked himself. What can I control? Decentralized and secure technologies do not lend themselves to such simple subversion, and my I2 clearance isn't very helpful with the other 4s they gave me along with it. The only option I might have available is to request passage through *Calendar*, he mused. But, how can I use this to my advantage?

The lift began moving automatically, called by

riders on other levels, and it offered a beep to indicate a last chance to specify the desired level.

"Level Ten," he said, keeping his face buried into the sand-coloured padding above the access panels.

*

After a moment to himself and after others had come and gone, Olen looked up from the lift wall, and said "Yes!" to himself. The only thing I can do is to try and get to the past, to disrupt her mission somehow, and harmlessly, that would be my only path. It's the only way to avoid any timeline alterations here. But first, I must convince them our model is worthy of a green light, otherwise I won't be authorized to go anywhere.

The lift came to rest on Level Ten and Olen rushed out and across to the treadway toward the sector's core. He began running at a slow pace, the travelator propelling him faster, as two Defense officers passed by in wonder. He nodded in the direction of the two, generals he thought, though it was hard to make out their squares as he ran. He continued on and quickly arrived at the core, slowing up a bit to calm down, then he bounded off the treadway at the foyer and walked quickly across the UNI seal, still trying to bring his heart rate down so that he would not break out into a sweat.

He continued to ruminate, but turned his thoughts onto the shield model, on how he could gain leverage in the timeline if he were sent to the past. I need to know more about the timeline than I do, he said to himself, and maybe if I knew more about... Wait a minute! The thought struck him and he almost stopped walking, paying little attention to the occasional passing Intelligence officers. There are several hundred teraquads of data which were sent with me on my original trip, he thought. I hadn't even thought of that possibility! The data should contain thousands... millions of...

"Call   the   lab,"   he   said   toward   his communicator.

He   started   to   walk   quickly   again   down   the secured corridor, feeling excited about his idea.

"Yes, Doctor," James said, "this is..."

"Mister Perkins, you are just the man I wanted to speak with, it turns out. I'm about to go into my meeting, but I was wondering if you would like to do me a very large favour?"

"Certainly, sir," he said.

"I need you to go into my office. Go to my desk and access the storage array I brought with me."

"The databases, sir?"

"Yes. I need you to do some surfing while I'm here," he said, pushing a few light buttons on his tablet, then slowly walking down the corridor toward the Meeting Hall.

"But I'm not authorized..."

"You are now," Olen said, pushing a remaining input in the sequence on his tablet. "I've just unlocked the array so you can access it from there. It's just a hunch, but I need you to look for a needle in that haystack, anything you can find on an RSF Major Milona Devon."

Olen felt a pause on the other end as he finally approached doors leading into the large room where his superiors awaited. Could Perkins have been the wrong person to ask, he wondered. If this leads me down a path into unauthorized territory, will James be an asset or a curse?

"Yes, sir," James said.

16

Peter found he had been reading the same paragraph again and again, still disoriented, unable to adequately concentrate, after awaking from a long afternoon nap in his deep red sitting room, in one of his favourite places to read, a dark leather chair in the corner opposite the dining room. He had again become distracted, thinking of Milona, and had decided to get himself up, putting off his re-reading of Kant's *Critique of Judgment* for some other time. He put the book down on a nearby black chair, which was stacked with other books and papers, and stood up, wearing only a pair of grey jockey shorts and a black t-shirt.

He leaned over and powered up his disc player and the amplifier, reflected for a moment on his CD collection, then inserted a favoured Rush album, *Counterparts*. He turned the volume up loud, and the first pounding drumbeats of the music seemed to reorient him. He walked around the house aimlessly, halfheartedly straightening things and looking over his familiar surroundings, eventually landing, staring into the open refrigerator, then he straightened a few things in the kitchen, and then popped out the back corner door into his back yard to look at his garden.

The light of the sky was in its last blue shades before going dark, and the cool air and ground felt good on his skin, the dirt and grass tickling between his toes. He took a look around, noting that his Barberry was nearly bare, but the Sycamore was just beginning to show leaf buds. His various herbs looked good, as well as the leeks and asparagus, and it might be about time to put the tomatoes out. Perhaps things are not as bad as I'd feared this morning, he thought.

Peter lingered for a while longer under the fading blue light, feeling the music inside, and he thought about how happy his little house made him. I wouldn't trade it for the wide world, he thought, as he slowly made his way into the garage, glancing at his bike collection, and then eventually back to the house toward his bedroom. He found himself vacillating between getting ready to go out and simply forgetting it all when the telephone rang. He turned around and trotted around into the sitting room, turned down the music, and then stepped to the counter bordering the kitchen to pick up the handset as it rang a second time.

"Hello?"

"Couldn't help wondering," Milona said on the other end, "if you wanted to go out?"

He was delighted, recalling they had forgotten to make plans earlier. I'd love to see her out, he thought, that kiss today wasn't nearly enough. "How'd you get my number?" he wondered.

"You're listed in the phone book," she said, "That's what they're for, right?"

"Right," he said, feeling a fool. "I just woke up from a nap, so I'm not quite here."

"Well, I was thinking about going out around ten. Is that too late?"

Peter looked over at the clock in the kitchen, which read nearly seven, then inspiration struck him.

"Actually," he said, "what are you doing for dinner before then?"

"What did you have in mind," she asked, "the place you mentioned?"

"No. I've got another place in mind, a brick oven bistro nearby. Why don't you come here first and we can take that walk."

"Where do you live?" she asked.

"It's listed in the book. That's what they're for, right?" he teased. "Actually, it's on..."

"I'll find it," she said, laughing. "How about eight, then?"

*

Milona sat poised at dinner, feeling like a picture of contentment. She wore her dark hair in a bun with two long aluminum sticks and simple makeup, modeling a silvery silk cocktail dress with a matching lined shawl and high heel sandals. Of course, she was well aware her duty was still to be done, but with Geof off doing his own thing until later, and with the evening all to herself, she could not avoid the temptation to experience whatever she could with Peter.

Sitting with his hair combed back, wearing a deep charcoal suit, black dress shirt with an open collar, black belt and shoes, Peter was amazed at the shimmering beauty of his dinner companion. He had enjoyed their walk to the restaurant only blocks away, offering his suit jacket. He had slipped it around her shoulders, and she gave a bright smile as he did so. It was such a nice evening, they both kept noting, and they each liked the idea of being able to walk home after a dinner out.

Each of them feared they were developing an "in love" aura about them everyone else could sense. The other people on the sidewalks, the hostess at the restaurant as they were seated, and the server himself, Milona thought, they all seemed to be tuned in to their disgusting display. Peter noticed this as well, but he did not care, preferring to take advantage of every instant they had with each other, never knowing where things could lead or how long they would last.

"I got some good news today," he said, taking a sip of the red zinfandel as they waited for their entrées.

"What kind of good news," she asked with a sip, then shifting in her seat to cross her legs.

"My paper on Metaphysics, on Time Theory, is going to be published."

Peter had almost forgotten what a joy that kind of news brought. 'My article is going to be published,' he repeated to himself.

"Really," she said. "Related, I take it to what was discussed at the end of the class today?"

"Basically. Yes. And I'm working on a book-length project, with that paper forming the basis for one of the chapters."

"I think that's wonderful," she said, trying desperately not to think about her duty, though realizing what this meant, that he had been working on these ideas for some time. "You know, my own book project," she added, using her cover story as a clever conversation topic, "is coming along slowly but surely."

"Great!" he offered, happy enough to be getting some personal details from her.

"I've just about got the plot settled, but it's coming along differently than I had imagined."

"Isn't that always the way," he quipped, thinking of writing in general. "What's the story about?"

"Well, I don't like to talk about works in progress, but let me say it's got plenty of intrigue."

*

Peter slumped over the edge of the bar in the busy, brightly coloured club in the trendy Vista area. He stared blankly at a television in the corner. *North by Northwest* played silently to no one, as the sound was muffled by the loud dance music, and everyone seemed consumed by conversations. Peter sipped on a gin-and-tonic and thought for a minute about his perceptions of Milona. I've never had someone come at me so directly, he thought. She's so straight-forward, but then, I'm not complaining of course, no man would. Yet, it does reinforce that "Russian spy" thing, and sometimes it really does makes me feel like I'm being watched. How strange it would be, he thought, to be tracked by people from another place or time. It'd feel like being hunted, I suppose.

Peter imagined a scene: He would get up from the bar, pay the tab, and step outside onto the sidewalk.

I would notice a man, dressed in black, of course, leaning on a dark car parked across the street. He would be watching me, Peter thought. Then from behind that man, another man would appear, walking around the first man directly in front of me.

'Professor Nexin?' the imposing dark figure would inquire.

I would nod, not quite sure if I should.

'Come with me,' he would add, 'I'm with the FBI. We want to talk to you.'

He would motion in the direction of the other man, toward the car...

Oh God, that's stupid, Peter interrupted himself. It wouldn't happen that way! It's too obvious, a little too Hitchcock, too hackneyed. Peter let out a small laugh as he took another sip from his drink, sitting up slightly more straight on the barstool, resolving to feel confident his mere philosophical ideas could never attract such dire attention.

Milona emerged from the back of the bar, her dress and low hanging shawl catching the complex lighting as well as many eyes. She approached Peter from behind and put her hand on his shoulder. He shook with the interruption of his thoughts and the tingle from her lightest touch.

"The back of this place is really interesting," she said. "There's a dance floor and the walls are covered in graffiti," she added.

"Yeah, I've been here many times," he lamented. "This bar has probably seen too much of me over the years, I'm afraid."

"Why do you continue to come here if you hate

it," she asked with a sly smile, taking a sip of her martini.

"I didn't say I hated it," he said with a smile, taking a second to soak her in, her dark hair and fair skin which seemed so soft. She electrified the room as no one else could, he thought. "You look so very beautiful," he added.

"So do you," she returned, placing her hand on his forearm, his skin tingling again from her touch.

"I bet you want to dance, don't you?" he toyed.

He gently slid his hand across her shoulder and then slowly moved it around to her back. She felt a tingle run across her as she looked at him, and the two stared doe-eyed at each other again momentarily as the metallic dance music played on around them.

∗

After arriving at Peter's house they said little, hopped out of the red convertible and walked to the front door, Milona wearing Peter's jacket. He invited her in, showed her around his house and garden, and he also showed her his bikes along with many other details of his life. She did not know he was a gardener, or that he had such refined tastes in the simple things around his home. Eventually, they settled down in the sitting room, as she hung his jacket and her small purse over a chair at the dining table. She sat gracefully on the black vinyl sofa and crossed her legs, looking around the dark red room, noticing the hardwood floor and large rug, the books and papers all around, and the sound system. Peter poured tap water into two glasses, noticed Milona looking around, and then thought to put on some music has he handed her a glass.

He showed her a few discs, to pick out something, Jazz and popular music, even classical, including Fauré's *Requiem*. She avoided reaction to the Fauré, but was impressed with his selections, many of which she had never known, and she decided on Ravel's *Daphnis et Chloé*, something he agreed with, then they sat back on the sofa to listen. Milona loved the old French music, early on and from her days at the ISB and École, but hearing it with Peter seemed to open it up from a completely different part of her. His mere presence in her life somehow taught her to relax and listen again, and in those few moments sitting in his comfortable home, to listen to herself. She knew she always longed for someone like him, someone who would provide intellectual challenges for her.

Peter began to feel this is what he always wanted. Here is a woman who already knew so much about him and could challenge him, who became more and more sexy and interesting with each new plateau. Her tastes in music, her mysterious charms, her timeless beauty, her seeming ease with herself. Peter knew he could easily sit there all night, gazing into Milona's blue eyes and hanging on her every hint about herself.

They slowly became uneasy underneath the surface, sitting alone in the dark listening to Ravel. They even moved to the floor, talked occasionally and held hands, but found that words were unnecessary. Milona thought about all the decisions from the Chancellor and senators on down, the mission Director

Zhang and Colonel Ford had prepared for her, the trips she and Geof had made, and now she sat at this turning point. She worried she was doing the wrong thing, being here with Peter, but felt she could worry about it no longer. She leaned in toward Peter, kissing him softly, then again with more distinction.

He edged the silvery shawl off of her shoulders, letting it fall to the floor behind her, and kissed her shoulders, her neck and her face, completely immersed in the desires for this mysterious woman he could no longer avoid. She slid the sticks out of her hair, letting it fall across her shoulders as Peter let his hand lay down on her bare knees, kissing her with a conviction he could not stop. She put her hand on his thigh and they began kissing even more passionately.

She smoothly unclasped and pushed off her sandals and gently stood up before him, pulling on his hands to stand with her as they continued kissing. He slipped the straps of her shimmering dress over her shoulders and let the garment slide down her bare body. She unbuttoned his shirt and trousers, revealing his strong lines, as he kicked his shoes and socks off, allowing them to continue their kisses. Their bodies ached for each other, as they slowly gave in to each other's powers. In these bare, naïve moments between them, Milona knew she might very well be in jeopardy, but also that her desires would never weaken.

17

After talking with James, Olen found himself nervous, anticipating his meeting with the Chancellors, senators, generals, and directors. Rightly so he mused, as he stepped up to the two Reconnaissance Guard lieutenants stationed at the doors.

"Colonel, Director Zhang has asked to send you right in, sir," the lieutenant on Olen's left said, and both of the guards nodded for him to continue on deeper into the hall.

"Thank you," he replied, continuing on.

"Welcome, Doctor Nadimov," Science Director Franklin said, reaching out emotionally to Olen as the saviour of their *Tempo Programme*.

"Welcome back to *Orbis*, Doctor," Director-General Lorentz said. The other chiefs and Operations Director Zhang nodded and said hello as they sat down. "You'll notice on the viewscreen behind us," he motioned, as Olen looked up to see the Chancellor and some of the senators he saw earlier during the parade, "we have conferenced in, and let me welcome, Madam Chancellor at the Planalto in Brasília, and Mister Vice Chancellor Jasthi, Chair of the Senate, visiting with the Chief Justice of the UN Court in Luxembourg, and

Senators Levy of France, who is Vice Chair, McCallum of Australia, Hassan of Iran, and Prikosh of India, all in the Senate Complex in Sydney,"

Lorentz deferred to each of them to nod or say hello, giving the extra details about them for the Doctor's benefit, who might not know all of them or how they fit into the situation.

"Thank you," Nadimov said softly, suddenly nervous and flush, not having expected such pressure.

"I realize that time is short," Lorentz continued, "so I will let Director Franklin update us. Director?"

"Thank you Director-General Lorentz. I thank all of you for meeting with us. As you may recall, I reported earlier that we had no success in our research through the *Tempo Programme*. Yet, only hours later, we could not be more pleasantly surprised to be flat wrong. Our Lead Scientist and Section Chief in the Particle Laboratory, Doctor Olen Nadimov, who many of you will recall authorizing for the Temporal Alliance Program in the past, has informed me this afternoon of their surprise success in developing the models." Franklin looked to him for some assurance that he was indeed ready, to which he offered a slight nod back as he keyed up several commands on his tablet. "With that, I turn the floor over to Doctor Nadimov."

"Madam Chancellor, Mister Vice Chancellor, Senators, Generals, Directors," Olen began, summoning up all the presentational skills he could find, "I am deeply honoured to be here speaking with you, as a scientist, as a time traveller and visitor here, and if you will, as a citizen of the world. This afternoon, we had a surprise in the lab, thanks to Doctor

Michelle Lambert, whereby she discovered a way to disrupt the threat this mysterious distortion field may pose before it ever reaches us."

He pushed a virtual button which started the program. It read Michelle's latest data from the laboratory and rendered it through the hall projection system in a huge display above the middle of the ring table, spanning nearly from floor to ceiling. Everyone winced at the sheer size of the hologram, as well as the subtle, deep sound cues which had been programmed by the assistants to increase the dazzling effect. A reddish cloud-like field rose up nearby the coloured models of Venus, Earth, Moon, and Mars, more closely resembling the scale difference between them than in the modeling lab. The display was also transmitted to render at different scales where needed at the Planalto, the Court, and the Senate complex, and it wowed their viewers as well.

"This," he continued, "is a reasonable and likely representation of what we feel could happen within a week if the field were to arrive as expected in our orbits without any action on our part." He pressed another button, calling the program to display the cloud approaching the planets, with multitudes of small, fiery blasts erupting all around them, the noises booming in the large hall and other meeting rooms. "The blasts you're seeing are the power grids, stations, and various crafts being overcharged by field intensity and simultaneously destroyed by field distortions." The cloud edged across Mars, slowly causing it to cleave itself and break apart, causing large blasts and distortions of the planet. "I'll stop it there," he added, assuming no one needed to see what happens to Earth, "as I think we all get the point." He then keyed in a different program quickly and continued. "Now, this is what we have constructed today," he said, as the cloud reappeared farther away from the planets with a large, flat matrix of yellow nodes. "The cloud approaches the matrix we will set up, actually far beyond the orbits near the Solar Heliopause." The cloud began moving. "Now, watch this," he warned. The cloud began to pass through the matrix, some two hundred nodes, but then it was dispersed, in such a way that increased as the field moved, which charged up the nodes. "These nodes will initiate the dispersal of the cloud energy effectively so that it no longer poses a threat. Then we power them down during parts of the cloud passage, allowing them to cool, so that we can employ them again and again if necessary. What we proved in the lab was that once this dispersion starts, if done in just the right way, it continues like a chain-reaction, and may not even require extra bursts from the nodes."

The program ended and silence fell on the room as everyone tried to digest what had been shown, what it meant, and what position they now held.

"A breathtaking presentation, Doctor," Director Franklin said, feeling overcome with joy that her team had come through, if seemingly a little late for the Chancellor's visit earlier.

"What do we do now about the other approach?" Senator McCallum asked.

"This is certainly a very promising solution!" Senator Prikosh suggested, "I think we should pursue this with expeditious preparation."

"We have already authorized the director's team," the Chancellor said, "so I suggest we pursue both initiatives."

"I agree," Senator Levy said, "it is wise to keep our options open."

"If there is nothing further, then," the Chancellor concluded, "I'm authorizing the scientists be given all command priority assistance they need to set this shield up and deploy it." Franklin and Nadimov both looked at each other with a smile. "But to be safe, I would like Director Zhang's team to continue with their operation," she added as Zhang also breathed a slight sigh of relief. "People, this is not a contest. Either or both efforts could mean our very survival. We need to pursue every available solution and technical advantage we can."

*

The small shuttle pulled into the Science Centre, and Olen hopped out and walked toward the doors, through to the lifts and then he rode down to Lower Level Two. He recalled with relish that Director Zhang had even authorized his request to briefly visit the past at a couple of insertion points, including the major's mission time, to conduct tests on the temporal subspace distortions from those vantage points. He thought it clever to work this into their experiments, but he also knew they only had a few hours to get what they needed together as the nodal systems were to be immediately configured for the actual attempt. 'You might even bump into Major Devon down there before she leaves,' he remembered Zhang saying. That would be rich, Olen thought, since they already knew of each other, in a manner of speaking. He arrived back in the Particle Lab and continued through to his office.

"Sir, as you requested," James said, startling Olen for a moment as he recalled why he had contacted Perkins, "I went through some of the data you'd brought from your original trip from the past. I must say, sir, this data could change everything for a lot of people. The rediscovery of family histories alone would..."

"I know, Mister Perkins, but unfortunately that is far beyond our authority to call, you understand. The Directorate has a whole task force working on it, so, just keep it to yourself."

"Of course, sir."

"Did you find anything, though?"

"Well, it took a while but I was able to retrieve information indicating the presence of a Milona Devon in that past."

"How old is the data?"

"Most of it dates from about seventeen years before your trip, sir. I turned up her name on a birth certificate," he continued, bringing up the certificate on the desk's surface, "here it is."

Olen looked down at his desk and was shocked to see the names listed as parents of the child in such an official way.

"Very good work, Mister Perkins," Olen said, visibly stunned as he gathered the words. "This would be around three years after the major's current insertion," he mumbled, thinking about the time frames, as I understand from the reports I got from Whitaker. "Carry on, then," he added, moving over to his lounger.

James returned to his work as Olen dropped his weight to the lounger to rest for a moment, looking up at the red-accents on ceiling panels. This would have meant something went wrong with her mission, he thought, or somehow things were changed drastically. The major seems to have gone to the past to stay, or did she come here to stay? She wouldn't be there and here at the same time, unless... there were some technical error, or just a coincidence with the data. Who knows? Looks now like the only way to ensure my past is safe is by helping her. I've been looking at all of this the wrong way. The major has to terminate her target! That must be what went wrong. This is the only way, I think. I have to spoof her.

"Are you okay, Doctor Nadimov?" James asked, returning again to his doorway.

Olen looked up at James and pulled a smile across his face. "Mister Perkins, how would you like to take a trip?"

*

"Thanks again, Sergeant," Olen said as he and James hopped out of Sergeant Werner's sedan shuttle carrying several items of field detection gear.

They rushed across the landing platform in the rain and down the stairs. Olen thought it looked like the rain could break, and he could see a bright golden mid day Sun beginning to stream through the lush trees of the forest. He led James into the Jackson Station facility, through the doors, and down the secured corridor. Olen waved his right hand across the scanner, then pressed a button to scan a visitor. He pulled James' right hand across the scanner and then the door slid open. The two stepped into the reinforced security lock, James still reeling but unresponsive.

Olen looked at his communicator, noting the time was near 11:00 am locally, 16:00 UTC, or 5:00 pm in Berlin. After the lift brought them down and the inner door slid open, they moved in toward the control room. James remained back in the hallway nervously, holding the gear as Olen continued inside. Although he could not see anyone right away, he thought perhaps he would see Major Devon again, but he also questioned that idea.

As timing would have it, Olen had arrived in time to stand next to Major Waters just as Milona was passing through to the past. They had only caught each other's eyes for a second, he recalled, but that was enough to send a chill across Olen's skin.

"Do have a nice trip, Major," he whispered quixotically, feeling a rush of conflicting emotions.

Major Waters and Lieutenant Mathis looked over at him and nodded just before Mathis turned to go through, to which Olen only returned a blank nod. Geof moved to the chambers on the sergeant-major's signal and was also transported to the past.

"Mister Chief," Major Waters greeted after Mathis cleared the chambers, interrupting Olen's thoughts, "we heard you would be joining us."

Waters did not wish to seem unwelcoming, not to a superior officer at that.

"Major, I didn't expect to be here."

"Not to worry, Doctor," Waters offered.

He turned and led Olen and James into the briefing room where Colonel Ford was awaiting on the viewscreen. We are having a busy day, Waters thought as the sergeant-major joined them, and then he closed the door behind them. Waters felt an odd energy as Major Devon, Lieutenant Mathis, and Doctor Nadimov all caught sight of each other in that moment.

"Doctor Nadimov, Technical Officer Perkins, Welcome," Ford said from the viewscreen, as the three nodded his way, each with 'Colonel'. "I will make this brief. You are cleared for two insertions. First, arrive in the past one hour before the major and lieutenant are arriving now. Avoid complications as much as possible with the active insertion. Second, arrive in the past one month earlier during a quiet time for a control measurement. Confer with Sergeant-Major Mitchell and Major Waters on the exact times."

Olen had a sinking feeling as he reflected on the possible dates of the time frames in the past.

"You will work with Special Agent Gibbs and Army Captain Oglesby as needed to set up Army covers, funds, or transportation as needed. You are expected back in Berlin ASAP, so you're instructed to request synchros no more than an hour from now using your timestamps here. This way, you may stay longer to conduct whatever experiments are needed around *Visitor*, that's the facility in the past, and even outside the Army base if need be, but come back quick."

"Yes, Colonel," Perkins said, feeling extremely nervous and excited at once.

"Yes, Colonel," Olen added, "we should be back at the Science Centre within an hour."

Olen felt very uneasy about visiting the past, but he felt confident in his overall plans and ideas for the shield, and to learn about the major's mission. He had already instructed James during their shuttle ride to stay in the past as needed to make a trip to the University and take readings from there, if for no other reason than to have comparison data regarding temporal flux and undulation. Olen had made it very clear to the young man that should he meet the RSF operatives, he should not interfere with what they are trying to do, except to ensure one small detail, if he could.

18

It was certainly after Midnight, Milona thought, and it was surely time for her to be leaving Peter. She lay quietly, curled up with him in his bed, trying to concentrate on what she needed to do. Geof would have made his way with our things to the car outside, she thought, but she could not be sure. She would have to find a way to leave Peter's home without it seeming odd, but before long, she found herself continuing to lay still, thinking of their beautiful night together.

She recalled their leisurely walk through the flowery neighborhood to dinner, their windy ride in the convertible to the club in the Vista, their dancing under the strobe and black lights, the music and their lovemaking. And now she lay here in his bed, she thought, feeling the slight breeze coming in through the open windows, the sheer white curtains waving back and forth in his soft blue room. What a nice feeling that is, she mused, when so much of my time is spent on a space station, a cold, artificial place compared to this lush, green city. The fresh air blowing across this room is itself such a simple delight, she thought.

Why, she continually asked though, do I have to do this? Why did I have to feel this way about him, conflicted about my duty and my emotions? Why did they ask me to come here, to erase this wonderful man, and why am I behaving like some swallow in a spy novel? I don't know, but somehow, this must be done. My orders are clear. Peter is the one.

"Are you awake?" he asked, still reeling from his day and their night together.

"Yes," she said, as her thoughts were pleasantly interrupted.

"What are you thinking?"

"I was thinking of walking," she quickly contrived, "walking across the Statehouse grounds today, looking around at the trees and sky in my mind. It was lovely."

Milona was pleased to be able to mask her true thoughts so well.

"Quite a symbol isn't it?" he asked.

"What is?"

"The Statehouse."

"Yes," she answered. "Americans think they are on top of the world. The culture, I mean."

"What does that have to do with the..."

"Well, that's the symbol I see. You know, like the ancient Romans nearing their end? The whole society is crumbling around them, but they only focus selectively on this crack or that one, vowing more money or the next election will patch it up, confident that their way is best. All the while enslaving much of the world economically..."

"That sounds strange, coming from you," he said. "Sounds like something I would say."

"I'm sorry, Peter. I'm in a mood, I guess," she

said, rolling over to lay her head on his bare chest, trying to cover her real thoughts with something very different.

"No, it's okay," he said, suddenly intrigued by the topic. "Perhaps one day, living with simplicity, and all kinds of other self-expression will be 'allowed' to exist without the sacrifices of mass commercialism. Maybe technological advance will be common without controversy, pollution, or inequity. Maybe uncorrupted, almost Marxist, democracy really will spread across the globe without assimilating every last traditional beauty into 'McCulture'."

"It will," she said, laughing at that last word. "Eventually, it will," she added. "I'm sure of it."

"I hope so. But in the meantime, I can only try to approximate it on my own. It would be unethical, I think, to live any other way than by that principle. There are just some things you can't get at the mall."

"You are so very different from everyone else."

"How do you mean?"

"You seem to me to be more alive. You know, alive with the kind of simplicity we will cultivate... need to cultivate... in my opinion. The way you live so simply, it's so different from the people around you, but it's the way everyone will need to live in order to... Well, to spare resources."

"Yes, I do live simply. Mostly by choice," he said, wondering again why this seemed to be bothering her, but he still enjoyed the impromptu discussion.

"It's all by choice, don't you see? You are happy in a way that many others cannot seem to fathom, because they cannot buy a product which will give them true happiness."

"Well, no, they can't. You're right. I see what you meant by 'choice', now."

Peter was struck to hear her speak like this. Usually, he would reserve such critical judgments until getting to know someone very well. However, it almost seemed to him that Milona was speaking rhetorically or to someone else. Perhaps not, though, he thought. I really don't know her well enough to say.

"I am falling in love with you," she said abruptly with a nod and without reservation, something she dare not even say to herself until now, not even in those lightest moments, when thoughts of the present were far away, but there it was, she said it, and it was out in the open. She picked herself up slightly, looking down at him. "But how can I do what I have to do, when I have these feelings?"

"I don't know what to say."

Peter was not quite ready to put a name on his feelings, but he was not able to deny them, either.

"I..."

"Don't say anything," she said, nudging herself in a little closer to him again.

She knew she could probably divulge anything at this point. Why would it matter? She wondered about Geof, and she knew he would, of course, point out that the lives of billions of people were at stake, people in her present and in their future. It was the present of the World, and it was also her present, her reality, she reminded herself, again and again. That present outweighs a single life in the past, no matter how authentic, doesn't it?

Overcome with frustration and anger at her situation for a moment, she imagined the house itself exploding, instantly killing them both, leveling the whole structure. The explosion happened slowly in her mind, and she also watched from outside as the two of them were killed, the house erupting with flames and debris, the present she knew and the distortion field immediately altered for the better in a great ripple of *Time*. One act of complete cruelty, she thought, in order to save a more developed civilization! She feared her thoughts would grow darker still if she did not leave now, right away.

"What do we do now?" he asked, after a few moments of silence.

"Well, I hope you don't take this the wrong way," she said, looking back up to him, "but I'm going to have to get going."

"Why? You can stay for breakfast..."

"No. I need to go. Thank you, but I really can't," she said, sitting up straight, nude, and continuing to look at him, nude as well.

"Well, okay."

He wondered if he would ever learn anything more substantial about this mystery woman. Did she have family? Friends? Where did she live? She seemed so independent to him, yet he also wondered if she might be too independent for her own good. Still, he wasn't about to offend her, and he found a way to understand her departure.

"You understand?" she asked, as she leaned down and kissed him, holding back emotions and tears.

"Yes. It's okay."

She got up from the bed and went into the front

room to gather her clothes as he lay silent, watching her disappear around the doorway, trying to listen for any clue-like sounds she might make as she slipped herself back into her dress and wrapped her hair up, pushing the sticks in to hold it. After a moment, he heard her heels on the floor as she returned from the sitting room. She pulled her shawl around her shoulders and sat down on the edge of the bed with her purse, leaning in to kiss him again, then again.

"Please don't get up, Peter. I'll see myself out." She sat up and looked at him in the dark room. "Peter, I want you to know I had an absolutely dreamy evening with you. I mean that more than you know. It was beautiful. I just need to go right now."

"I had an incredible time, too, Milona," he said, sitting up to kiss her again.

"I hope to see you again."

"I am powerless to resist. Of course you will."

"Then go back to sleep," she said, smiling. "Tomorrow is a new day."

Milona stood up, and with one last look at Peter Nexin, slipped out of his bedroom, through his house and out his front door, telling herself over and over again that everything was okay, that she was going to be fine, that she just needed to leave. 'Tomorrow is a new day,' she recalled. It's a total cliché, but it seemed truer for me than him. She forced herself to continue, closing his front door quietly remembering to leave it unlocked, then down his front porch steps, and back to the car. As she arrived at the car door, she could barely make out Geof sitting under a large bush between houses, near the passenger side of the car. He wore a black outfit of trousers and a thin turtleneck sweater.

"Major," he whispered, acknowledging he had seen her, tuning out how striking he found her in her silvery cocktail dress.

"I got what I needed," she whispered to him, aware of the deep and bitter irony, then slid into the driver's seat, pushing hard to keep her feelings down.

"Stop worrying," he whispered across to her, trying to keep his voice down. "I suggest you drive away, come around the block."

"Okay," she returned, with tears now coming to her eyes.

"Major?" he inquired.

"Lieutenant, you are a go!" she whispered sternly as she wiped away tears.

Milona knew this was her final authorization for the action they had planned. She started the car and drove away, trying her best not to look at Peter's house, but she failed again, taking in one last glance.

Geof moved out of the night's shadows and sneaked over across Peter Nexin's yard and onto his front porch. He quietly slipped the door open, sliding into the house. He could hear his heart beating in his ears as he stepped quietly across Nexin's sitting room, checking for sounds, moving onward through the house to the door of Peter's bedroom. He noted the professor appeared to be dozing, or hopefully, he was asleep.

*

Milona eventually drew the car back to the curb a few car lengths further down the street, suppressing her urge to look at the house. Tears continued to stream down her cheek, and she was unable to shake off her cruel and selfish betrayal, unable to stop thinking of the sweet, innocent man now dead in that house. She could see Geof sneaking his way back toward her in the corner of her eye, and then she began to cry openly, the reality of what they had done now unavoidable to her.

She also found herself thinking they may have to remain here in the past, if the present was altered enough by this break in the timeline. If it were enough to erase the time chambers, she wondered, or something along those lines, then this would mean staying here in this time, for who knows how long, every second of it without Peter. I'll only have tonight, and my betrayal, she thought, still crying uncontrollably.

Down the street, Agent Gibbs had patiently watched events for hours, tired from a long day of being patient. He had watched as Nexin entered the house with Devon, and then sometime later, he noted Devon's eventual exit. He saw Mathis make entrance, and Devon return in the car. He now watched as Mathis crept across the professor's front yard. Mathis took one last look around, and then slipped down the street and got into the car with Devon.

Gibbs thought he could see her putting her head down once or twice, but after a moment or two, saw that the car began rolling again toward him. Maybe she dropped the keys, or something, he thought, dropping himself down as they quietly passed by. They had seemed to be surprisingly unaware of his surveillance once again, he noted, while slumped. He waited for a few seconds and sat back up.

Wait a minute! he thought. I see what's happened here! Devon didn't drop any keys. She might have been crying. And Mathis, what with all that sneaking around, surely he didn't go into the house to use the bathroom! These people are... This whole thing has been a...

"I don't believe it, Cornea!" he said, the radio receiver picking up his voice for Special Agent Tanner and the others on their secure loop.

"Bulldog, what are you talking about?" Tanner asked him.

"I think we've got a Vic!"

19

The red convertible took them under city streetlights, a starry sky, and through the cool night air as they drove silently through the neighborhoods toward the base. Geof slipped his black turtleneck off, revealing a black shirt underneath, and then threw the sweater and a pair of gloves into a commercial trash area as they passed by slowly. There was very little traffic on the roads at the early hour of the morning, and the sounds of the engine and gearbox, wind passing overhead, kept them both entranced. Neither really felt they should say anything, preferring to keep their own internal reflections to themselves for the moment.

Milona felt as though she were in a full shock, struck dumb by the disjunct between the wonderful evening she had with Peter, along with the realization that he was now dead. Everything was a reminder, the very wind itself which now mussed her hair, her last moments with Peter in his bedroom with a fan breeze flowing over their bodies. Geof tried to avoid feeling personal remorse for killing Nexin, not because he thought he should not have remorse, he mused, but because he found remorse was difficult to reconcile with their duty and the kind of society the UN sought after, both in the present and the past. He sat still in his seat as she drove the car, steering surely enough through neighborhoods and onto the base. He simply leaned his head back, looking through the passing streetlights and trees, up to the star-filled heavens for guidance. She knew they needed to hurry to get back to *Visitor*, get back before being caught, but she dreaded returning all the same. Assuming *Calendar* is even operable, she mused, but we have to try.

To Geof, Milona obviously seemed very disturbed about losing Nexin, but he couldn't blame her for a second. It was a terribly difficult position for anyone to be in, he thought, not that his wet role in the mission had been any easier than hers. He could never allow himself to forget the gravity of what they were doing, as if it could be forgotten, and his duty to his major helped keep him focused when even that faltered. He recalled an afternoon when he visited the Executive Services offices on the base. He remembered looking at the plaques commending the Special Joint Services Program, an administrative cover for many classified operations such as the Temporal Alliance Program, and he wondered how these good people in the past would view what they had done.

"You did your duty," he finally offered, looking over toward her, noting her blank stare.

They pulled up to the fence line near *Visitor*, and she solemnly shut the car down as they got out.

"I know, Geof, but why do I feel so terrible about it? Don't you feel the same way?"

"Of course I do," he agreed. "It wasn't easy, what you and I did."

"We followed our orders. I know. We would follow them again and again. But, I just wasn't prepared for how morally questionable this would be." She leaned in over the door of the car. "Are we such a superior culture if it takes a covert trip to the distant past to politely remove someone based only on pure suspicion of their ideas? I'm sorry. I just wasn't ready for how I would feel about all of this... Not to mention how I feel about..."

"Milona," Geof said, grabbing his bag from the back seat, "Peter was a very unique individual. I realize that, too. But keep in mind, if we make it back, and if what we've done has solved our problem, maybe there is a chance we could find a way to bring him back, somehow, or find some other way to keep this field from threatening us."

"Those are big 'if's'," she said, grabbing the bag containing her other clothes from the back seat, tossing her small purse back inside it and shutting the door. "Let's just see if *Visitor* is operational as a first step."

*

Devon and Mathis were cleared through the secure fence around *Visitor* by the guards on duty at the gate, and once they were on the inside, the installation personnel on duty saluted them. They returned the salutes by simple nods and rank greetings, and proceeded down the steps and into the control room. They could overhear one of the engineers reacting to their entrance, and their odd mix of clothing.

"Make sure the hole is clear, Corporal. We've

got two more guests tonight."

"Staff Sergeant? You said two more?" Milona asked. "What other guests tonight? I'd like to review your logs, if you don't mind."

"Yes, ma'am!" he returned, saluting her. He walked over to a small desk and picked up a clipboard. "Major, here are the logs for the last ten days."

"Thank you, Staff Sergeant," she said softly.

The engineers tried not to stare at the major in her revealing clothing or the lieutenant in his suspicious black outfit. Milona thumbed through the pages and showed them to Geof as well. She looked up and down the list, made up mostly of entries by herself, Geof and Colonel Ford over the last few days, but then she noticed two other names she did not recognize and stopped on them abruptly:

Olen Nadimov, UNI
James Perkins, UNI

These entries, she thought, referencing their times, show their insertion and then a synchro by this Nadimov before our own insertions that morning, with Perkins seeming to stay in the past after their insertion.

"That first name seems somewhat familiar," she said, showing the lieutenant the logs again, "but I can't place it. Maybe it's just an anomaly in my head. Still, who would these people be?"

"Never heard those names before," Geof said, doing well to cover the fact that he felt he had briefly seen a lieutenant colonel standing next to Waters that morning before he came through to the past. He shook off his deceit by reasoning that these two were likely only scientists, and whatever they were doing probably would not impact their mission. "Probably scientists," he offered.

Milona knew the controllers in the past would know nothing they could reveal. No one we've met goes by these names, she thought to herself. Why does it seem one of them is apparently still here?

"Are we the only operatives using this insertion?" she asked, knowing their answer would not be helpful.

"Maybe they just came to do maintenance or something, Major," Geof offered, nodding to the others to ignore her concern. "This facility doesn't belong to us, personally," he added, as the controllers snickered.

Milona looked at Geof, wondering if maybe she was only looking for something to concern her, to take her thoughts away from Peter and the mission.

"Carry on, Staff Sergeant," she said, shaking off the concern.

"Yes, ma'am," he returned.

"Well," she said, turning back to Geof, "the facility obviously seems to be intact..."

"Ma'am," the staff sergeant noted, "I will be requesting the synchro now."

"Thank you," she said, adding, "let's request a two hour delay after insertion, Staff Sergeant."

"Yes, ma'am."

The controllers in the past initiated synchro communications with the future from *Visitor* by making an entry into a secured optical storage LED readout device. This device sat in the control room through

Time, while messages saved would instantly notify the engineers in *Calendar* right after the operatives had left the present. They would read the entry, log the timestamp and other headers, requested delay, and other information in the message body. Only then could they know when to schedule and initialize the chambers to retrieve the operatives, in this case, two hours after they had inserted. It was considered by the officers on both ends to be a simple, yet a clever and effective way to hail and synchronize return trips. *Calendar* engineer's responses to these requests were usually quick if no local delay was requested, but this time seemed a longer wait than usual, which made both Milona and Geof nervous, Milona fidgeting by straightening her hair as Geof tapped his fingers, but the staff sergeant and corporal both knew it was normal.

*

Gibbs had conferred with his handler, after seeing Mathis leaving Nexin's home, then he had called in Columbia's Police to the scene. As a result, he now had little time to rush onto the base, hopefully where Astros would be waiting. TAP's group of JSOC operatives, Delta Force, Force Recon, Night Stalker, Ranger, Seal, Special Operations, and others under CIA, NSA, and SOG Command would often pose as military personnel or civilians and conduct various operations as needed. Gibbs and Tanner made up names for them, Alphas, Frogs, Prowlers, Astros, Walruses, and Specks, for cover, and the CIA and DOD leaders felt the US should be prepared for anything possible from their temporal visitors.

Gibbs felt they had activated too late, as he hoped he could try to confront or stop the Morlock murderers, pleading with them for an explanation, anything which could solve this mystery, but it seemed to him he was going to be a few minutes late.

"Special Agent Gibbs?" he answered, bringing the phone to his ear as he drove across the base.

"Detective Jameson. We verified the shot. Single bullet through the temple. A nine-millimetre Beretta in the left hand. Residue inconclusive, no sign of forced entry," the detective said.

"Any sign this was a setup?"

"Not yet."

"Thanks, Detective. I'll get back to you," Gibbs said, then ended the call and checked with Tanner through the radio loop. "Cornea, are you there?"

"Read you, Bulldog."

"Well, Vic is leaking from a nine-B. Still no clear signs."

"Bulldog, we are authorizing you to detain either or both of these visitors for questioning. Hopefully they have a pretty good explanation, but do tread very carefully."

"Understood, Cornea."

Gibbs pulled up near the red car sitting at the fence line, and immediately feared he was too late, feeling his blood rush from the excitement, but he could not see his men. Without them to back him up, Gibbs feared his actions would be seen as irrational to Oglesby's Intel people.

"Where are my Astros?" Gibbs called out loud,

jumping out of his brown sedan, rushing toward *Visitor*'s security gate. But just as he arrived, a green and dusty utility vehicle drew up behind the other two cars and slid to park nearby them. Three armed Ranger operatives in generic black uniforms and berets jumped out. "Come, on!" he urged, under his breath.

✱

Finally, Milona and Geof were relieved by the familiar chamber noises after what seemed like many minutes of waiting.

"You go ahead," he said.

Milona looked at Geof, thinking how kind he had been to her, and stood up next to him.

"Go home, Major, I'm right behind you."

Milona studied her trusted junior as the loud clap shook the control room of *Visitor*, then she stepped across the control room and into what was now an initialization chamber, becoming visible to the control crew at *Calendar*, and then almost immediately she faded away, materializing inside the opposite chamber and back in the present. Geof watched her, and then waited for the clear signal from the corporal so that he could go through.

✱

Gibbs and the Rangers had rushed through security, flashing their ID's, and were saluted by the personnel as they ran onward to the steps leading down into the control room. Gibbs was very surprised to find only Morlock Mathis standing in the control room, just as the lieutenant was about to move into the chamber.

"Prepare to shut it down, Staff Sergeant," Gibbs said, signaling to the controllers to standby, who understood the Special Agent's authority was to be considered at least as high as Captain Oglesby's, though none of them knew his full credentials.

"Yes, sir," the staff sergeant responded.

"Restrain Lieutenant Mathis, Colonel," Gibbs ordered one of the Rangers.

Lieutenant Colonel Donald, senior of the three Rangers, nodded to his two majors and they quickly seized the strong Lieutenant Mathis, who did not resist, holding him firmly in place. Gibbs slowly paced across the control room.

"What is this all about!" Geof demanded.

"Lieutenant, I don't think this is what our top brass had in mind when they set up the Temporal Alliance Program," Gibbs said.

"What are you talking about?"

"A little felony called murder. It's wrong where you come from, too, I hope?"

"Of course it's wrong! But, it's not what you think," Geof pleaded.

"Not what I think? I tracked you entering the home of one Professor Nexin, a target which had been softened, if you will, earlier this evening by your lovely Major. Local PD tells me the professor won't be making it to class tomorrow." Gibbs took a moment to walk closer to the lieutenant. "So, did she kill him in his bed, or did you?"

"You don't understand," Geof said.

"I'm sure I don't, Lieutenant Mathis, and that's just the point." Gibbs spoke more surely now, happy that his hunches were panning out, but uncertain of the repercussions of this unprecedented detention. "You see, our government isn't going to like the idea that people from the future just slipped into our world, used us for access and resources, killed an innocent American with no explanation, and then tried to sail off without any consequences."

"How do you know anything about..."

"We have followed your investigation of Professor Nexin very closely," Gibbs said. "Don't you imagine we can track cars and listen to conversations and do all kinds of amazing things with our 'ancient' technology?"

Geof struggled against the restraint of the Rangers in frustration, angry with Gibbs for following them all along.

"You can't do anything about it," Geof said, "don't you think my superiors will notice I'm missing? They will send someone to..."

"First," Gibbs interrupted, motioning to the staff sergeant with a finger to his neck to end the synchro, "let's close this open tunnel, shall we?"

20

"Sergeant-Major Mitchell, it's nice to see you again," Milona said, with a sigh.

She stepped away from the chambers now that she was back in the present and moved nearer to the engineers at their control stand. As she awaited Mathis, she thought the control room looked exactly the same to her. But if our mission was successful, she asked herself, how could all of this be the same?

"You know my name, ma'am?" Mitchell asked, looking at his staff, wondering why they had requested he come in to greet a civilian woman who looked dressed for a night on the town. The other engineers stood silent in their amazement of her, but also because there was no corresponding synchro to correlate, and no record of her name being associated with any synchro.

"Of course I do!" she said. "I was last here two hours ago, before lunchtime, among many times being here, Sergeant-Major."

Mitchell was interrupted by a signal, and held his finger up to excuse himself. Another message was appearing directly from the controllers in the past requesting to end the synchro, authorized by someone named UNR First Lieutenant Mathis, the reason given was he was delayed indefinitely. Mitchell nodded toward one of his engineers, who initiated the close of the wormhole, which then brought the resolution chamber back into synchronization with the present by collapsing the warp generation. All of this confused Milona greatly, as the past disappeared from the resolution chamber, as the chambers made their sudden noises and her awareness returned to the present.

"Sergeant-Major, why are you closing down the synchro? My lieutenant is still back there."

"Ma'am, there was a secure request from the past to do so."

"But Lieutenant Mathis... Please resynchronize so we can..."

"Ma'am, Lieutenant Mathis was the one who authorized the disconnect," he said. "Unfortunately, I'm going to have to request you wait in the briefing room over here," he asked, pointing toward the room nearby, "until Colonel Lindsey arrives."

"Colonel Lindsey?"

"Warrant Corps, ma'am."

✳

Milona felt nervous and reflective. She had pulled her watch out of her bag as she sat quietly in the cold briefing room, and it indicated nearly three o'clock. Even with a two-hour delay in the requested synchro, she could not easily reconcile the lost relative time-of-day difference after coming back through synchro. While it should be one in afternoon, locally, it would be 18:00 UTC in her normal mode. She was confused enough as to why Geof would be delayed and request a disconnect, and even more so when Mitchell did not seem to know her. Ah, this outfit, she thought, having forgotten herself, I must look very... different to them. I've never come through here dressed like this! More than anything, though, Milona was still disturbed by her mission. She found herself missing Peter's company, as she also felt displaced from her real life in the present. At length, someone finally arrived.

"Good afternoon, ma'am," Colonel Lindsey said, a Reconnaissance Warrant officer, as he quietly opened the briefing room door and closed it behind. He was a dark-skinned man of average height, and proudly wore his duty uniform coat and trousers, rank and decorations, red-on-silver investigator badge showing a magnifier depiction, all setting off his black Recon uniform. The gentle Zimbabwean seemed unfazed by Milona's appearance, her disheveled hair, her revealing dress, even though he could plainly see she was a very beautiful woman.

"Colonel," she said, standing up at attention.

"At ease," he said slowly, confused as to why this seeming civilian was being so formal. "I understand you've arrived from the past?"

"Yes, sir. My lieutenant and I completed our mission and were to return to the present.

"Your lieutenant?"

"RSF First Lieutenant Geoffery Mathis, sir."

"And you are?"

"RSF Major Milona Devon, sir."

"I see," he said, again with a slow voice. "What kind of mission were you completing with Lieutenant

Mathis, and who is your CO?"

"Our mission is highly classified, sir, I'm sorry. Our CO is RSF Colonel John Ford." Milona was sure at this point that she was being tested, not debriefed. She felt there was no reason to divulge anything more than was asked, yet she also wanted her other bag.

"Ma'am, please wait here," he said.

"Sir, if you let me retrieve my other larger bag from a locker over in the changing room, it has my communicator, duty uniform, and a work pad..."

"That won't be necessary. But you may get your things if you wish. I will still ask you to wait in here, though. I'll be back with you momentarily."

"Thank you, Colonel."

She crossed the hall and stepped into the locker room, finding her larger bag was not where she had left it the previous morning. She looked around the room and lockers, around in the hallway, and drew continued strange looks from the staff as her heels clapped the floor. Where did it go? she thought, returning to the briefing room frustrated.

After a minute or two, the colonel reappeared from down the hall, along with Major Waters dressed in a plain suit, and he closed the door behind them.

"Major Waters," she nodded, of course recognizing the man as Intel Station Chief of *Calendar*.

"I'm sorry," he said, "I haven't had the pleasure, ma'am," looking at her head to toe as if undressing her, then leaning in to shake her hand. She slowly shook his hand, but read nothing different in his face.

"Is this a joke, sir?" Milona asked the colonel, increasingly angered and confused. "Lieutenant Mathis is unexplainably delayed, and my duty gear is missing from the locker..."

"Ma'am, Colonel Ford is waiting," Lindsey said, then nodded to Major Waters.

Waters looked over to the blank viewscreen on the wall and pushed a code sequence on his datapad to activate it. Colonel Ford appeared on the screen in his service uniform.

"Colonel, sir," she said, nodding and relieved to see her commander.

"Ma'am, I understand you're claiming I'm your CO, but I don't recognize you. Is this some kind of hack or spoof?"

Colonel Ford, already briefed by Lindsey, was beginning to suspect that this Devon woman was somehow infiltrating from the past.

"No, sir!" she urged. "Sir, I'm an RSF Major. Lieutenant Mathis works with me, and he would be here right now but he apparently requested a disconnect before returning from the past. I'm sure the sergeant-major can..."

"The past? What mission were you on, then?"

"Sir, as you know, it was an XT for *Operation Tempo, Mission Progenitor*, under the supervision of Intel OD Zhang. I went to the past with my entry officer, First Lieutenant Geoffery Mathis."

"Ma'am, Second Lieutenant Mathis is not under my command, but I do happen to know that the lieutenant and his captain are on training missions I cannot discuss with you. He does not report to any Major Devon, though."

John was surely curious now, because from afar

he had been eyeing Mathis for recruitment, and he also knew Director Zhang was not a name someone casually dropped the way she did.

"Sir, we were XT to alter the timeline to avoid a massive destructive subspace distortion field fast approaching our orbit."

Milona was beside herself. How could this be happening to me?

"Yes, ma'am, I'll verify that," John said, "since you seem to be grasping at straws. We have, I'm told, what seems to be a possibly harmless magnetic field approaching orbit, but the only plan I know of is one developed by our scientists to disrupt this field with some kind of particle array, or something. That's all I know about it."

"Yes, sir," she said. "It was my understanding that because Science Director Franklin's team had not perfected their solution, we were being sent in for a more direct intervention... but we all knew that it could have consequences."

"Now, I understand you are serious about your claims," he said, "but I need you to understand, ma'am, this mission you speak of is not recognized. There is no such particular *Tempo* mission to my knowledge, and your name and rank are not coming up in any records. In short, Miss Devon, and as far as we are concerned, you do not exist." Everyone was silent for a moment as he paused. "However, Director Zhang may be able to clear this up. So, I'm going to request Colonel Lindsey authorize you be shuttled up to *Orbis*. I suppose you know what *Orbis* is, too, ma'am?"

"Of course, sir. The UN Command Orbiting

Superstation. In fact, my own quarters are in Recon 4A aboard the station."

Ford, Lindsey, and Waters looked surprised at this claim, but Milona began to see a glimmer of hope, since in all of his denial, the Colonel did not deny he was working under or knew the Operations or Science Directors, and he would not have suggested just anyone to be shuttled to the station. He also did not exactly deny that there was an *Operation Tempo*.

"My shuttle will be on the way, then," Colonel Lindsey offered.

"Thank you, Colonel. I request you accompany Miss Devon to Intel and continue your investigation with Director Zhang."

*

Led out of the time machine facility by Colonel Lindsey, Milona recognized everything around her, from *Calendar* itself and all of its supervisors, to the landing platform, to the clearer skies after the rain. A shuttle ride followed, up and around the planet into the sunset and then toward the station. Nothing seems out of place, she thought, sitting silently in the rear seat of the sedan shuttle, Colonel Lindsey taking advantage of the short break to doze up front. The present seems different in some ways, but mainly the same. Maybe it's exactly the same, she thought, maybe I'm only noticing things more.

She soon realized this was probably no mere test, and it surely was no joke. Checking in with more of my commanders, she thought, would likely mean most, or none, of them will know me, since the colonel surely did not. I just don't understand how I could have disappeared from the system, when all we did was terminate Nexin. And why did Geof not return behind me? There must have been a contingent modification of the timeline, or some kind of glitch, she thought. And whose names were those in the chamber logs at *Visitor*? Also, why would the colonel not even know me? She turned these questions over and over in her mind, paying little attention to the views out the windows of the shuttle or the cool temperature, as she pulled her shawl around her a little closer.

Before long, the shuttle arrived at *Orbis* and she was escorted by Lindsey away from the small hangar at the Security Sector and down to Level Two, where he had already issued temporary guest quarters for her. Lindsey then left her to herself so that she could freshen up or take a nap, and then he went on to meet with Director Zhang. Milona merely paced around the small room again and again, kicked off her heels, and turned her questions over and over. She remembered Colonel Ford had mentioned the UN scientists. This led to her remembering her father, and it occurred to her to try to search for what information she could find. There should be some basic network clearance through the viewscreen, she reasoned. I need answers! she thought.

"Access the Public Internet," she said in the direction of the viewscreen.

'Welcome to *Orbis*,' the familiar voice said as the screen lit up with the historic UN emblem and the ring insignia of the station. Milona was relieved to hear that same soothing international tone of voice. 'Your privileges are Guest Level,' the voice added. Milona sat near the viewscreen on a thin brown lounger, keeping her shawl close around her shoulders.

"Find the UN Science Centre," she said.

'There are twenty-two thousand seven...'

"Refine search, Nadimov," she interrupted.

'There are seventeen results,' the voice said.

Milona scanned over the summaries, her eyes falling on one looking like it described research ideas.

"View Number Six," she said, and the display changed the readout to the selected page.

She read over that page, which seemed to describe for public information the various programmes ongoing. She found one paragraph describing Particle Lab Research, then stopped on one name, one of the leads, who seemed to be the director of the lab:

Dr. (Lt. Col.) Olen Nadimov, UN Intelligence
Section Chief, Particle Laboratory, UN Science

Milona knew she would have no deeper access in these quarters if she were not to be found in the databases as Colonel Ford had said. After staring at the screen for a moment, she began feeling sleepy, just then realizing how long and difficult her day had been.

"Close," she said, and the screen went blank as the calm voice responded, 'Goodbye.'

"Thank you," she mumbled, mimicking the voice as usual.

She stood up, moved over toward the plain bed, realizing how tired she was, and she thought it had been quite a long time since the colonel left. She looked down at herself, thinking she must have seemed strange or provocative to all those men in her cocktail dress, heels and mussed hair. There was only the other outfit in her in bag, and she had no sleeping clothes. Since her duty bag seemed to disappear, and since she could not get to her own quarters, she decided to simply toss her shawl off and slip out of her dress and shoes, tossing them all onto the lounger. She let her hair down fully now, dropping the sticks onto her shawl. Then she crawled into the little bed naked, the sheets feeling cold to her touch, and a tingle rolled over her skin as she slipped herself in tightly. Eventually, she warmed up as she continued to fret about her problem.

So, she mused, a scientist, Nadimov, and presumably his assistant or technical officer, were visiting my insertion, but why? Maybe he's working on the shield and nothing more. Wait a minute! He must somehow be working with the US Government in the past. Maybe he did something to the timeline to mess this all up? Of course, he is the reason why I've disappeared from my world. What a fool I've been! All along, he was either working to spoof me, or to set me up as a throwaway, and I've played right into his hands.

As her thoughts finally began to calm down, in her emotional and physical exhaustion she began to forget all about Colonels Lindsey and Ford and the mistake everyone was obviously making. Her eyes became increasingly heavy and she began to think irrationally. I suppose Major Devon's career is now derailed, she thought. She would have to start all over, she said to herself, start all over with the UN and then start over and over...

"Peter, I miss you. I had you murdered, Peter," she mumbled to herself. "I don't even exist, they said... I'm sorry, Peter..."

Crying openly on this last thought, tears rolled down her face and onto the crisp white sheets of a guest room in the Security Sector of *Orbis*, across the station from where her own quarters should be. As she eventually fell fast asleep, she was deeply disturbed and depressed by her unusual and unexpected situation. She felt as powerless as a butterfly to change anything that mattered to her.

PART THREE

21

Milona walked across a green field. There was a pond in the middle of an open area. The wind was blowing, grazing the top of the grasses and water, swaying the distant trees. It was as if there was no *Time* passing. A man then appeared on the opposite side of the pond, but she could not see who it was. She motioned for him to come to her...

"Yes!" she responded, just then startled awake by the beeping of the viewscreen in her small guest quarters.

"Hello Major, this is Security Administration Lieutenant Whitaker, assistant to UN Intelligence Operations Director Zhang," he said, his image and voice coming from the screen.

"Audio only," she said as he spoke, trying to conceal her nudity, as the screen went blank. "Sorry Lieutenant, but yes, I know who you are."

"Major, the director would like to meet with you at zero-eight-hundred."

Confused and still half asleep, Milona looked up and around the quarters, trying to see a clock.

"Lieutenant, what is the current time?" she asked with embarrassment, then realizing she could have jumped up and looked at her watch, or asked the screen after the call.

"Ma'am, current time is zero-seven-hundred twenty-one, UTC."

"Thank you... On my way, then, Lieutenant," she responded, wrestling her weight from the bed, beginning to see that this was all a good sign.

"Yes, Major," Whitaker said, closing the connection.

In the flurry of waking up, she seemed to forget what it was she had been dreaming, and tried to remember as she stood up and walked nude across the guest quarters. But wait! she thought. The lieutenant addressed me as *Major*! Yes! Perhaps this has all been cleared up! "Finally!" she said aloud to herself. "Now we're getting somewhere!"

She pulled herself together with a renewed purpose, then. Looking around the small bathroom and beginning to fully remember where she was, she now figured she had plenty of time to take a shower and make use of the spartan but functional toiletries guest quarters offered.

*

When she later emerged from the steamy lavatory, Milona thought about how good it felt to be clean, the drops of water running off of her hair and down her face and body. However, she mused, I'll still have to wear my clothes just as they are. She quickly toweled herself dry, leaving her hair slightly wet, dressed back into the insertion clothes from her bag, the khaki pants and checkered shirt, the ankle boots, leather jacket and the watch.   Regardless of being aboard *Orbis*, she knew it was either this eclectic outfit or the revealing dress and heels, snickering to herself and scooping up her things from the lounger. She hung the dress and shawl in the small closet, placing the heels with them, and she thought of Peter again as she returned to her bag, picking up the hair sticks putting them in with the purse inside the bag. She then made up the small bed and put her bag on top, all reflexive actions as she continued to think to herself.

Ever more eager to visit Intelligence and meet with Director Zhang, she walked toward the metallic door and was startled when it slid open in front of her to reveal an RG sergeant waiting for her outside. The young woman looked quite imposing, tall and rugged looking, with dark brown skin and wearing a black duty uniform coat and trousers, the silver badge quite visible on her chest, and a sidearm and utility belt across her midsection.

"Good Morning, Sergeant," she said.

"Good Morning, Major, I am Sergeant Jwahir with the Reconnaissance Guard. I'm under orders to escort you to Intelligence, ma'am."

"Please proceed, Sergeant."

*

Milona was led around to Intelligence Level Five, and on to the familiar large Mess Hall in that sector where Director Zhang awaited, and then she wondered why he had her brought here, specifically.

Zhang took a moment to look into Major Devon's blue eyes, reading in them an honesty which seemed genuine to him, she thought. After all, as he was thinking while motioning for her to sit, such a story she offered would be extremely unlikely if she were not part of an alternate timeline. But, how childlike she seemed as she sat down in the nearly empty mess hall, her eyes darting around and determined at the same time. Yet, the major was no child, he could see, as she had a deadly serious tone about her, somehow, and she also reminded him of his own daughter, Cassie, down in Shanghai. Obviously, the woman was caught in a vulnerable and troubling situation.

"Carry on, Sergeant," he said to Jwahir.

"Yes, Director," she responded, turning and walking well away to leave them alone to talk.

"At ease, Major," he said, bringing his eyes back to Milona, "Are you hungry?"

"Extremely, sir," she said, lowering her head.

She was inwardly very pleased the lieutenant, sergeant, and director had all addressed her by her rank. Perhaps they really did believe her, she wondered, as Zhang now motioned for the server already standing by to come over and take their order.

"Major?" he offered.

"Yes, Specialist, I think the mushroom melt special and fried potatoes will be fine, with an orange soda," she said timidly as she ordered, "one of my favourites," she added.

She felt slightly embarrassed, now suddenly in a comparably intimate situation with such a superior officer, one whom she had only formally met the day before in her timeline, and today, he doesn't even know me at all, she noted.

"Make that two, please," he said with a smile, realizing as he looked back again at the major that she had not actually looked at a menu.

"Yes, General," the server said, and rushed away across the large open space.

"Please, Major Devon, I hope you will be able to relax and stop worrying about the situation. I apologize for what happened down at *Calendar*. Colonels Lindsey and Ford, Major Waters and Sergeant-Major Mitchell are all well-intentioned officers doing their duty, but honestly, it's not really surprising they were unprepared for this kind of eventuality."

Milona's heart raced and she thought that perhaps this was all a test or a mix-up after all.

"Actually, I wasn't prepared, either," he continued with a laugh, "but we old spymasters have our moments."

"Sir, what about Colonel Lindsey? Isn't he..."

"I wanted to meet with you alone. Recon Guard and the Warrant Corps now see there is no threat."

"Director, I'm surprised you're taking me so seriously, sir. I'm very happy for it, of course, but surprised... I mean, why would you so easily believe what I've said?"

"Well, it's very elementary, Major. Someone appears from a time machine we tightly control, whom we do not know. You emerged from a highly secured covert area on an Army Base in the distant past, you requested a two-hour delay, and you have knowledge of the present that is very unlikely to be gained through Special Agent Gibbs or Captain Oglesby's staff. While UN Command does not tell the Americans in that time frame everything about what we're doing, we are at least reasonably sure they are not sending infiltration agents our way. There's a certain order to things in our Temporal Alliance."

"I'm very relieved, Director."

"You'll also be happy to know I've verified from *Calendar* that your First Lieutenant Mathis did authorize the end of your synchro, which if accurate, means he exists in both the past and the present, but with different ranks and duties. I've also talked with our Second Lieutenant Mathis, who reports he has never heard of you, nor has he yet met Colonel Ford. There really is just no way to fake all of this evidence," Zhang said, "unless you really are on a mission of some kind from the future, not the past, in which case, just like the Americans, we have little choice but to coöperate with you."

"Unbelievable, sir," she sighed with relief, impressed with the director's reasoning and kindness.

"I'd like to think we're sophisticated enough to know these kinds of consequences could be likely complications from our temporal research," he whispered as the server brought their order. "Thank you, Specialist," he added.

"Thank you," she chimed.

The two sipped their sodas and began eating, each measuring their thoughts about what would happen next. Eventually, Zhang broke the silence between them.

"Major, I want you to know I'll be presenting everything to the Director-General shortly. Are there any other details you want to add to what you've already told everyone?"

"Well, sir, I will gladly say, the only mission I'm working on is from the present, authorized by you, called *Mission Progenitor*, a part of *Operation Tempo*." She spoke plainly and calmly, trying to hide her emotions. "We were to find out everything possible about a Philosophy Professor, Peter Nexin, who in that past we suspected of innocently initiating key particular subspace and temporal research leading to time travel itself, which had only been theoretical before then. It was our temporal work over time that seems to have attracted an odd distortion field which is feared will destroy us all. So, after I verified, Mathis and I were to... well, remove Nexin from the timeline, and return. We trained for weeks and visited the past many times changing nothing. Lieutenant Mathis and I went XT only after meeting with the Command Chiefs, yourself and Director Franklin, a number of senators and Chancellor Kitamori just yesterday. Then... we did... execute the target, we left the scene, and here I am. I don't have any idea why Mathis was delayed, or why everyone here would not know me."

"You said the Chancellor?" he asked, "I haven't actually met her in person yet."

"Sure, you... Oh, of course... She only took office recently and they came to the station in part for us, this mission," she mumbled, "and so if that reason were taken away..."

"We met here, on *Orbis*?" the director asked, "I

think I would have remembered that like it was yesterday."

"Well, sir, it was yesterday for me," she added with a hint of sarcasm, and they both laughed at the turn of events.

She continued with a few more details about her life for the director as they continued with their lunch. By the end of the meal he was even more convinced, and the two had hatched a theory, as he would put it. Something very subtle must have happened to influence Peter Nexin's contemporaries to pursue their ideas, they reasoned. Nexin's suggestions were taken up and quoted by innovative scientists, thus leading eventually to various temporal experiments. This had been the key to all of their confusion, but why did their execution fail, though?

"The whole modern history of the problem," he said, "must have already stemmed from one of Nexin's students or friends at the time you were there. Maybe they felt a duty to take up the mantle after his death?"

Unfortunately, Milona could not remember or report anything significant about any of the students or others she had observed, stopping short of admitting to the director that her focus was perhaps a bit too strong on the professor. Ultimately, they could reason no more, but before she left the Mess Hall with the sergeant, she pleaded with the director to let her return to the past.

"Sir, I can only ask you to let me go back and fix all of this somehow, to put it right, sir. *Tempo* was put off course, and *Progenitor* eliminated someone wrongly, only because we concluded that Nexin was the only one to execute, that it would be the end of the story. Peter Nexin must be allowed to live, sir, because his death has obviously not changed anything at all we set out to change. It was wrong for us to murder him."

*

Sergeant Jwahir was quiet again as she escorted the mysterious major back to her guest quarters. Milona finally felt as though she could relax and breathe, turning the conversation with Zhang over and over in her mind. She thought she had told him everything that could help, and she was now filled with hope that this would all be worked out as they now stood still on the treadway. Jwahir remained quiet as Milona looked about the familiar station blankly.

Once alone again in the guest quarters, with nothing else to do but wait, Milona started to wonder about which other parts of her life may have been affected by this mistake on their part. Forced to settle down and relax, she began thinking of her parents, about Jennifer, Geof, Jon, and the shadowy Nadimov figure. If I've never existed in this present timeline, she thought, then they wouldn't know me, either. She looked over toward the blank viewscreen, then plopped herself down on the small lounger in front of it.

The system reported that her clearances were upgraded to level 1 across the sectors, which told her everything. However, only minutes into her searching she found she was not enjoying this trip down memory lane, because she could find no information on her mother or father, even though a Doctor Gotthard Devon

should be in the UN system. But wait! she recalled.
My mother was Belina Courcoux before marrying. A
search on that turned up results describing a Belina
Courcoux married to Pierre Tourbier, living in Paris.
My stars! she thought. So, my father didn't exist, and
my mother is married to someone I've never even heard
of! No wonder I don't exist!

She quickly tried to find Jon Martin, learning he
was living in New York, listed on a biography page as
working for a quantum technology research firm in
Manhattan for the last two years. He was married to a
Linda and had two children. Milona then faintly
remembered him mentioning someone named Linda
once, after he attended a technology seminar in Berlin.
Linda was always trying to get him involved in that
field in America, Milona recalled, or maybe it was
London, but anyway, our relationship, such as it was,
seemed to keep him in Europe as a therapist. He just
wanted so much more than I could give, regardless.

Now in frustration, Milona stood up and walked
over near the window, pushed a button to open the
blinds so she could see outside, across the inner ring of
the space station and the blue Earth below. "It's true,
then," she said aloud, "I was never born, I never lived,
and even the bloodline leading to me on my father's
side never happened. My own mother would not even
recognize me if I called her right now, nor would Jon,
or Geof, or Jennifer, or anyone else!"

She looked out around the ring of windows,
again to the planet below and up to the black of space
above, again wishing she could be in her own quarters.
I could curl up on my own lounger listening to music,

or better yet, get into my own bed and just sleep for a week. Let's see, my quarters are right across there, she thought, leaning closer to the thick glass, pointing slightly and looking across to the opposite Recon Sector of the massive station. She followed the rows of windows, up from the bottom to Level Four, then clicked off in her mind which ones she thought were hers. Or are they mine? she asked herself, unable to avoid her disturbing situation. There appeared to be a dim light on in one of those windows, but she could not see any activity. It was too far away to see any details. Is it me in there, she mused, or some other Recon officer pretending to be me, or living their own life?

Just then, the viewscreen behind her beeped with an incoming call, and Milona welcomed the interruption this time, turning to answer. It was Director Zhang, calling her directly.

"Major, I hope you have been resting."

"Not really, sir."

"I think I understand," he said. "I wanted to tell you myself. I've met with Director-General Lorentz, and then we briefed the other chiefs and the Chancellor. After some deliberation, you'll understand, they have decided to agree with our assessment. It must have been one of Nexin's students who took good notes, or there is some other explanation to cause with Nexin's death nothing more than your own disappearance from the present."

"Sir?" she asked, unsure where he was leading.

"Major, you are therefore authorized to return to the past through *Calendar*..."

Milona jumped with excitement as Zhang

continued.

    "...Report to the Meeting Hall in the Intelligence Sector at ten-hundred, and we will all discuss your new mission in more detail then with all the players. You are likely to leave right away."

    "Yes, sir!"

22

"If Major Devon's testimony is true," Director-General Lorentz said, "then the best option is for the major to return to the past, to some point in time before she had ordered First Lieutenant Mathis to execute Professor Nexin."

The large group had been quickly assembled in the Intelligence Meeting Hall on *Orbis*, as well as where Lorentz was, at the Senate in the Chair of the Senate's meeting room. At the Senate were the Chancellor, Vice Chancellor, and the key senators, with the Directors of Science and Information, as well as General of Defense Whitney, all of whom were already meeting on the shield matrix. The group on *Orbis* included the Directors of Operations, Counter-Intelligence, and Analysis, as well as RSF General Venda, and RCT General Frederickson. Both groups included advisors and other generals.

Science Director Franklin, at the Senate, began to feel nervous, while Director Zhang and RSF Colonel Ford, on the station, were intrigued by the possibility. They had all just heard Devon complete her long description of events to them, and now sat silent for a moment of reflection.

Milona was very nervous, and feared she would have to meet strong objections from many division officers, senators, and Chancellors, but she repeatedly urged herself to calm down, given the respected Director-General Lorentz and Director Zhang were indeed on her side.

"I suggest the major simply track herself," General Venda added. "Major Devon would be well aware of her own movements in the past, and could easily do what is necessary to prevent the XT without further disruption."

"But Generals, is this even physically possible?" asked Colonel Lindsey, who Zhang had asked to be present to continue following the case as normal investigation. "Can there be two Major Devons in the same time frame?"

"Actually Colonel," Milona replied, as all heads turned toward her, "Aren't I living evidence that once transmitted through a temporal tunnel, matter cannot be controlled by timeline discontinuities? Obviously, this can have drastic consequences, if neglected."

"Major," Director Franklin asked, "will this affect our research in the Particle Lab? The shield is being readied as we speak."

"When I originally left, ma'am, your team was very close to a solution, and from what I can tell, those events are entirely unconnected to my timelines. So, I presume this proposed action will not affect your mission in the least."

Director Franklin was put at ease by this comment, even though Milona felt she had glossed over the fact that Franklin's plan had been sidelined due to failure, at least according to the last information Milona received. There must have been great progress while she and Mathis were away, Milona thought, or perhaps a whole different chain of events has occurred.

"Well," the Analysis Director said after a pause, her red duty uniform's decorations catching the light as she turned, "it does seem a bit outlandish..."

"But quite interesting, you'll admit," the Counter-Terrorism General added, who sat adjacent to Milona in his black camouflage battle fatigue jumpsuit. "I mean stopping yourself from performing an XT which had previously somehow erased you? Talk about being beside yourself!"

Milona and most of the two groups laughed for a moment at General Frederickson's quip, and the tension lifted from all of their faces.

"I'll agree," Director Zhang noted, "this seems very irregular from our perspective, but I think we should go forward. Major Devon has been questioned again and again by Colonels Ford and Lindsey and myself. Her knowledge of things, details from our here-and-now, is all sterling. We also know that the executive action she described changed nothing with respect to our problem, so we have an ethical duty to let her... restore things."

"I agree as well, "Senator Hassan said. "If we murdered someone in the past and it didn't even change the problem, then we simply must correct that error!"

"I agree, too," Chancellor Kitamori said.

Milona felt everyone in the meeting seemed to be taken aback by her story and the proposed solution, but she also felt they were nevertheless going to agree.

She could somehow tell they understood what was intended by herself and Director Zhang, but she also began to lose her full concentration. All the worry over Peter and the ensuing complications had weighed her down, and now she was deeply exhausted. The rest of the meeting seemed a blur to her, and lucky enough for her, she was not called on directly for any further details about the proposed mission she would call *Rewind*. She nodded and said yes when necessary, but eventually, when the Chancellor called for a show of hands and everyone agreed, Milona was a picture of relief. They would be sending her back to the past to correct what had happened. She would save Peter.

*

After napping for a half-hour, Milona slowly opened her eyes and saw a plain ceiling of the guest quarters. Little by little, she roused herself off the bed feeling slightly better rested and beginning to regain her clear thoughts. She barely remembered the details of returning to the room on the director's recommendation she get a little more rest after the meeting. She knew she could have slept much longer, but the weight of things kept her from slipping into a deeper sleep. She stood up slowly, wiped her face, and made her way to the lavatory to splash herself with water. She wiped her wet hands on her face and ran them through her hair, straightened her shirt and trousers, and checked herself in the mirror. How drained her face now seemed, as she studied her rather gaunt appearance and near ashen complexion. When this is all over, she thought, I'm going to sleep for a week and eat myself fat! Perhaps they will grant me some vacation time. I'll be able to visit my Mother in Paris. Boy, will I have a story to tell! Except I can't tell it, of course.

She walked over to the small closet, pulled out her silver cocktail outfit and walked over to the bed where she had thrown her bag, packing the things as neatly as she could. She thought about how pleased she was to be allowed to go back and prevent Peter from having been killed. I may not be able to stay in the past, she thought, but at least his death will be avoided. I will be so excited to see him again, but my personal feelings should not hide the fact that the situation is now more complicated than ever. It will certainly be a strange thing to confront myself in the past.

She looked down at her old watch, noting she had a little less than an hour before she was to depart back to *Calendar*. But turning over her thoughts, something still bothered her about Doctor Nadimov. Why was he visiting her insertion before? She picked up her bag, turned and grabbed her leather jacket off the back of the lounger, and then took a last look around. She felt it unlikely she would be back to these temporary quarters again, and then headed out the door to meet Sergeant Jwahir, who had patiently waited outside. She requested the sergeant take her to the Reconnaissance Sector before leaving the station.

*

Sergeant Jwahir nodded to Major Devon, indicating she was clear to enter Master Sergeant

Collett's office.   Milona took a breath and braced herself, stepping in through the open doorway, hoping at the last second that all of this would have been a mere hoax, and that Jennifer would immediately recognize her. Maybe there would be at least some connection to her life in the present.

"May I help you, ma'am?" Jennifer said, standing at her desk in a duty uniform coat and skirt, curious as to whom this visitor was that the RG sergeant brought to her.

"Jennifer?"

Milona paused. She was instantly crestfallen, stung by Jennifer's obvious lack of recognition, suddenly pounded in the chest once again by the weight of her situation.

"Excuse me, ma'am?"

"No... excuse me," she said, tearing up. "RSF Major Devon, Master Sergeant. I suppose you don't recognize me do you?"

"No, I don't, ma'am. Should I?"

"My name is Milona, and if you check your files on today's Intelligence briefings you'll know at least something about me."

Milona was crushed, and tried in vain to hide it. It was one thing to be unknown to a bunch of men she worked with and barely knew, but that her best friend did not know her one whit beyond the regular reports of the day was too much to take.

"Ma'am, I don't have access to that kind of..."

"Jennifer, with your Administrator clearances I'm going to assume you know just about as much as anyone about a mysterious woman who appeared from nowhere and was brought to the station. Look at how I'm dressed. I know this all seems very odd to you right now, but you and I..."

Jennifer was moved as the major paused, and Milona thought it now mattered very little if, between her tears, she simply came out with what was on her mind. Jennifer would keep it confidential, she thought, and perhaps she could get some information on Doctor Nadimov beyond public access.

"You see," Milona continued, "in a different timeline, we have been friends for many years. We met when I was a first lieutenant training in Washington DC, where you grew up. You were recruited as a corporal before later attending college."

"How do you know all of that?"

Jennifer was becoming very uncomfortable as the major reminisced. This was moving, she thought, but it must be some kind of a joke or test, she wondered. Who is this woman? she wanted to ask, looking to the sergeant outside the door. She had seen some of the briefings but tuned them out, assuming they had nothing directly to do with her office.

"I know a lot more," Milona said, wiping her eye. "You're up for sergeant-major this month, possibly even a jump to command officer grade, because you've run *Orbis* Recon by yourself since the lieutenant colonel was reassigned to *Mars 5*. Your fiancé, Will, is up for captain himself, and might very well be stationed at UN Treasury in Hong Kong by now. You and I had lunch, just yesterday in my timeline, down in the Level Five Mess."

"Ma'am..." Jennifer started, but sat down at her

desk, crossing her legs and resting her head on her hand. How could this Major Devon have anything to do with me? she asked herself, quickly pulling up the briefings onto her desk's surface.

"Milona. Please," she asked, sitting in the nearby chair across Jennifer's desk.

"Milona, then. Just what do you want from me, if you don't mind my asking."

"Well, I admit I'd wanted to see if you would recognize me, but that not being the case, I also came to request a 201 on a Doctor Nadimov." Jennifer rolled her eyes, but Milona continued, speaking faster. "He's a UN Science section chief in Berlin, that's all I need, nothing more..."

"Why?"

"It's a long story, and I hope you'll just understand and trust me. I'm not asking for anything beyond your clearances or discretion. It's just that for the time being, I'm merely a guest on station..."

"If this comes back to bite me..."

"It won't. Believe me."

*

Milona walked with Sergeant Jwahir away from the Recon office, away from seeing Jennifer, and the tears filled her eyes again, rolling down. She had the distinct feeling she had failed, and if given another chance, she would definitely try to be a better friend.

"Sergeant, do you think I did wrong?" she asked Jwahir as they walked.

Milona thought she had nothing to lose, since

no one knew her. The RG sergeant may as well be my friend from some other timeline, she mused.

"Ma'am," she said, "It is not my place to judge."

"But, Sergeant?"

"Major, I think you did nothing wrong, if you must know my opinion. Sometimes the rules can be bent a little."

"I appreciate that, Sergeant. I suppose I did bend them somewhat, and perhaps Directors Zhang or Franklin would have given me the same information if I had only asked? It's just that... Well, it's..."

"She was your friend."

"Yes. She was my friend," she said, beginning to tear up again with emotion.

She was my best friend, Milona thought, really my only friend, since I've moved to the station and pushed Jon away, and since Mother seems to get along fine with my being gone for long periods. I suppose she got used to it with father gone on so many scientific missions. I didn't realize how important everyone was to me until now. Peter, who should have been merely a target, had become my most intimate friend, and look how that turned out! I mean, I come back here and not a soul knows who I am!

Milona brought her hand up to her eyes to catch another tear from rolling down her cheek. The irony now is that in order to get them all back, I have to go to the distant past and risk never returning to see them. But, even that means more to me now, just to put things right, than to make it easier on myself somehow. Yes, Sergeant, Jennifer was my friend, Milona thought, as Jwahir led her down the corridor toward a hangar, pretending not to notice the major's crying.

They walked the rest of the distance quietly, through the corridors around the observation deck, on their way to one of the Intelligence Sector shuttle hangars, where a ship awaited them for the flight to *Calendar*. They got to the hangar quickly enough, Milona thought, and as they had marched on, she began to feel better about the mission. She realized it would not be much longer before this whole ugly mess was cleared up, one way or another. As they passed into the small hanger on Level Three, she took in the curvature of the Earth beneath the station and the view of the Moon in the distance outside the hangar's airlock shield, wondering how she had become so bound up with the fate of things.

23

As the olive drab shuttle lifted off of the landing platform at *Calendar*, Sergeant Jwahir looked on as Major Devon stopped in her tracks on the industrial-styled staircase. Of all the things to notice on the short trip down from the station, Milona found herself now moved by the quietness of Jackson Station as the shuttle's whine faded away. While here was a powerful hum from the microwave receivers and the power station over to her left, the lush green trees of the forest in the early morning sunrise with blue sky overhead, she felt it all seemed so peaceful. Now lured by the movement of a deer in the trees, she took a moment to step back up the couple of stairs she had come down, back onto the platform, then she walked over to the edge. It was just a chance to simply breathe the fresh air, take in the scents, and relax, even for just a few seconds, she mused.

"Major?" Major Waters called from below at the station door. "Are you okay?"

"Just a second, Waters," she answered, holding up a finger to indicate pause, wondering why she didn't seem as mindful about these things more often.

Oh, I suppose I always have been, she thought,

but the last day or two has just been too crazy. How nice it would be to go for a hike, not far from here in the Appalachians, or go for a run on the sands of the Andean beaches, or discover some corner of the globe I haven't yet seen, she mused. Somehow, she felt she might not ever be able to return home. With a sigh, she reluctantly turned back toward the power station and made her way down the staircase toward Major Waters. She noticed he was eyeing her as usual, even if he did not know her in this timeline, and perhaps that made it even more glaring.

"It's really quite beautiful out here. Isn't it, Major?" he said, leading she and the sergeant into the station, down the corridor to the security lock, toward *Calendar*'s control room. "Perhaps you could stay long enough for a coffee sometime, if you come back and everything is okay."

She thought Waters was the one person she had encountered in all of this who did not seem any different by not knowing her. The major didn't skip a beat, she laughed to herself, but perhaps it was due as much to how she toyed with him from a distance.

"Now, Colonel Ford has briefed me on the situation," he continued, "and let me offer my assistance in any way you need."

"Thank you, Major," she said curtly, more concerned with the time, noting by her watch it was nearing twelve o'clock, which was 12:00 UTC, or 7:00 am at the station. She could reset her watch for the past when she could firm her ideas up on what time she was going to target for insertion, but then it occurred to her that noontime might be best, anyway.

The three then waited quietly for the inner door to slide open, and then stepped into the control room to find the sergeant-major and his crew awaiting them. The crew had been alerted by Colonel Ford about this new mission as Major Devon was shuttled down, and they were instructed to give her all assistance.

"Welcome back, Major," Sergeant-Major Mitchell said. "We are ready for you, ma'am."

"Thank you, Sergeant-Major," she replied, smiling, and then she turned to acknowledge the other engineers, "Master Sergeant, Corporals," and then she nodded to the physician, as well, "Lieutenant."

She assumed the doctor would take the normal precaution, while the lieutenant would not have remembered giving her the injection just the day before. Doses were usually effective for at least a week, but no matter, she thought, preparing to receive the nearly painless injection again. Two in as many days probably wouldn't hurt anything. As the lieutenant inspected her, a small telltale was noted of a very recent injection, and the lieutenant nodded to Waters. Maybe the major really was telling the truth.

Remembering her reflections during the shuttle ride down from the station, Milona considered again what time she should target, and again tried to recall the flow of events during her previous day in the past. As everyone else fidgeted about at their stations she knew it would be necessary to meet herself somehow before she had sent Geof into Nexin's home to murder him, of course, but when? She considered what might be the best path to herself without complications, and after a moment, she figured the general time between Peter's two classes would be best, but she still did not know what precise moment would be right. Perhaps, it would be best to confront myself... say after that lunch with Peter, but before the introductory class later in the day. Yes, I know the perfect moment to approach her... me... Uh, myself!

"Ma'am," Mitchell asked, "I hope you have had a chance to think about what time you'll be visiting?"

"Yes, Sergeant-Major. On reflection, I think the best time will be seventeen-hundred local time in the past on the same day I'd arrived from." She didn't quite know exactly what she was going to do yet, but twelve o'clock would give her a roomy window to complete her mission.

"Will do, Major," he said, dialing in the chamber control settings himself with a nod.

*

The Army staff sergeant and his corporal who were manning the control room seemed confused to see the major again, and stood at attention in their fatigue uniforms after hearing the usual noises and seeing her appear. 'Busy day,' the staff sergeant mumbled to himself, saluting Major Devon as she emerged from the chambers. I'm pretty sure she is still here, he mused. I know she hasn't gone back.

"At ease," she said.

"Welcome, ma'am," the controller said.

"Staff Sergeant, I need to speak with Captain Oglesby. Is he available?"

"Yes, Major. I'll contact him, ma'am."

"I'll just wait over here, Staff Sergeant."

"Yes, ma'am."

She looked around the spartan control room where things had become so confusing with Geof and she reflected on the flow of events during their day.

"Ma'am, I've got the captain on the line, but he may not be available to meet with you right away. Is there something we can help you with?"

"Oh, sure," she said, "I only need a ride into town. It's a long story..."

"Sir?" the sergeant asked the captain, "Major Devon just needs a covered lift into town. Sir, she apparently does not have the car." He paused, listening to the captain tell him he would send out his lieutenant. "Yes, sir," he said, hung up the phone, then nodded to the major. "Ma'am, it won't be a problem."

"Thank you..."

"The captain is sending Lieutenant Jeffers, ma'am, and the lieutenant will gladly take you into town. The lieutenant should be here in around fifteen minutes, ma'am."

"That will be fine, Staff Sergeant. I've got nothing but time," she said with a hint of a smile.

The staff sergeant wondered why the major would be so concerned about needing a ride. It was their sole mission to give her just about anything she asked for, short of any threat to national security. A lift into town was nothing to them, he thought, but then he tossed his concern aside and returned to his post, as the major was always very polite. He was sure she had a good reason.

Milona sat down and waited patiently for

Lieutenant Jeffers, continuing to turn over in her mind the best way to handle this business of approaching herself and Geof. I mean, what do I do? Walk up and say, 'Hello, Major,' or something? 'Get this, Milona, I'm you, about a day from now?' Perhaps I could just kill myself somehow, but that wouldn't be any easier than killing Peter, in fact, how would that possibly work? What a strange form of suicide, that would be!

✳

"Mind if I ask you a question, Major?" First Lieutenant Jeffers asked as they drove.

"As long as it's not personal," she joked.

"No, ma'am," he said, laughing.

"Fire away, then."

Jeffers sat relaxed in the driver's seat of an unmarked black utility vehicle, driving down the streets of the base, toward the city's downtown blocks. His civilian clothes looked new, she thought, and his reddish sandy hair appeared from underneath a baseball cap, which he adjusted again and again.

"Where you come from, Major... I mean, in your time, is our country... is the US still the most powerful military force in the world?"

"Let's call that a personal question, Lieutenant," she said, under strict instructions not to divulge such information to people in other time frames.

"Please pardon me, Major, I..."

"Oh, it's okay, Lieutenant," she said, falling silent as she looked out the window.

She knew his question was as innocent as it

could be, but she still could not answer it, now matter how interesting to him and obvious to her the answer would sound. It would violate several TAP regulations if she even indicated in the most minor way to the lieutenant that the United States was not a notable power in her time. No member of the United Nations can be as singular or powerful as the US once was, especially because of the myriad problems the US empire created. It is tempting to discuss, however, because while this young man will be retiring, decades away from his point of view, his proud country will be going through a cascade of political and economic failures imploding its strength in the world, and all other developed nations will eventually find similar conditions as a result.

Recalling her History, she was suddenly intrigued by the facts from this perspective. For decades, she remembered, during the last failures of typical Hayekian Capitalism, US Presidents would struggle to keep allies in peace as they formed the Federation of the Americas. The struggle would take years though, faltering through slow world-wide depressions into the final trade wars between the nations of the Federation, African Union, Islamic Consulate, European Union and Pacific-Asian Federation, all of it during the heights of disease and terrorism. Nearly all nations, and international institutions such as NATO and the IMF, finally shed their ruse of globalization and achieved a sustainable world government in a new United Nations. It all happened in part because of US arrogance and failures in policy. Never again, one of her professors had said, would any UN member nation ever be allowed to lord such vast powers over other nations. Never again would wars based on Religion or Nationalism even be possible. Though there will always be problems with terrorism and separatism, never again would one class of society be allowed to enslave the rest for profit.

Of course, she thought, glancing over at the lieutenant, I hadn't even had cause to think about all this until his question, but how strange it is even to visit the US during this time frame, at the start of their long collapse. All at once, this is like visiting military Sparta or democratic Athens, imperial Rome during its slow decay, or London before the colonial revolts. What a History lesson this is now becoming! A natural, inevitable evolution of society and history is happening all around, and the people of this time are too close, or too proud, to see it.

But, it wasn't all bad, of course. Without the long history of world empires like the US economic empire, the pervasive freedom of nations enjoyed in my time might not have developed. We might not have been able to build a world military, standardize networks and protocols, or spread humanitarian and medical advances. Though hundreds of languages are still actively spoken and promoted, and traditional cultures have again thrived, there has been an undeniable impact of American and Western values on the world. So, maybe the lieutenant's question wasn't such a terrible one, after all.

"Tell you what, Lieutenant," she said, smiling. "I'll give you another chance to ask a question. Better make it a good one." She looked at the younger man with a smile.

"Thank you, Major," he said, smiling back, taking a moment to reflect. "I guess I have been wondering, ma'am... does it hurt?"

"Hurt?" she asked.

"I mean, going through that wormhole, ma'am, travelling years, decades, or centuries in a spit-second. What's it like?"

She considered there could be little risk to UN interests or US national interests in this topic, and she was relieved to be able to respond to Jeffers' need to connect with her as someone from the future. She tried for a moment to think of a good analogy to her trips.

"So, have you ever had a chance to try bungee jumping, Lieutenant?"

"Several times, Major. I'm paratrooper trained, as well."

"Good," she said, looking at him, "It's a lot like that, in a way, then. A leap of faith. It doesn't hurt, really, but there is a definite tingle. The physicians," she continued, thinking of the Security Medical officers whom she could not mention by position, "they tell me my whole body just stops still, for just a micro-instant."

"Really, ma'am?"

"It just freezes or solidifies in place, I guess, because I instantly pass through the temporal tunnel at a much higher mass, but it doesn't do any harm because it happens so fast. My watch stops, too. So, if I weren't thrown through so fast, I'd probably die very quickly."

"Wow!"

"You just have to trust these scientists and engineers, that they've got it right," she said.

Milona looked out the windscreen, over the shiny black hood to the pavement rushing toward them, holding her arms slightly outward and sitting up straight in her seat with her eyes closed.

"And then, you just jump."

24

Only a few more papers to grade, Peter noted, having put most of them off for his lunch with Milona. After a few minutes of trying, he found he was looking over one of them again and again, then realizing he wasn't concentrating on it at all. He recalled walking across campus earlier with a noticeable spring in his step, looking forward to meeting her. He remembered their short walk around the Statehouse grounds, to get their lunch, and then eating under the shade. He remembered Milona kissing him, and then he was quite sure he was not concentrating on the papers at all. His day, he thought, was definitely beginning to revolve around Milona, and he felt powerless to stop it.

He sat motionless in the empty shared office, the other adjunct professors elsewhere, his bookbag sitting on the guest chair and the computer at his desk filling the room with its humming white noise. He rested his head in his hands for a moment, staring blankly at the wall, which displayed several arts posters and a calendar, and then he allowed a smile to roll across his mouth. Milona was beginning to pervade his every thought, a welcome addition, he admitted, but he had so much work to do!

Looking away from the wall at the computer in front of him, he ran his fingers down his blue and gold checkered tie, and thought perhaps looking at his mail would jar him back into concentration. He hit "F12" on the keyboard, launching his email program on the screen. Looking across a couple of email messages, he nearly passed them all over without noticing a message from a journal editor he had been awaiting for weeks. His eyes opened fully as he read the message, which was an informal notice that his paper on Temporal Theory was to be published in their next issue. He was very excited about this news, leaning back in his chair for a moment to savour it, but was interrupted by a knock on the door. A look up revealed his Department Chair, Jarvis Beard, and just the sight of him, dressed in a grey sweater and brown jeans, seemed to drain Peter's happiness away.

"How's your day going, Peter?" the pale-looking academic administrator asked.

"Well," Peter happily reported, "I've learned my 'Metaphysics of Time' paper is to be published!"

"That's great, Peter. Where?"

"*Phainomena*," he offered.

"Ah," Beard replied with his usually smug academic undertone.

Beard thought such an obscure European journal might not really count as 'published' in his proud view. Beard always enjoyed looking down his nose at Peter and the others, never giving them an ounce of encouragement, not since he made tenure decades ago. The only way to succeed in Academia, he thought, was to stay with the mainstream topics, focus on the grants and other administravia, and try not to take Philosophy too seriously. He learned this the hard way, and actually took delight in watching his juniors trip up on it in their zeal to set themselves apart.

"This means my new book won't be such a hard sell," Peter said, very pleased his ideas could become an easier read for editors, and he was feeling a shot in the arm as a philosopher.

"Are you sure you want to go down this road?" Beard quizzed, unable to get on board with Peter's motivations. "I mean, I wouldn't use the term 'Metaphysics' today, and Philosophy of Physics isn't at all mainstream either. Are you sure you have the background for it? Maybe you should crack a few more important journals with reviews and critical pieces in and around Realism or Compatibilism."

"Well," Peter mused with anger, though not wishing to insult his Department Chair, "I'll have to think about that."

Peter fumed below the surface at Beard's series of put downs, but struggled to keep it all to himself. He had no interest in toeing the party line of academic mediocrity. This is *Philosophy*, after all! I'm supposed to ask difficult questions, right? A true philosopher doesn't just adjust their ideas to fit what is fashionable this season! Maybe that's the problem with all of our institutionalized Education. It just leads to algorithms of boredom.

"Okay," Beard returned dismissively, "but you don't want to be an MA Adjunct forever. You might think about getting into a doctoral program, and what they might like to see on your CV, acceptable topics, good letters, and so on."

"I'll think about it," Peter repeated, with no intention of taking the Chair seriously. "Thanks."

"Oh, I expect you'll be here tomorrow?" Beard said, as he turned in the doorway. "You'll help us with the grant applications and course plans for next semester?"

"Sure," Peter said.

Peter threw Beard a shallow smile, while Beard offered back an equally fallow grin. Beard then turned and made his way down the hall, finding himself surprisingly concerned about Peter's career, but at the same time, unable to avoid relief that one more half-hearted fundraiser for the department would be pushed out of the way. That's all professional Philosophy is today, he mused, fundraising and irrelevant discussion. Perhaps I'm only jealous of Nexin.

Empty academic! Peter thought, watching in absolute disgust as Beard navigated his hallowed hall. He's in Humanities purely for the credentials, for the climb up the administrative ladder, the would-be Dean or Provost, all while people like me do real Philosophy the hard way for the ideas! Grant applications and begging the rich departments for funding, that's the most important task here. What happened to Philosophy? It died in Academia.

Looking back at his email, Peter knew that true advances in the History of Ideas and inspiring teaching were long gone from American Education. That's a laugh, he thought. Paglia was right, the Humanities in America really were dying. Philosophy has been dead for a long time, just another bureaucratic department at

University, killed by mediocre academics, sucklings on a state tit, scared of ideas, their job to justify their own existence in the budget against all the other more successful and relevant departments that were actually born out of Philosophy over the years.

One day I'll make the move and be out of here, working on my own, publishing whatever I like, not having to constantly justify my existence, justify my very ideas, to these mediocrities. Doctoral work is a laugh all to itself, I have no use for it. More and more specialization in an increasingly evaporating field? What is the point? Assuming I could hack the massive competition and deceptions, and assuming they would accept me at my age, I'd rather be more free than less free. Just one or two more pubs, that's all I need to keep them happy. Then, get my book out, maybe, and then I can be independent. His thoughts trailed off in anger as he tried to get his mind back on the real success at hand, and away from his negative feelings surrounding what he variously called "Acanemia" and "Agonemia". Jack will understand, he thought, reaching within himself to overcome his frustration. I think I'll tell him. Peter opened up a new email window and quickly typed it out:

> *Jack,*
> *Good news!   :)   My Time paper will be published next month!   This is very cool!*
> *Maybe you and I can grab a beer and chat sometime in the next day or two?*
> *Nex*

"You Humanities people," Jack said at the door.

Jack happened to appear while Peter was typing and knocked on the doorframe just as Peter was sending the message. He wore with ease his dark blue suit coat and trousers, yellow tie and white pinstriped shirt.

"I was just emailing you," Peter said, surprised, if not ready to fight, after feeling shot out of the sky.

"I'm done for the day," Jack said, "I just had a lunch with my Chair."

"Ugh," Peter moaned, then whispered, "mine just left, the wasted flesh. I hope the Physics Chair isn't as... you know what? Nevermind, I don't even want to finish that sentence."

"Well, I think I know what you mean. And the answer is no," Jack said with a smirk.

"As you said, Professor Crowley, we 'Humanities people'. The stakes get lower every year."

"Okay... so anyway..." Jack interjected with a laugh, understanding of Peter's frustration, but trying to cheer him up. "I was in the neighborhood, and I wanted to know if you would come hear me give a talk."

"Sure, when?"

"Tomorrow, over in Jones."

"What time?"

"Two o'clock."

"Well, I have the one class earlier, and I have to help out here with some paperwork, but I think I can swing it."

"Great, I could use the audience."

Jack had been making strides in recent years, Peter thought, getting his experimental evidence together and giving talks in support of his theories. He had been building up to publishing a larger paper or monograph, but he knew it was something which needed to be done methodically and based firmly in experimental findings.

"Oh, guess who I had lunch with?" Peter asked, as Jack looked blank. "Milona Devon. You know that smart beauty I told you about?" Peter lowered his voice again, this time playfully mocking that he did not want anyone else to overhear them.

"Really," Jack said in a matching whisper, picking up the cue, plopping down on the guest chair against Peter's bookbag and mimicking a gossipmonger. "Do tell! Did she talk? Did she pay? Did she..."

"She kissed me. That's all I'm gonna say."

"Ah yeah," Jack said with a laugh, drawing his words out as he noticed how smitten Peter seemed to be with this mysterious woman. Jack then let is thoughts trail away for just a second, thinking about his own recent breakup with his girlfriend, but then he felt hopeful since he was just starting to see someone new, an artist both he and Peter had met at a party. He decided to press Peter for more details. "Alright, cowboy, you can't leave me hanging on that..."

"It was really nice. What can I say? She's still an enigma, of course, but I really like that about her, the mystery and all."

"When are you going to see her again?"

"We mentioned doing something tonight, but..."

"Movin' in fast, I see..."

"Well..."

"Alright, I'll drop it... Oh, what were you mailing me about?"

"I almost forgot! My paper, you know, the one on Time Theory, it's going to be published!"

"Sweet!" Jack said, proud to hear the news. "That's really cool, man!"

"It won't come out for a while, but in the meantime I can work on some other papers, and of course, my book is coming along, little by little."

"That's great, Peter," Jack offered.

"I owe it all to you, buddy."

"What are you talking about? All I did was teach an Eighteenth Century Philosophy guy everything he knows about Physics," Jack said, laughing. "Of course, I didn't teach you everything I know, you see, so that's where I set you up, son."

"You're killing me," Peter said, exaggerating.

"No, seriously, man, I didn't do anything. I'm just a guy working on Quantum Entanglement and Inequalities. Whatever you came up with, it's all you. Besides," he said, lowering his voice, "don't worry about what these pinheads think. They're not philosophers. From what you've told me, you've really got something there."

"Well, thanks," Peter offered, then the workload of papers came back to him. "Now get out," he joked, "I've got a couple more papers to grade before my afternoon class."

"So, try to come to the talk tomorrow, and if not, I'll have you taken out," Jack joked, pointing at Peter for effect as he stood.

"I will do my best to get there, man. Oh, what

are you talking about?"

"I'll be showing how Quantum Entanglement occurs with respect to two distant electrons, but how it might underpin Classical Temporal Theory and Engineering."

"Very interesting. So, this 'action at a distance' is a way of understanding how things actually happen up at the Newtonian level, from orbits, to fields, to all kinds of distant and temporal influences?"

"Yes, that's what I'll be talking about," Jack said. "Try to act surprised, now."

"I'll probably be there," Peter said, "as you know, I'm very interested in the subject."

"What do you say to another ride soon? Maybe, in a couple of days? Maybe we can go out through the Fort, like yesterday?"

"Yeah, that sounds cool," Peter said. "Hopefully the weather will hold out for us."

Jack tapped the doorframe and left, but then returned, sticking his head in. "How was that kiss?" he inquired, realizing Peter wasn't thinking about biking.

"See ya', Jack!" Peter kidded.

Peter then tried to get back to his last papers at last to grade them before class, still thinking in the back of his mind about how nice it felt to have his own paper published. He picked up the remaining papers and realized how grateful he was for Jack's visit, not to mention his friendship.

25

Lieutenant Jeffers pulled the black vehicle into the Pickens Street entrance of the Pendleton Street University garage, rolled down its length, and then up and onto the next split-level just as Milona had requested. He slowly brought it to a stop as the passenger door opened, and then she jumped out, turned, then reached in to grab her bag.

"Thank you very much, Lieutenant."

"Yes, ma'am!" he returned. He was proud to do anything for their visitors, and pleased, as he felt very lucky to have had a real conversation with one of them, especially such a beautiful lady as Major Devon. "Do you need me to wait for you, ma'am?"

"No thank you, Lieutenant. That won't be necessary. I'll catch back up with Lieutenant Mathis from here. Thanks again for the lift."

"Have a nice afternoon, then, ma'am," Jeffers offered, feeling as though he were talking to a celebrity. "Remember me on your next jump, ma'am," he added with a smile.

"Will do, Lieutenant," she said, returning the smile, pleased to have such a genuine interaction.

She then shut the door and watched as the

vehicle rolled away, around the end and back down the ramp, then she noted by her watch that perhaps her timing really was going to be perfect. We hadn't arrived yet, she remembered, walking over to the edge of the garage, to the concrete railing lined with overgrown plants, looking out toward the University's buildings through the trees, then back toward the stairwell. She hoped this whole thing would work without incident as she grew more nervous and awaited herself and Geof.

*

Outside the garage, Agent Gibbs then drew up in his car from Pendleton to Bull Street, confident Devon and Mathis had not noticed him as he followed.

"I'm in place at the playground," he said, shutting off the car engine. "I'm near a parking garage. They just went inside."

"Bulldog," Tanner said over the radio earpiece, "I repeat, you are not to interfere with them here."

"Understood," Gibbs said, keeping his eyes fixed on the garage, hoping he could only figure out why this professor was so important before something terrible happened.

*

Inside on Level Three, after only a few minutes of waiting, Milona saw the red convertible enter from Bull Street just as she remembered, and her heart raced even faster. Looking down the row of columns, she watched as they crossed and drove down the length on the same level where she was standing. Geof stopped the car abruptly and the tires let out a screech as both he and Milona recognized Milona herself, standing mere yards away near the corner.

"Geof?" she said, as both of them sat still, shocked, "are you seeing... what I'm seeing?"

"It's you, isn't it?" he asked. "What the..."

Milona walked from the edge of the terrace, moving nearer to the red car, as Milona noticed from the passenger seat the other was wearing not a similar, but her exact outfit and carrying her same bag.

"Major? Lieutenant?" Milona said, "This is just what you think it is. Please, don't be alarmed."

Milona sat quietly in her seat, her mind racing to think of what could possibly cause two of her to exist in this same time frame. Was it even possible? For a moment, though, she thought she knew the answer.

"Is this some kind of a trick?" he asked.

"No, Geof. I'm her, and she's me!"

"Yes, I'm you. Just hear me out."

"Was there some kind of accident... with *Calendar*?" Milona asked.

"No, there was no accident," she said, moving to stand next to the passenger side of the car. "I'm here under orders." She reached out for the other major's hand, hoping the gesture would prove she was real. "I'm real," she offered, as the major took her hand, and then it pulled away, disturbed by the scene.

"Just what the hell is going on, here?" she asked.

"Look, I'm real, and I know you're freaked out.

I'm only about a day older than you, but fortunately, about five minutes wiser," she said with sarcasm. "They sent me back to correct a... mistake we made. I'm here to ask you both return to the present right away. *Progenitor* is aborted. This is *Mission Rewind*."

"What mistake?" Geof asked.

"That XT you both have planned for later? It will not be effective."

"What happened?" she asked.

She quickly gathered her wits and got out of the car, and Geof jumped out of the driver's seat at the same time. He noted a young lady passing through the garage toward them before the two majors did.

"Are y'all twins?" the young student asked them.

"Uh... yeah," she said, thinking it would certainly have been believable as the other shut the car door, throwing a look over to Mathis.

"That is so cool," the student responded, "and you're identical, I see. I have a twin sister myself, but we stopped dressing alike years ago."

"That's great," she said dismissively, standing next to herself as the young lady stared for a moment, and then walked off in a huff.

"Anyway," she said, almost allowing herself to laugh at the sheer oddity of it all, "both of you will need to return to the present immediately. I will stay behind, at least for a few hours or overnight to make sure Nexin is safe, that he does not suspect anything. I'll go to this class you are headed for, then I may inspect *Visitor*, but I won't return to the present unless and until requested to do so, because you'll be there."

"This comes from Colonel Ford?" Geof asked.

"Yes. Actually, it comes from the Chancellor on down, after we had a briefing which included the directors, generals, senators, and others. You see, you removing Nexin from the timeline tonight will do absolutely nothing to affect the distortion field, which makes the XT an even more unjustified murder."

"I've had my suspicions," she said.

"Yes, I know," she returned, "but there's more. The present that I returned to after we removed Nexin was exactly the same to everyone else, except for one big difference."

"What was it?" she asked.

"I didn't exist."

"How do you mean?"

"I mean, I never existed! There was no record of a Milona Devon ever living, or Father. Geof and I carried out the mission," she continued, holding a hand out toward Mathis, then waving it around, "and then I went back. For some reason, Geof, you were delayed in the past and ended the synchro. But when I got back to the present... It was as if I had never been born or lived. I wasn't in the system at all. No one knew me! I had to stay in guest quarters on the station and plead with everyone to take me seriously. Fortunately, Director Zhang and Director-General Lorentz did, and so here I am. I don't know what I would have done without that."

"I wonder why I was delayed?"

"We don't know, Geof," she replied, studying herself for a second. "Can I have a minute... with myself?" she asked.

Geof nodded, and moved away from the car to walk around, keeping his eyes on both of them so that he could continue to tell them apart. He struggled to do so because they were exactly the same, and he certainly did not want to be confused, in case this was a test. I'm just happy there aren't two of me! he thought.

"Look, Milona, maybe the SM people can merge us later," she said, making up a reason to help her other self continue with the decision at hand.

"But I do not wish to return, or be... 'merged'," she retorted, unsure as to what that could have meant.

She knew very well from her training that if an operative were to meet themselves in the field on an insertion, then the authority fell to their other version. Yet, temporal protocols practiced in training, she thought, were never quite as terrifying or disturbing as this is in reality right now!

"I think I have feelings for him," she continued as she brought her voice down.

"That's an understatement."

"I'm supposed to kill him, but I don't think I want to leave him!"

"I know," she assured herself, looking to make sure Geof could not hear them clearly. "Remember, I'm only slightly older than you with all of those same feelings, so I'm right there with you. I didn't want to do it, either. Worse still, it didn't even work."

"I guess not," she said, "Of course, you would know everything I feel."

"Well, I know just a little bit more," she replied, with a pause. "Listen," she continued, holding her by the shoulders, speaking slowly, "I did not think I could go through with it, hurting Peter, but I did. Geoffery may have pulled the trigger, but I had done the damage. I was selfish about him, and now, even though I'm here to stop it from happening, even though Peter is over there in that building safe and sound as we speak, I still carry the memory, the hurt. I will pay for that deceit as long as I live. It didn't change anything but to destroy an innocent man, and the only difference in our present was that I and our bloodline didn't even exist! *Mission Progenitor* didn't exist." She stepped back from herself. "To learn that you never existed, that your father never existed, that nobody knows who you are, and that you've just terminated the one person you thought you cared most about... It has all been very disturbing, you'll understand."

She cried as she wondered if maybe she should not have said all of that, but it appeared as though her other self was not fully listening, anyway. Perhaps it didn't matter, she thought, as long as I can convince them to return without a causing a big scene, drawing attention to us all. As long as I prevent Peter's murder, then I've done my job here.

"Then you go back!" the other yelled, frustrated, but then lowered her voice. "You can go right back to the present and leave me here to ensure his safety."

"No, Milona. This is why you have to go. To you, the present should be the same as it was before you left earlier today. There's no telling what would happen if I went back. You will explain the situation in your debrief, and everything will be fine."

"But..."

"Your mission is terminated, Major!" she yelled at her, losing patience with herself. "*Rewind* takes precedence. Remember your protocols. Remember your duty to the UN, all those billions of people! Remember your friends and family, and go back. Go now, please. Take Geof. Take the car. Go back to the base at once and return to the present! That is an order! Everything will be okay for you both, but you cannot be the one to stay."

She began to accept what she had to do.

"But, keep in mind, some things are going to be complicated."

"Complicated?"

"Well, there is a sec-chief named Doctor Nadimov. Look him up in Berlin. He may have other plans for you when you get back," she emphasized.

"What plans?" she asked.

"He's working on Director Franklin's scientific solution," she said, unwilling to divulge the solution was nearly deployed when she left, as they will return the day before she left. "Even though this whole thing should be about beating that distortion field, he seems to be far more personally involved here than it appears. I didn't have time or clearances to find out anything further, but I do know that he visited this insertion today. Check the logs at *Visitor* and *Calendar*. You should also have your full 2's when you return, your duty bag in the locker, your quarters on the station. So, see what you can find out about him quickly and quietly. I've told you everything I can." She paused for a moment, ensuring everything she said was sinking in. "One more thing."

"What?" she mumbled, looking up.

"Thank Jennifer for helping me."

"Okay," she said, giving up her last objections.

"Geof?" she said, waving at him to return.

He quickly made his way back to the car. Having watched the two of them closely, he could not be sure what they were saying, and the major's love life was probably none of his business, he thought, but he was sure they did not change places on him. He found it impossible to tell them apart except for their behaviour. One was down and in shock, and the other, the one who surprised us, seemed much more confident and clear minded.

"Lieutenant?" she added.

"Yes, Major?".

"I realize this is all very confounding to you both, but your mission is aborted and you are to stand down. I'm ordering you to escort Major Devon back to the present immediately and to brief Colonel Ford."

"Yes, Major," he said, getting back into the driver's seat of the red convertible, as this major slowly got in after him with a blank stare on her face.

"I would also take care to keep this from Agent Gibbs if you see him," she said, leaning on the passenger door as she pushed it shut. "Goodbye," she added, looking at herself. "Goodbye, Geof."

"Goodbye," she returned, watching her as Geof nodded and turned the car around and drove them away, down to an inner ramp, up to the next split-level, then out the far exit back onto Bull Street.

As they emerged from the garage, Agent Gibbs picked them up again, watching and ducking as they drove past.

"I'm making them again," he said.

That was odd, he noted to himself. Two went in, and two came out. He continued to follow them at a distance, moving away from the garage and down the streets of the University area.

*

Milona took a moment to recover as they drove away, remarking to herself at how easy it had actually been to meet her other self and Geof and order them to return. I was expecting it to be much more difficult than that, she thought, but I suppose adrenaline took over. Now what do I do? she wondered, turning again to head out of the garage. I suppose I've got a class to attend, she said to herself, suddenly happy to be able to see Peter again alive and well. She continued to the corner near the terrace, heading down the stairs and out the grey metal doorway to the sidewalk, blinded momentarily by the bright light outside. With every step, though, she wondered if she were going to be met by another copy of herself, or some other operative. She continued across Pendleton and down the walk, enjoying the breeze blowing through the trees.

26

Geof appeared from the past behind Milona, stepping out of the chambers into the control room at *Calendar*. She felt glad to be back safely, but she was also concerned about Peter and her other self. It seemed so strange even to think about, she thought, but she supposed it was all too real. Geof shook off another tingling passage through the chambers.

"Welcome back," Sergeant-Major Mitchell said.

"Thank you, Sergeant-Major," Geof said.

"Everything seems normal," she said, as Major Waters came in through the opening lift door.

"Sure it is, ma'am," Mitchell quizzed. "That seemed quick, ma'am," he added.

Waters noted the message and timestamps as he arrived in the control room. He wondered if the major may have seen Doctor Nadimov because they would not be able to let them know anything. Nadimov had used their insertion and returned less than an hour later, not long before they arrived. At the same time, Waters was also unsure as to why the major and lieutenant returned so soon, based on the past timestamps.

"How long were you gone?" he quizzed.

"Well," she said, "it was about six hours, but

still, you're both right, it was quick. We were cut short, actually, and we need to contact Colonel Ford on a secure loop."

"Right away," Waters said, as they all looked to each other, "why don't we go into the briefing room."

Milona and Geof followed Waters, and the sergeant-major joined them straight away after ending their synchro and adjusting other station controls. Major Waters closed the door behind them, looking to the viewscreen as he tapped his code in, which brought the blank screen to life with a secured Intelligence interface and insignia.

"Contact RSF Colonel Ford," Waters said, and a small indicator on the interface sequenced through an animation representing the search and call as they all watched blankly. The screen then showed the Colonel as he answered from his office on the station.

"Yes, Major Waters," the colonel answered, then he saw Devon, Mathis, and Mitchell in the briefing room behind Waters. "What's happened?"

"Colonel," Milona said, "we were ordered to abort our mission and return to the present."

"Who ordered you, Major?"

"Sir..."

"Who authorized your abort, Major?"

"Well... I did, sir."

"Major?"

"Only it wasn't me, Colonel. It was another Major Devon... from a different timeline."

"What?" John said, his thoughts trailing off, confused, as Waters and Mitchell also mumbled similar reactions.

"Colonel," Geof said, as Milona nodded in his direction, "we were approached in the past by an exact double of the Major, sir, in fact, she was the major herself, from an alternate timeline. That Major Devon told us she was coming from around a day in the future from today, that she was under orders from as high as the Chancellor, that our mission was not going to be a success regarding the distortion cloud, and then she ordered us to abort and return under *Mission Rewind*. We had little choice but to comply due to protocols, and that senior Major Devon said nothing much further in detail, only that removing Nexin accomplished nothing except that when she returned, Major Milona Devon had never existed in that alternate timeline, the one she was coming from. For them, there was no such *Progenitor* mission under *Tempo*."

"I think you both should get up here right away."

"On our way, sir," she said.

"Major Waters and Sergeant-Major Mitchell, keep a tight lid on this conversation until we can clear everything up, please."

"Yes, Colonel," Waters said, looking to Mitchell and then to the major and lieutenant.

*

"Let me see if I've got this right," Director Zhang said, now standing across from Ford, Devon, and Mathis as they stood at attention before Zhang in his office. "The two of you were in the middle of your day, on track with Professor Nexin and your cover stories. You pulled into a garage, I suppose to drop the major off, but there was another Major Devon, exact in every way, who explained that she had come under orders, not just from me, but as high as the Chancellor, to stop you from executing Nexin."

"Yes, General," Milona said.

"Were you about to execute Nexin at that particular point?"

"Not yet, General. We weren't sure exactly when... We were still formulating a plan, sir."

"Still formulating a plan. And then this second Major Devon said, that from her point of view, she and Mathis had already executed Nexin, that she had returned to the present while Mathis did not, but the XT did nothing to affect our approaching field, and the only real thing that had changed was that Major Devon had ceased to exist in the present, in that timeline?"

"Yes, sir," she repeated.

"Lieutenant Mathis, you had no reason to doubt the reality of this situation?"

"No sir, General. Given where this was, sir, I would highly doubt it was any kind of simulation, and the two of them interacted in a way which could not be programmed. They even touched each other with no effect. I could not tell the two of them apart on any possible feature of their appearance or clothing. They were literally the same person. I had to watch them very closely for behavioural differences."

"Such as?"

"Sir, the other major was very confident in her orders. I've known Major Devon long enough to know the other... version was real, just as real, I mean. It was her, sir, it was a real Major Devon standing next to another real Major Devon. I'm sure of it."

"And Colonel, you did not issue these orders?"

"No sir, General," Ford said.

"Nor do I recall," the director continued, "being in any meetings authorizing this kind of abort." Silence fell on the room as the director considered the situation. "At ease," the director added, realizing he had quizzed them long enough, and he sat down at his desk, rubbing his chin as he thought. Ford, Devon, and Mathis each stood at ease, wondering what the director was thinking. "Perhaps the distortion field isn't dependent upon our temporal experiments in the first place?" he mused after a long pause. "Dismissed," he said, "Oh, and thank you."

*

Milona sat quietly in her quarters on Level Four of the Reconnaissance Sector. She felt let down about her mission, since they had not removed Peter, but she also could not forget her feelings for him. I wish I could return to the past, she thought, but then I kick myself for allowing these feelings to take me over. One thing is clear, though, it's all out of my control, now.

Why, she questioned, changing her thoughts, should I have disappeared from any timeline? Why was I apparently the only changed element of that entire present? The only way that would happen is if Peter were my ancestor, which would mean that... I could have been my own ancestor, my own great, great, however many generations back, grandmother! That's it! I must have been the one who completed this whole circle! That's as possible as anything else, she laughed. Since so many records were lost during the world's depressions, many of us are completely unsure of our ancestry. But, I grew up in Europe, so why would my ancestors move from the Southeastern US to... Then again, it could make sense, with so many people fleeing the collapse of the US during that time. Who knows?

There must have been a reason she approached me in that garage before that second class, she mused. Perhaps, we were about to do something in the afternoon which would have complicated matters further? Or maybe something was going to happen in that class which later led to the published papers on the subject of time travel, which led to early experiments? Or maybe it was just the best place for us both to be concealed. So, by killing Peter sometime later in the day or night, the experiments were unaffected, but it somehow took out my ancestry and nothing else? Rubbish! she thought, as she got up to make a cup of tea. What nonsense! She then paused on her way, and for a second looked outside her windows, settling on the idea that perhaps it was just simply the right moment to have approached herself. That garage was perfect, really. Maybe I'll just take a hot bath, she mused, looking out onto the far windows of the inner curve of the station and the Earth below, following the arc around and around.

*

During her bath, she could feel the strains of her day dissolve as she listened to a soothing recent

symphonic work by Turkish composer Anik playing
through the viewscreen. For a few minutes, she lay
there with the back of her head submerged in the hot,
soapy water, taking in the warm amber glow from a
candle-like lamp, as the reflections off the water were
passed to the walls. She thought of Director Zhang's
surprise in hearing about the other Major Devon, then
she recalled how disturbing it was to see herself, as she
slowly sat more upright, recalling every detail of the
conversation. Her other self had mentioned this Doctor
Nadimov, who filled her thoughts as she listened to the
wiry thin instrumentation of Anik's *Winter Symphony*.
Eventually, she emerged from her bath wearing a thick
camel-coloured robe, feeling far more relaxed.

      She walked into her small, functional kitchen
and pulled out her favourite teacup, a large, black-
glazed oriental mug. She selected a sweet green
variety from a tea box, scooping the leaves with a
stainless, ring-shaped infuser, snapped it together, and
poured the near boiling water over it from a service
tap. She walked barefoot across her Afghan rug while
Anik's music still calmed her spirits, and she looked
across her bookshelves. She then picked up her shiny
personal tablet loaded with a book she had been
meaning to read, a new suspense novel by R.T. Ropat,
and then finally she settled down, curling up on her
lounger.

      She wondered, though, if the director would let
her return to the past again, and found herself worried
about Peter. It's only insecurity about my feelings, she
thought. I guess I'm going to have to accept that I will
never see him again. Still, she thought, as the wheels

turned in her mind, fantasizing about throwing caution to the wind, I could defy my current orders and return to *Calendar*. I could lie to the sergeant-major, order them to send me back to that day. I could find a way to get rid of the other me if she were still around. I could just run out of here, leave my quarters, run through the residential section toward a hangar, tearing down the halls on my own mission...

However, she laughed at her own thoughts. She stopped her seeming fantasy and turned her head to look out the windows again, marvelling at her own silliness, laughing out loud at herself. Even if I could get a shuttle authorized, and even if Defense Command or Security Patrol would let it land, the sergeant-major and his staff would have to report being ordered to set up the chambers. All of this assuming Colonel Ford didn't chase me into the past himself and have me hauled in front of the Security Judicial Generals. It's all so stupid, she thought, laughing at herself again. As she checked messages and reports on her tablet, she realized she hadn't even tried to read her book.

*

After a few minutes, across the room her viewscreen beeped with an incoming call, automatically lowering the music volume. She worried about being seen in her robe. Even though it was only around 18:30 UTC, she was not entirely sure if she were still on duty, and she wasn't given to simply parading around on station half-dressed! She sat up and made sure she was covered, at least.

"Audio only," she said as it beeped again. "Hello?" she offered.

"Major Devon, this is Lieutenant Whitaker. Please hold for the director."

She thought this would certainly be important, running through her mind as to why the director could be calling.

"Video on," she said, just as the image of Whitaker came onto the screen, then was replaced with one of Zhang.

"Major, at ease," he said, "Please forgive me. I'm sorry to trouble you off duty, but I'm glad to see you're getting some rest. It has been quite a day for you, I'm sure."

"Yes, sir," she agreed, also relieved to know she was indeed off duty as far as he was concerned.

"I've got new orders for everyone on the Colonel's team, but because of your involvement, I wanted to talk with you first. You are to leave the past as it now stands. Nexin is to remain in the timeline."

She looked somewhat confused. She was happy to know that Peter would be allowed to live his life, but she began to worry about how they would solve the problems of the approaching field, the other Milona either being abandoned in the past, or her trying to return, and then there was that missing scientist she had found referenced in *Visitor*'s logs on the other Milona's intriguing suggestion.

"What about the field, General?"

"The *Tempo* wizards have perfected their model," he continued, "Doctors Nadimov and Lambert have been working day and night, and they've nearly finished figuring out how to mod up a set of satellite nodes, it seems. They will be launching within a day to deploy, they hope. DG Lorentz wants UNI to focus on that plan," he said, wondering how they could simply leave it at that.

"General, we still have a slight problem."

"You've got to be kidding."

"No sir, General. Not only is there another me in the past, there is also a scientist, or a technical officer, who accompanied Doctor Nadimov into my insertion. He seemed to still be there, as far as we knew, sir."

"Yes, they were cleared to visit."

"He hasn't returned, sir. I just checked not long ago, and I'm sure he was expected back by now. If he is still there, sir, I've got an idea about how to handle it, and how to deal with my... other self being in the past."

"This sounds interesting, Major. I think we better talk in person, right away, as soon as you can get here. My apologies for ruining your time off."

"Thank you, sir," she said, the viewscreen image going blank, leaving the default interface with its UN emblem and *Orbis* logo, then the music returned to the previous volume setting.

Now, she reflected, what is behind this plan Nadimov has? She shifted her weight around, recalling herself warning her about the section chief. She had said he was more involved than it seemed. She looked back at the viewscreen for a moment, wondering if she had time to eat something, before leaving to see the director. Earlier, she considered a call to Jennifer for dinner, but that would now have to wait. Instead, she focused on the mystery, and decided to search for information on Nadimov, hoping she could figure things out. She took a sip of her now lukewarm tea, then put it down.

"Access Intel," she said.

'Welcome to the Intelligence Directorate, Major Devon' the familiar voice said as the screen lit up with its imagery. 'Your clearance is I2, and your cross-clearances are R2, D2, and S2.'

"Find Doctor Nadimov with UN Science."

27

Milona could not believe how strange this felt, as her thoughts were still floating somewhere between the disturbance of meeting herself as a separate person and the elation of seeing Peter alive again. It was along her way down the quiet sidewalks of the campus that everything took on some otherworldly significance, she thought. In her mind, she could feel the breeze on her face and through her hair, she could see the trees, the buildings and myriad of young students passing her. She could see herself walking into the Humanities building, taking the stairs, and coming right into the classroom, saying hello to Peter. She was seeing it all as if it were some presentation on a viewscreen, and now sitting through the class, she thought of nothing else. The world almost seemed like some distant show being played out beyond her reach.

Peter almost seemed like a puppet on a string, but maybe, she wondered, it was she who had been the puppet? Toward the end of the class, she watched as Peter listened to the young student who was posing her question, and slowly came into better awareness of what was happening around her. She knew the clock was ticking on the class time, and she wondered if something was going to happen afterward.

She thought Peter displayed an obvious concern for the discussion, and seeing him safe and sound, right here in front of her, was she still found such a huge relief after an awfully long night of worry over his well-being. But, I've never felt more conflicted, she thought, because I'm not sure if I will even be here much longer, but somehow I think I would like to stay. Peter certainly seems as though his patience is being taxed, though. But he also seems genuinely interested in getting these young people to think for themselves.

"But if we can travel through time," Keisha said, straightening her back in the plastic and metal student desk, "doesn't it have to do with the speed of light?"

"Perhaps," Peter replied enigmatically, smiling at her and the others with approval, but also concentrating on the problem as he stood from leaning on the desk to pace over to the edge of the room closer to her for emphasis. "Perhaps it is possible that light speed, which seems incredibly fast to our minds, so fast that we can't really even get a feel for it, maybe that super-speed is just a slow trot to some of the more hidden forces and effects of the Universe?" He then moved to the board to begin to sketch an idea.

Milona was still taken aback watching Peter in the same situation again, unable to get over the fact that he was right there in the room, looking into his eyes for the first time since she had left him in his home. Or has that happened yet? she wondered. Despite the technical confusion in all of it, she was not prepared to feel this way, and in all the hurry, she had assumed that meeting herself before the XT would simply mean that this hadn't happened. Those words to myself in the garage just came out, she thought, but they were so true. Now as I sit here, the execution hasn't happened, but I still have the memory of doing it. The deceit is still with me.

She watched Peter interacting with his students, deep down hoping he would notice her, but this time, to absolve her somehow of the guilt she was feeling. Peter and Milona then looked at each other, and he allowed a small smile to pass across his face, but then he continued. He tried to send no signals to the students about me, she thought, but I'm sure they have their suspicions. She felt much better after his smile, slowly allowing herself to become interested again in the class material.

Lenny found all of this more interesting than usual. He looked around the room to see if others were interested in the topic. Most of the students seemed bored or confused to him. But, there is that older babe, he then thought, looking toward Milona. I bet she's his girlfriend, because I noticed that they just looked at each other. Professor Nexin smiled right at her! Wow, I'm jealous. She's really hot.

"So," Peter continued, "let's say we instantly took off from where we are standing, say in a ship or whatever, and shot off to the Moon, or to Jupiter, or the edge of the Milky Way, and then came back in less than a blink of the eye. Perhaps then, we would not only appear to ourselves to have gone nowhere, but would we have also travelled backward in time within the same split-second?"

The students, he often thought, seemed positively awestruck by this proposition as he continued to keep up the pressure. Each of them sitting still, either looking at the professor or slightly away, all wrapping their mind around the problem, or so he chose to believe. Peter knew this kind of topic was slightly above the heads of those coming into an introductory course, but he also felt that once in a while, he had to give them something to reach toward, in that way, something very hard to figure out. He wanted to push them with something difficult or strange when he could, rather than simply settle for them memorizing historical materials or attaining low standards.

"Of course, the problems of how this is going to happen, and how the human body can withstand such forces, must be challenged, but scientists can figure those problems out," he said.

Milona could not help thinking of the irony. The double irony, the triple irony! Of course, I agree, she thought, as she listened on, and she enjoyed recalling her feelings for Peter the first time she was here in this same moment. She found herself feeling less guilty for what she had done, now falling in love with Peter all over again, taking delight in the fact that his eyes were still bright with life, his mouth was still speaking, his body was still pumping blood and breathing. Peter gestured as he paced around the front of the room proposing his ideas to these young people, and she felt she could watch Peter engage in this ritual all day long. But, will the Directorate let me stay here?

"But," he added, "why do the official accounts of this temporal shift assume that '*Time* slows down'?

How is it that *Time* slows down due to the incredible speed of travel?"

Peter looked at Milona while she was just then finally looking around the room instead of at him. He hoped her eyes could catch his, because despite his ability to focus on the discussion, he found himself falling for her, unable to avoid it.

"What are you talking about?" Lenny quipped, jarring the professor, Keisha, and others, who allowed themselves to snicker to relieve tension.

The young Physics major had studied with the professor before, and knew that he liked to get the students going. He was already working on an honours paper on these topics, too, so it was good to work out the ideas as best he could.

Milona remembered thinking she had witnessed a certain intellectual power in Peter she had not quite seen before. He had been much more conservative in all the other interactions she had with him. She felt her instincts the first time might have been correct, and their beautiful night together was clear indication of that. Oh, our beautiful night, she swooned, I will always have that, I suppose, even if I have to leave right away.

"Why," Peter answered, while attempting to impress Milona, "does the idea that going fast necessarily involve the dilation of *Time*?"

"Because," Lenny said, "that's what the experiments you talked about showed, right? *Time* ran slower when the clock on the plane was brought back." It was obvious to Lenny that science had proven Einstein right. Einstein was right about everything, he

thought. Professor Nexin is pretty sharp, but who does
he think he is to challenge that?

"Yes, the airborne clock showed a shorter
timespan, if you will, by fractions of a second," Peter
said slowly, "I'll give you that." Several students
smiled and laughed, anticipating a clever wiggle out of
this. "But all which has ever been observed, or proven,
is that the apparent time measured had been shorter, not
that *Time* itself was dilated." The room again fell silent
as brains computed this, and Peter felt they were
pausing on his suggestion correctly. "The 'Concorde
Experiment', which we talked about the other day,
seems to definitely show that one clock slowed down
due ostensibly to the speed of travel, as do our
numerous satellites in Space every day, but does that
really mean that *Time* itself flowed slower inside the
airplane?" Peter then paused for a moment, allowing
the students to reason, "Or, could it just be, that the
very real forces of Magnetism which made up the
surrounding air, the seat and dinner tray table, and so
on, that they physically slowed the clock down?"

"But the clock was atomic," Keisha chimed,
"not physical."

"Yeah, that was an atomic clock, not a
wristwatch," Lenny added, several other students
laughing.

Milona recalled finding Lenny cute to watch, a
tall, dark, and handsome young man full of youth, and
full of himself, as he struggled with Peter's logic, but
his comment was indeed funny, and she considered that
her favourite little watch had been through quite a ride
these last few weeks. Certainly it showed minor

discrepancies, she knew. If it were accurate enough, or if the time spent at those speeds were long enough, they would add up to more than incredibly small changes.

"Atomic clocks," Peter asked, "are not part of the Universe? Atoms don't respond to forces?"

Peter smiled with a satisfaction of having achieved his goals for the class as silence again fell on the room. The students were all focused on the problem, and Keisha was coming out of her shell quite nicely. Milona could again see that Peter had managed to get most of the students to focus and forget worrying about what they sounded like.

"True," Lenny stubbornly admitted.

"See, an atomic clock is still very much a part of the physical system in which it sits, just as much as any wristwatch," Peter explained. "In fact, I could argue it may even be easier to affect it through Electromagnetic forces, since its elements are not as bound with other physical systems, like the wristwatch could be. But that part aside, the question is why did the clock run slower? It's not because *Time*, this mystical 'dimension' no one has ever shown exists, was itself slower by the hand of Man, in some equally mystical way which has not been shown. Isn't it likely the clock simply found more resistance to ticking, if you will, given the forces acting upon the atoms as they were hurled across the Atlantic on a Concorde at supersonic speeds."

The room was again silent, but Peter could also sense that ticking clock in every classroom just before class time is about to run out. "Next time you're in a car, stick your hand out the window and think about it." He paused for a moment longer to let this last sink in. "See you next time."

✳

The students all began moving out of the classroom, but Milona sat still for a moment, thinking she might simply blend in with those students who were leaving and sneak away without speaking to Peter. She lingered for a moment or two longer, remembering the first time this class meeting happened, trying to decide what to do this time.

Last time I waited around to ask Peter a question about the class discussion, she thought. Yes, I remember that. But, this time I might just cry off, and go somewhere to get my head clear. Surely, I don't have to play out every second the same way, do I? I'm anxious about what might be awaiting me outside this room, too, and I'd rather deal with it head on. Something keeps bothering me about this whole situation, it's just underneath the surface of things, and I need to solve it, or at least try. I can't help wondering if Geof and my other self made it back alright. Perhaps I should just go out to the base and make sure everything is fine? I can try to catch up with Peter later, assuming I'm not scooped up by then and pulled out of this time frame by Colonel Ford or something. She waited for most of the students to file out, and then motioned to Peter as she stood up that she was going to leave.

28

Even though it would be later in Berlin, Milona wanted to satisfy her fascination and try to reach this Doctor Nadimov at the Science Centre. She stepped out of her kitchen and into the closet, took off her bathrobe, then laid it across the khakis and checkered shirt. Humming to herself, she thought she should look presentable for Nadimov, but not too formal for the director. After a few minutes, Milona stepped out into the main room wearing her black duty uniform skirt and long black boots, with a white duty pullover, noting the thin UN emblem at the center and rank squares near the high neck looked straight. She ran her hands through her hair, and continued to the lounger, picked up a work pad she had already prepared, stood in front of her screen and placed the call directly to the laboratory. To her surprise, Nadimov himself answered the viewscreen from his office. Her pulse quickened and face became flush for a moment.

The section chief had been working all afternoon and evening. He and Michelle were alone, and he'd realized she was napping. It was looking to them to be an all night effort, he recalled, sitting on the lounger. His red duty coat was across the armrest, and he had been reading over their notes before the viewscreen beeped.

"Hello, this is the UN Science Particle Lab, Doctor Nadimov speaking..." he said, then realized who was calling.

"Good evening Doctor," she said, with a certain tone in her voice, he found, "or would Commander be more accurate?"

"Major Devon? This is an honour, even at this hour," Olen said, bemused by her timing.

"I can see you've been working late, Doctor, but I have too. You see, sir, I've been trying to piece together a mystery."

"How can I help?" he offered.

"Well, I pulled up your 201, sir."

"Boring night, Major?"

"Olen Pavlushka Nadimov," she started, referring to the tablet. "Born before the global depressions, now thirty-five, the second son of Russian immigrants to the United States, early enrollment in college, Doctorate in Particle Physics from MIT, Commander with Naval Intelligence, later a section chief with the CIA DS&T, selected for the Temporal Alliance Program, and assigned by Doctor Franklin to the prestigious Particle Field Labs at the Science Centre to work on the *Tempo Programme*."

"Where do you find the time?" he asked, still somewhat surprised to hear from her, wondering how she was back on the station so quickly. "I could return the favour, Major, I've got your information around here somewhere, but I am a bit tired. We've been trying to save the world down here, you'll understand."

"You've been the one directing this shield research all along."

"Of course, but it's not just me," he said with a hint of a smirk, "we are a team down here."

Olen looked over toward Michelle, who was still asleep at her desk in the next office in the row. Michelle had started working even earlier than he, as she tried to finish modification commands for their nodes. They would have to be replicated over hundreds of units before delivery out to meet the slowly approaching distortion field.

"I imagine you've had help," Milona continued. "Who is it? Some innocent junior officer?" she quizzed, "an assistant scientist hoping for higher clearance and promotion?"

"Major, I'll ask you to watch your tone with me. I may be a visitor here from your perspective, but I still outrank you."

"Of course, Colonel. My apologies. My frustration with all of this has gotten the better of me. I'm sorry."

"Now," he said, accepting her apology, "we have been quite successful, on short notice I might add, in perfecting our shield model. We've had to put in some hard hours and stumble across some unforeseen solutions, but our shield will work when implemented."

"And the Science Director is very impressed, I assume," she said.

He was standing up from his lounger, looking out the window to the night lights of Berlin, then turned back toward her as she spoke, unsure if she had intended sarcasm.

"...Well, I know Director Zhang is impressed, sir. Is that why you visited my insertion today?" she recovered, realizing her insolence too late.

"Major, if you must know, we needed to take some readings of the temporal distortions to inform our modeling. We had to do it quickly, and per Colonel Ford, your insertion was the best active one we had to compare," he replied. He did not wish to let on that his technical officer was still in the past. "Director Zhang knew we were there, if that is where you are headed."

"But why the competition with me, sir?"

"Well, it's all been a little too easy for you, hasn't it Major?" He was tired from a long day, but he also felt rubbed the wrong way by the major's apparent lack of perspective. "You glide through your schools, your UN training, travel the world in minutes, grow up with luxurious technologies, get a once-in-a-lifetime mission."

Milona began to recoil from Nadimov's harsh and judgemental words.

"It's not just you, though," he continued, "it's just about everybody in this future." Olen moved closer to the viewscreen. "You lost your father," he said, surprising Milona with his familiarity with her background, "and for that, I'm sorry. And sure, there are still social problems right here and now, probably always will be. But you don't know, none of you know, what it is like to watch your family slip further every day into inescapable national poverty, your community, region and nation, and eventually the whole world degenerating around you into brutal inequities and increasing political chaos.

"You haven't lived in a world when nearly all of the population is either destitute or sick, and medical technologies cannot help because few people can even afford them. You don't know what it is like when every nation struggles to survive under a growing decades-long world depression, constant terrorism and war, dissolving institutions and governments. People in this time lament the loss of their family histories and other data, many of their historical treasures and buildings, but deep down, they don't want to think about how dark the past actually was."

"You want to stay here, sir," she said, wiping a tear from her cheek. She had welled up with emotion, moved, as she should have been by his words, yet still finding herself focused on the mystery. "You don't want to go back home. Beside saving us all, Doctor, you also hope this shield will put you in a position for a permanent place here, and who could blame you?"

"I'm glad you understand, Major," he said, now relieved. "You see, I really do not have a home to go back to, not in that way. I now know too much about this future to exist in my past. Most of what I loved is gone, anyway... I think of what my life might be like here, in this world I've seen, and I know I couldn't go back to that cold and desperate time. You're damned right I want to stay here!"

"You were the one who set off the research race to build a working time machine, weren't you, sir?" she asked, surprised at her supposed sudden insight into his motivations. "And so that's why it didn't matter if Nexin lived or died."

"I was sure you would figure it out on your

own," he said, wiping his face of tension and perspiration, pausing to consider if he should say more. "If given enough time, Major, I knew you would have eventually understood, if you didn't already, that Professor Nexin was a speck of dust in academia, that is, at the time you were visiting. His work was incredible, and it changed my life, but my colleagues at MIT would never have referenced a lowly MA Professor in Philosophy, if it were not for my urging the study of his works. Actually, though it rarely happens, that is the only aspect of the academic world I do miss, the collaboration of the best minds to solve the biggest problems. I guess that's why I've sunk my teeth into this shield research."

"Myself, I miss the École, sir," she offered, recalling her days in Paris after the Academy.

"I see," he returned, not having anticipated that side of her coming out. Just then, his viewscreen immediately displayed a secure textual alert, and he knew he needed to cut the call short. "Well, Major, I very much appreciate your call, I hope we can do this again sometime soon, but I have an urgent message and must..."

Milona's viewscreen went blank, and she looked around her now quiet quarters, where she stood frozen. She checked the tablet, and it had also gone blank. She wondered why communications seemed to be down, and listened for a moment longer, intently to the wider area around her, and after a minute the power flickered and the tactical alarm began to sound all over the station, which startled her.

*

After a second or two, Milona could hear a few small explosions erupting from what sounded like another part of the station, and visual blasts could be seen at transformation stations outside her windows beyond the station. She leapt toward the glass to get a better view. From security beacons to points on the Earth's visible dark side surface, she could make out many fiery blasts. All around were the now fading sporadic reactions of satellites, transports and power grid generators. The distortion field must be approaching, and approaching faster than estimated! she thought. Whatever Nadimov's team figured out, it came too late, and my mission was of no use!

We were all wrong! she worried, as she ran out into the corridor, down toward the lifts, to check communications from an access panel. When she arrived, she found the panel was blank. Several others, half-dressed in their uniforms or in off-duty attire, were wandering the corridor trying to understand what was happening.

"What's going on?" someone asked.

"Are we under attack?" another yelled.

The distortion field was very powerful, and it was pushing a Doppler wave of subspace energies far out ahead of it, which quickly overloaded all manner of circuitry and electronic equipment. The station gravity fields were interrupted, and everything around the station went silent and dark, some items floating for a few seconds, as systems fell offline, backup systems compensating.

Milona froze as her ears began ringing from the shock, feeling weightless several times as she slowly returned near her quarters, but the gravity fields stabilized. Crashes could still be heard, and dozens of officers began to file through the corridor, asking each other if they knew anything about what was happening. Eventually, communications and other systems returned to normal across the station, and everyone was able to find updates on the wave. She went back inside, grabbed her duty coat and communicator, and headed back out to meet Director Zhang.

*

Olen sat frozen on his lounger, listening to explosions, as Michelle suddenly woke up from her nap. Several systems in the building flickered, the lights outside the windows showing similar reactions all around the city. Michelle and Olen could hear several large explosions and blasts which sounded vaguely to them as though from overhead. Michelle jumped up from her desk and ran into Olen's office, throwing herself next to him on his lounger.

"Is it an attack?" she worried.

"It's a forward density wave ahead of the field!" he yelled over the noises.

"A forward wave of energies? Must be surging through circuits, power systems..."

Michelle was interrupted by a blast in the laboratory itself, as one of the modeling systems overloaded.

"I saw secure Intel from *Atlantis* just before this

all started." he said.

"And it's not the distortion field?" she checked.

"Not yet!"

"I hope the nodes are safe at the facility down in Gibraltar!" she said, speaking of the assembly site where their matrix of nodes were being collected and loaded before configuration.

"I think so. They're all powered down."

"We are definitely running out of time!"

"Should be over in another minute or two. This means there will only be a day, two at most, to get the matrix in place." he said, thinking of the likely distance of the forward wave and speed of the field.

"I hope it works!" she said, nervously looking up toward the windows.

29

Leaving the classroom, she found her curiosity hard to ignore, and decided to get to *Visitor* right away. Milona's concern over the fate of the present was too great, and she could not be sure if she should press her feelings about Peter any further, particularly if she were going back. She had made her way out of the room, hoping to leave Peter talking with his students then rush on her way off campus.

"Peter, I'll see you later, I have to go," she managed to interject in passing, hoping he would not think it strange.

"Are you interested in all of this time travel stuff?" another young man then blurted out to her.

She turned to see a darker black-haired young man with a thick accent wearing canvas trousers and a white shirt. Unavoidably suspicious, she realized who he was, and then she looked at Peter, who seemed along with the others to be equally confused. After all, she thought, given events, I certainly don't know what is going to happen from one minute to the next! She stared at the young man for a moment, and confirmed she had not seen him in any of the classes she visited. Then again, she thought, she did not catalogue the students, either, so maybe he was there and she just didn't notice.

"I'm sorry," she said, looking toward the young man, as well as Peter, "I really don't have time to talk right now."

She turned to walk away, throwing one last glance back at Peter, wondering if she would ever see him again, and then she threw herself down the hallway, trying not to be moved to tears. She was still perplexed by the strange young man, who seemed equally perplexed himself, but then it hit her before she reached the stairs. Doctor Nadimov was personally involved in their previous insertion because he is personally involved right here! He must be! That name, 'Nadimov'. I knew I'd heard it before, maybe in one of Peter's roll calls!

"Olen?" she mumbled, first thinking of the mystery young man, then one of the others. She turned around and walked back toward them. "Olen?" she repeated, looking down the hallway toward them. The darker young man stood silent, watching her. "Olen," she said again, more sternly.

Olen was surprised as he turned to look, because no one ever called him by his actual first name, except his mother. Everybody called him Lenny. "What?" he said, turning, but then he saw who was calling him. Why is the professor's babe calling me? he wondered.

"Uh... nevermind," she added, shocked at Lenny answering, but then she tried covering herself. "I'm... mistaken. Bye again."

Everyone seemed dumbfounded about what was

happening, and stood still for a moment. Peter was confused as to why Milona would care about Lenny at all, or other unknown man. Lenny looked away from her and back to the professor, shrugging off the strange situation by returning to his worry over an upcoming test.

The other young man, James Perkins, found it difficult to discount the question and looked back on the conversation, realizing the young student standing right next to him was Olen Nadimov himself. James couldn't figure out why Major Devon waved nervously and turned to slip back down the hall. Maybe, he thought, this is what he wanted me to do? Maybe I'm supposed to make sure something happens here?

"Never underestimate an inspired student," Milona said sarcastically, almost under her breath, as she walked down the hallway quickly toward the stairwell door. She turned back for another glance toward the classroom and saw TO Perkins coming down the hallway toward her.

"This is a brilliant plan, Laurent, Major!" Director-General Lorentz said. "Giving the other Major Devon something to 'chew on', as you put it, it is the best way avoid breaking the circle, and your presence should be all the authorization they need."

"Thank you, sir," Zhang said.

"Good work, Major Devon!" Lorentz added.

"Thank you, sir," Devon said with a smile.

Zhang ended their secure call and looked out

one of the slot-windows of their craft, an RSF/RCT flat-black scout-class eight-metre ship assigned to Ford's team. RSF General Venda recently cleared the new scout from Mexico City's UN Engineering and Transport Complex, to ease the need for shuttle trips used by Ford's section officers, and now the brushed aluminum landing claws lifted off the deck and the special craft lifted off from *Orbis*. Ford turned and sped downward into the atmosphere.

"Recon Central sure gave us a beauty, Colonel," Geoffery said, referring to the Reconnaissance Centre.

"Absolutely, Lieutenant," Ford said, Devon and Zhang nodding in agreement while the craft curved and lifted hard into a flat run across the Southern and Atlantic Oceans.

Zhang thought it fortuitous speaking earlier with the major, and now found himself taking them to rendezvous with the *Nording Sea Group*, as they trained in the Atlantic off the East Coast of North America.

During their short trip from the station in the sleek, highly mobile stealth craft, they perfected Devon's plan for *Cut-Time*. She first described it in Zhang's office based on new information he supplied, and now they all reviewed it together as they arrived on deck at the *Nording* command ship, hovering with the carrier, corvettes and destroyers. Once there, they were greeted by Sea Group Commander Defense Command Brigadier General Kagiso, who happened to be one of Zhang's old friends.

General Kagiso authorized use of the *Nording* for staging going forward, along with any standard silver-blue Defense scouts or fighters needed. The team eventually climbed back into their craft and sped across the ocean and forests toward Bragg Station, another remote power transmission cover facility for the highly secretive *Schedule,* a twin machine of *Calendar* yet tightly controlled by Intelligence Counter-Intelligence and Reconnaissance Counter-Terrorism. The director had already alerted the station, and the team now landed near the remote facility and were escorted inside.

The target time was a point near when Devon and Mathis returned from the past, and each on the team stepped through to *Mirror*, an equally secretive installation on Fort Bragg in the past, controlled by a covert joint CIA and JSOC cell, separate and unknown even to the *Visitor* crew, including Gibbs and Tanner. Likewise, Ford and his operatives had known nothing of *Schedule* until now.

After meeting with the Special Operations commanders near the *Mirror* site, Lieutenant Mathis was put onto a helicopter which would get him to Columbia quickly enough. The two Night Stalkers flew Mathis into the city and dropped him atop the parking garage, establishing counter-intelligence ahead of their arrival by having their locals pose as photographers working on a film.

*

Milona slipped through the stairwell door and down the first half-flight of stairs, as James made it to the door after her. He called out the question again.

"Aren't you interested in time travel, ma'am?"

Both he and Milona paused in their tracks, and it was suddenly clear to her this man was the missing scientist from *Visitor*'s logs. Of course! she thought, recalling the whole scene she had made before her return. She looked back up at him. He doesn't know what he's supposed to do!

"TO Perkins!" she called up the stairwell. "What do you think you're doing here?"

"I mean you no harm, ma'am," he urged. "I was only supposed to make sure you asked your question. At least, I think."

She knew something about this was all wrong. This guy is just not very well trained at all, she thought, taking off down the remaining stairs and out the door. He chased her, but she was far more quick than he anticipated, and he found himself racing out the doors, bumping into others, running down the sidewalks, toward the Pickens footbridge, eventually chasing her flat out down the long path behind Sloan and Barnwell.

She could feel him struggling to keep up behind her, and then stopped cold in her tracks to surprise him, turning on the young man to give him a chance, but he kept coming at her. She gave him a fast, wide kick to his face with her right leg. He ran right into her kick, and fell over past her, right across from where she stood. He managed to roll over quickly, righting himself, and she hoped he would give up, but he got up to come at her again. She tricked him with a fake turn and gave two quick punches to his chest, attacking him again with a blow to his face, then a clip across his throat with a kick to the back of his knee, which put the young man back onto the ground with a hard, dead-weight drop.   He looked up at her, but could not manage to pick his body up from the ground.

This kid is just way out of his league, she thought, looking around, as she could hear a helicopter, and felt watched.

"What's going on here?" she said, "why is such a green operative interfering with me?"

James struggled to speak.

"Look, I don't know what you're doing here, but I'm going back to *Visitor* to get some answers."

Devon rushed away from Perkins, and as she made it out of sight, Mathis, wearing blue jeans and a black leather jacket, then appeared from behind a row of bushes not far away.   He had been watching the building, saw them running nearby, and then ran over to Perkins, waving off several people who seemed to want to help the young man.

"We have to get back, Mister Perkins," he said, dragging him up and across his shoulders, James bleeding from his face and rolling his shoulders inward.   "But a word of advice for you.   Never attack an RSF operative."

"Who the... hell are you?" James asked, wheezing as he regained his breath.

"An RSF operative, Mathis, and if you don't do what I say, you won't believe what I will do to you!"

James' eyes grew very large as he stood and took in the size of Mathis, then became faint as he wondered what he had gotten himself into, his chest and face now throbbing in sharp pain.

"She's going back... to the base," he said.

"Slider, this is Harley. We're ready down here," Mathis said, noting the time on his watch as he continued with James down the sidewalk.

"Roger, Harley. We're on our way," Colonel Bingham said over the loop from the circling helicopter. "Spinner," he added to his co-pilot, "let our paparazzi know we're coming back in over the city."

*

Lieutenant Mathis pulled TO Perkins up into the roomy Blackhawk helicopter, the waves of air pressing against James' skin as he rose. After Perkins was pulled in, the craft lifted above the parking garage, with the photographers down below pretending to film the event and quell any other immediate interest from potential passersby or local officials. Colonel Bingham guided the helicopter out across the streets and away from the area, speeding back toward Fort Bragg.

When they were back on base near Fayetteville, Mathis had a medic give Perkins more attention than they could, and requested a synchro from the control room of *Mirror*, which Major Devon had carefully timed out to avoid any further loops. Mathis and Perkins shortly emerged from the chambers at *Schedule*, met with the others, and the team headed out to the landing platform, boarded the awaiting scout and returned again to the *Nording*.

After discussions the directors, and even the Chancellor two days later, Milona was sent back to the past through *Calendar* to *Visitor*, to talk with her other self before she might return to the present. The targeted time was just before Milona would arrive at *Visitor* after she had attacked Perkins, per Mathis' assessment. The timing of the events was close enough that as Milona was nearly on the site, the tunnel used would close with the claps of noise signaling a visitor.

*

        "Thank you again, Lieutenant Jeffers," Milona said as they pulled up near the secured fence at *Visitor*.
        "You're welcome, ma'am," he returned. "Nevermind the noises."
        "I thought I heard small explosions! Is that what it sounds like farther away when we come and go?"
        "Every time, ma'am."
        "Well, there's my car there," she said, reflecting.
        She was glad to see the captain's staff had not put the red convertible away. She thought about the military helicopter she had seen over the city, and the untrained operative. She got out and approached the fence line, thinking that maybe everything was okay. She moved down the path, was waved through the security fence, walked toward the control room, but just then the other Major Devon approached her from inside. Dressed in a black Recon service uniform jumpsuit with boots and a hat, with her hair pulled back into a tail, she also carried a large black shoulder bag.
        "You!" Milona called, shocked to see her again.
        "It's been a couple of days for me," the other said, as they approached each other, "and they want me to speak with you before you do anything from here."

"Has the timeline been altered again?"

"No, it hasn't. It was apparently restored as you intended by preventing our XT. When we got back, everything was the same as when we left."

"*Mission Rewind*," she mused aloud.

"Clever name."

"Didn't I just see Geof back at the University..."

"Well, there was a mix-up with all that, and we're sorry it was confusing."

"I'm sorry about Mister Perkins."

"So, I can't tell you much, but I can say that my being here right now is an overwrite of my mission, *Cut-Time*. Two days ago, we left you guessing. We disabled this facility as you arrived just now, at least temporarily. We had Perkins posted here all healed up to give you some closure, but it was just no good, and so the Chancellor wanted to do this instead. She calls it *Snow White*."

"What about another rewind mission to prevent our doubling?" she asked after a small laugh.

"It was discussed, but it's already been too long, hasn't it?" the major explained to herself. "Think about it. Which of us do we save?"

"And which one gets erased," she nodded, realizing the emotional and ethical implications.

"Milona, they want me to make it very clear that you can return to the present anytime if you so choose, but there would be two of us, living in the same time..."

"...And trying to live the same life," Milona said as she began tearing up.

"On the other hand, you can also stay here in the past with Peter," she continued, also tearing up, "and everything will be okay, with full support from TAP, CIA, Army Intel. I can bring you just about anything you need from the present. What's mine is yours, of course." She reached into her bag and pulled out a smaller purse, showing it to herself. "In fact, I've brought you some clothes and a few mementos."

She noted the purse with a short look to realize it would be a few small keepsakes from her life.

"I've also brought you this," she continued, pulling from her bag a metal and glass display box with the UN Blue Star inside. She pulled the star and blue ribbon out and hung it around Milona's neck. "I hope I get this right," she laughed. "On behalf of the United Nations Chancellor Nishiko Kitamori, who cannot be here at this time, the United Nations Blue Star is hereby awarded to you, RSF Major Milona Kaatje Devon, for your bravery and sacrifice. Inscribed with the solemn phrase, 'In the Service of Peace', the Blue Star is the highest honour of any UN award or star we can bestow. It is quite an honour."

Both Milonas' lips trembled as tears rolled down their cheeks.

"The decision whether to stay or go is yours," she continued, "and either way the UN will not abandon you. This is from Madam Chancellor Kitamori herself. I won't abandon you, either."

Milona broke down for a moment as it all hit her, and the major steadied and hugged her as she swooned and sobbed. She knew things were likely to have been worked out in the present, and they couldn't have disabled *Visitor* forever, either. Regardless, either I stay, be with Peter, and give up my entire life, or give up Peter and go back to share my life with my other self like we were twins.

"If I do go back, which one of us changes her name?" she snickered as the other did as well. "I guess I knew this would happen as soon as I came here to stop you both," she said, wiping her eyes with her jacket, taking the bag the major offered. After a few silent looks between them, she put her hands on the other's face and looked at her. "Thank you, my friend."

Milona then turned in sobs and walked away from her other self and *Visitor*, back toward the fence.

The major cried openly as well, watching herself walk away, and she knew this would be the biggest challenge of her life, both of their lives, and one they would have to relive every day. She was leaving for now, and without incident or any great scene, so the major turned and walked back into the facility to request a synchro.

Satisfied and resolved with her emotions and her logic for the time being, Milona put the Blue Star in the bag and walked on to leave the secured area, relieved in a way to be able to think this decision over in her own time, rather than be rushed and troubled further by larger problems in the present, or that alternate timeline. She knew this wasn't going to be something she could easily decide, and either way would involve sacrifice and deep hurt.

30

"Major Devon," Agent Gibbs said, leaning on the convertible as he waited outside the fence for her.

She noticed the black utility vehicle still sitting on the other side of the car, Lieutenant Jeffers in the driver's seat, with a look on his face which made her wonder if he was merely under orders, or if he was more deeply involved.

"Agent Gibbs," she said, surprised to see him, but thinking again, realized she wasn't. "Lieutenant," she added, nodding to Jeffers.

"Ma'am," he saluted.

"I was just called in," Gibbs said, "but I couldn't tell if you were coming or going, so I waited."

"Yes, it's very strange, but I often have the same problem knowing which way, myself."

"The thing I can't figure," he quizzed, "is why you're here at all?" She looked at him with a perplexed expression. "See, I know you and Mathis went back, through, a couple of hours ago. But here you are."

Milona knew she could not tell him the whole story, but she just had verification that he had been following her all along, as suspected, so she quickly thought on her feet, remembering Zhang's comments in the Mess Hall. She owed Gibbs no allegiances, and she had committed no crimes.

"How'd you get back?" he added.

"Maybe I never really left today, Agent Gibbs, or maybe I got back just now." she said.

"But how could that be? Don't you know?"

"To be honest, I cannot tell you anything I may or may not know about it. I am not at liberty to discuss anything which may compromise operations, any more than you are, Agent."

"Operations."

"Yes. I'm sorry, but there it is."

"So, what are you going to do now, Major?"

"Well, I'd hoped I could return to the hotel downtown and relax, but is there anything I need to do for you here?"

"I meant that... you're here all by yourself. What are you going to do?"

"There isn't anything I can do, really. If my government needs me they will send someone to bring me back, at some point. Otherwise, I have to consider this a longer trip than I had planned. I would hesitate to call it a vacation, but hey, we all need a break."

"I assume you will need the car, the phone and hotel, the money, and the paperwork?"

"As long as the CIA and Army Intel are coöperating with the Temporal Alliance Program, yes, Special Agent. Operatives could show up any second, or not for years. Right now, there is honestly no way for me to tell. But I wouldn't want to have to say the good folks here didn't play nice."

"I'll keep an eye on you, then," he said, not

wishing to cause trouble with his own superiors. "If anything changes, I'll certainly let you know, or someone on the captain's team will let you know." He glanced over toward the lieutenant.

"Thank you, Agent Gibbs," she said, then looked over at Jeffers. "Lieutenant?"

"Yes, ma'am?"

"Remember me on your next jump," she said, with a wink. He smiled and saluted the major, as she walked toward the driver's door of the car, dropped her bags, and hopped in. "Oh, and the same goes for me."

"What's that?" Gibbs asked.

"If anything changes, I'll certainly let you know." She started up the car, spun the wheels slightly pulling it back onto the main road, and then sped off and away.

✳

She turned off the Fauré disc she had playing in the car as she drove downtown. Maybe the crucial changes they were looking for had happened in that classroom, she thought. She visualized the young Olen Nadimov, who had been waiting to speak with Professor Nexin as she left in a hurry, but then she had paused at the door and called out. It must have been in that instant, she thought, while everyone else was filing out of the room, when Perkins simply walked up at the right second to blend in. Certainly Peter wasn't the progenitor, but perhaps it was Olen.

She parked the car just off Main Street, on her way toward the hotel, and walked sluggishly, catching herself in the reflection of a glass store window. She paused to look at herself, to wonder what she will do now, who she will be, how long she will be here. Are they coming for me right now? she wondered, looking over her shoulder as a car passed, then she continued down the sidewalk with a laugh, because she knew she was on her own if she wanted to be. What a couple of days! It's all like a memory I can recall, and yet also like a feeling that it is not quite mine. I have a history in the future, a possible future in the past, and it's all too much, really. I have no idea what my future is, now. As the French used to say, I suppose I'll cling to my history, since that is all I have. Perhaps this was all a part of my destiny, in a way.

As she went through the motions of checking in with the hotel desk, boarding the lift, stepping into the hotel room, taking little notice of her surroundings, closing the door behind her, dropping her bags and throwing herself onto the bed, she she began to wonder. She she lay spread out looking up at the white ceiling. She thought about her past life, friends and family. They won't know the difference, because she is there, she mused. If I stay here, how is this now my life? What purpose would I have in this time? Is this past now going to be my present indefinitely, or forever? It's making me feel stuck here more than liberated. If I ever return to the future, or the present, then would it help or hinder my career to have been on this strange mission away? How would the two of us live as twins, anyway? So, examining this past, living in it, it's the only thing I can do. In a way, I'm timeless. Perhaps, I will never know what happened when the major... when I... when they returned. Also, I can't know if I will ever return, but I suppose that is okay, in some way. After all, I have saved Peter Nexin, and TAP seems to do a good job of setting us up for longer stays, if necessary. What about my career in the UN? What about Jennifer? What about my Mother?

Milona's thoughts became more and more cloudy, and she felt herself fading, thinking a part of her had somehow died in all of this. Perhaps the weaker part of me, she mused, the part which was so unsure of everything? Yes, this is now my life, and I am free to do what I will. The whole thing was really like a bad dream, an ugly nightmare. Removing Peter seems now to have been less than real, a betrayal in secret, something which should never be discussed, because it can never be shown? Perhaps, I'm safe now. She crawled into the bed and drifted off to sleep.

*

Having slept deeply for several hours, Milona slowly awoke not quite sure of where she was. She rolled up to a sitting position and looked around, noting the peach coloured walls, light wood furniture and deep gold upholstery of the hotel room. Ah, yes, she laughed as she thought. How could I forget? She glanced at her watch, which read nearly twenty before seven o'clock, and she thought that if there was a problem... but there wouldn't be any more problems, would there be? Is this a new form of freedom or imprisonment? On the other hand, how would two of me live in the same time, anyway? I suppose we could do a loop to prevent the doubling, I could go back and convince them of that, but would it create more unforeseen issues, and where would Peter fit in to all of that? I need to get myself together, get something to eat, maybe get some new clothes. But wait! I should call Peter and see if he would like to go out again. Of course! I could relive our beautiful evening together, or better yet, do some things differently to suit my own feelings, rather than satisfying a mission plan. That seems so strange, now. There is no mission plan!

She got up and pulled the silver dress and shawl out of her bag, remarking that the garments did not look too bad considering they had been balled up in the bag all day. She thought about getting another outfit, but first, she decided, she should call Peter, and worry about clothing later. She remembered his home number, and dug around her bag for the cellphone, surprised that it was still in working order. She dialed the number as she threw herself into a chair near the window, running her fingers through her hair.

"Hello?" Peter answered.

"Hi Peter, this is Milona," she said, diverging from her approach the first time. "I... wanted to apologize for that strangeness earlier today, you know, after your class."

"I'm not quite sure what was going on."

"I wasn't sure, myself. That one young man had been following me, I think, and I got confused and thought his name was Olen," she offered.

"Lenny? No, he's another tall, dark, and handsome intellectual who's too full of himself. Don't know who the other guy was, maybe a friend of Lenny's? I'll ask..."

"...Maybe we can forget it happened? I don't think it makes any sense or difference, anyway."

Peter paused and reflected that he didn't really care about what happened, but it had been a strange day all around. Not only did he feel like he was being followed, earlier, but more than anything he wanted to know more about Milona. He couldn't tell if this was the end, or if she wanted to see him again.

"Sure, no worries," he offered.

"I'm glad."

"So, I was wondering, then, if you'd like to go out, like we talked about at lunch?"

She felt a rush of emotion course through her, and simply whispered to him, "yes." He could feel her somehow through the phone, and couldn't avoid the memory of her kissing him after their lunch. She hoped he would suggest getting together, and how wonderful it felt to say 'yes' instead of being forward. Peter looked over at the clock in the kitchen, which read nearly seven, and then inspiration struck him.

"Milona," he said, "how about dinner?"

"I'd love to. What did you have in mind," she asked, taking care to sound surprised at his upcoming suggestion, "the place we... that one you mentioned?"

"No. I've got another place in mind, a brick oven bistro nearby. Why don't you come here first and we can take that walk."

*

For a few minutes after their call, she savoured her emotions, and she even had a laugh at how scripted some of it seemed, while she had done what she could for some form of spontaneity. She got up and looked in the bag the major had brought her, which to her delight contained a few of her favourite dresses and a number of other things. She pulled out one of them, her perfect little blue dress, along with a pair of gold sandal heels. She took the dress along with the silver dress and shawl and hung them all in the bathroom. She figured she would give them a steam as she bathed, and drew her bath, hung her khakis, checkered shirt, and leather jacket in the bathroom as well, putting the boots nearby. She put the watch on the counter, looking forward to the hot water.

Getting dressed after her bath, Milona studied herself in the mirror as she styled her hair loose. She told herself that even though tonight may be a *déjà vu* experience, it was still apparent that her future was an unknown, a mystery, just as it is to everyone else. Perhaps it always was, she considered. Well, now it seems I should enjoy everything more, feel things more deeply, listen to things and see things more clearly, enjoy Peter's company, and just see what happens between us. She knew she would enjoy the evening to come, because she needed to quiet her mind and live in the moment. Until I fully decide what to do, life is right here to be lived! Now, stop thinking about all of this! She took one last look at herself in the mirror, checking her makeup, the short blue dress and tights, pulling her heels on, and then taking one of her small purses, she slipped out of the hotel room.

*

"Ever have this feeling," Peter said, almost slumped over the edge of the bar as Milona approached him from behind, noting the cut of his dark suit, "like something bad might have happened to you? Maybe it was going to be minutes or hours away, but then you do something differently, and so it doesn't happen?"

"What are you talking about?" she quizzed. She sat back down next to him, looking over his face with a degree of incredulity. She worried that he might know more than he has let on, but she could also see their drinks taking effect after a dinner in Shandon and dancing now in the Vista. "Do you mean those choices we make to avoid danger?"

"Yes. Sorry, I've just had a... complicated day."

"Ha! You don't know the half of it!" she quipped, playfully, realizing what an understatement that was in her case.

"You too?"

"In a word? Exceptionally," she said heavily.

"Well," he said, remembering her calling out to Lenny earlier, but then tossing it out of his mind, "it's not like a single word can really change anything. But actions..."

"Actually, I think a word or conversation could change everything," she emphasized, offering a small kiss to his cheek, and remembering that this very conversation did not happen the first time. What other choices will we make, and what will those change?

"Nevermind me. I'm just thinking too much. I

could really just sit here forever," he said, looking at her, finding himself falling into her eyes, "just to be with you."

"Never say forever," she said flatly, then she looked at him again with a slight smile to let him know she was teasing.

"What does that mean?" he retorted, equally incredulous at her remark, then softening. "Anyway, do you ever think about what the future might hold, or even, what tonight might hold for us?"

He winced as he then realized how forward that had sounded, but she only smirked at the irony of his words. After all she had been through to fight for him, she could only feel grateful to be there, in the past, but safe and sound. She leaned over with a serious look which he also returned, and they kissed each other lightly, and then again, with a long lingering look into each other's eyes.

"Let's have another drink," she offered, changing her her tone to playfulness as he smiled at her. "The future can wait."

TIMELESS
A NOVEL TRILOGY

APPENDIX

FEATURED CHARACTERS
FEATURED JOINT OPERATIONS
EMBLEMS AND INSIGNIA
SHIPS AND TRANSPORTS
TIMELINES BY CHAPTER

FEATURED CHARACTERS

<u>UN Chancellery</u>

Chancellor
Nishiko Kitamori (Tokyo, Japan)

First Gentleman of the Chancellery
Kyo Kitamori (Tokyo, Japan, CEO of Nanokina)

Chief of Staff
Fernando Mendoza (US, New Mexico)

Deputy Chiefs of Staff
Operations Director, Le Heng (China)
Communications Director, Indira Sakki, (Japan-Turkey)
Security Director, Gen. Kona Azuma (Japan)

Vice Chancellor
Kyle Jasthi (New York, US)

Chief of Staff
Security Director, Zuri (Kenya)

Special Guard
Gen. Kona Azuma (Japan)
Col. Tod Huntsman (US)
Col. Brumbi (AU)
Guard Details
Chancellery, Secretariat, Senate, Treasury, Court

UN Secretariat

Secretary-General
Renzo Berlasi (Italy)

Department Secretaries
Energy, Labour, Health, Development, Trade, Justice,
Transportation, Education, Planning
Deputy Secretaries

UN Senate

Chair of the Senate
(UN Vice Chancellor)
Speaker/Vice Chair
Henri Levy (France)
Majority Leader, Minority Leaders
Committee Chairs
(World Affairs, Intelligence, Finance, and others)

Senators
(one per nation, one vote per nation)
Key Senators Featured
*Henri Levy (France), Shira Prikosh (India), Charlie McCallum
(Australia), Saeed Hassan (Iran), William Sherman (US)*
National Representatives

UN Treasury

Minister of the Treasury
Samuel Maddox (Wales, UK)

Ministers
(Banking [*Timothy McKaid*], Policy, Finance, Currency)
Deputy Ministers
National Directors/Ministers

UN Court

Chief Justice
Willard Pierce (Zurich, Switzerland)

Deputy Chief Justice
Christa Knezevic (Criminal Court, Serbia)

Deputy Justices (20)
Chancery and Justice Courts
Equity, Criminal, Civil, Appellate
National Judges

UN Command

Chair of UNC
Director-General of Intelligence
Nicolai Lorentz (Russia)

Vice Chair of UNC
General of Defense
Sandra Whitney (Canada)

General of Reconnaissance
Richárd Vadas (Hungary)

General of Security
Jana Sunari (South Africa)

UN Reconnaissance Corps

Division Officers
(Brig. Gen.+)
Guard (RG), Security Dir/DCoS, Special Guard (CG/SG)
General Kona Azuma (Japan)
Special Force (RSF)
General Nadira Venda (Bangalore, India)
Counter-Terrorism (RCT)
Maj. Gen. Hans Frederickson (Switzerland)
Warrant (RW)
Brig. Gen. Eliza Shelley (Australia)

Command Officers
(Lt.+)
RSF Colonel John Ford (Chicago, US)
CG Colonel Tod Huntsman (US)
SG Colonel Brumbi (AU)
SG Colonel Adams (US)
*RCT Lt. Col. Brigette Olsson (Stockholm, Sweden,
also DC Cpt. Bridget Owen)*
RSF Major Milona Devon (Amsterdam/Paris)
CG Major Takara Akiyama (London UK, US)
RCT Captain Nasir Rohani (Iran)
RSF 1st Lt. Geoffery Mathis (London, UK)
CG 1st Lt. Madura
CG 1st Lt. Feroz
RG Snd Lt. Lentin

Staff Officers
*Physics Student James Perkins (Aberdeen,
Scotland, UK)*

UN Defense Force

Division Officers
(Ground, Sea, Air, Orbital, Solar, Station, Space)

Generals
Command (DC)
General Donald Tenon (UK)
Logistics (DL)
Development (DD)
General Deterich Leopold (Germany)

Lieutenant Generals
Solar Command
*DC Lt. Gen. "Admiral" Bjorn Madsen (Sweden),
also Commander, Haley Space Group*

Major Generals
Atlantis and Stations
DC Maj. Gen. Nafisi (Iran)
Orbis
DC Maj. Gen. Taylor (US)
Centurion and Orbital Systems
DD Maj. Gen. Radha Khouri (India)

Brigadier Generals
Nording Sea Group (North Atlantic/Arctic)
DC Brig. Gen. Kagiso (Japan)

Other Groups
Forsythe Air Group
Chen Air Group
Putin Sea Group (Pacific)
Bahadur Sea Group (Indian/Southern)
Continental/Regional Ground Groups
Divisions

<u>Command Officers</u>
<u>UN Defense Centre</u>
DC Colonel Vitti (Italy)
DC Colonel Willis (US)
DC Lt. Col. Vicario-Padilla
DL Lt. Col. Steven Grant (US)
DC Lt. Jason Lance (US)

<u>Staff Officers</u>
DC Sgt. Judy Werner (Lincoln NE, US)
DC Spc. Maria Garcia-Gomez (Mexico)

UN Security Corps

<u>Division Officers</u>
(Lt. Gen.+)
<u>Patrol</u> (SP)
General Michelle Olanda (Australia)
<u>Response</u> (SR)
<u>Medical</u> (SM)
<u>Judicial</u> (SJ)
Brigadier General Javier Menendez (Chile)
<u>Administration</u> (SA)
General Vorley (UK)

<u>Command Officers</u>
SA 1st Lt. Whitaker (UK)
SR 1st Lt. Will Fulmer (US)

<u>Staff Officers</u>
SA Msgt. Administrator Jennifer Collett (US)

UN Intelligence Directorate

<u>Directors</u>
(Brig. Gen.+)
<u>Operations</u> (IO)
Lt. Gen. Laurent Zhang (Beijing, China)
<u>Information</u> (II)
Lt. Gen. Jeremy Stockbridge (London, UK)
<u>Science</u> (IS)
Maj. Gen. Jil Franklin (Calgary, Canada)
<u>Analysis</u> (IA)
Maj. Gen. Anna Topolski (Russia)
<u>Counter-Intelligence</u> (ICI)
Brig. Gen. Ikenna Yaradua (Burkina Faso)

<u>Region Chiefs</u>
(Col.+)
(Americas, Asia, Europe, Africa, North Polar, South Polar, Lunar,
Mars, Stations, Orbis)

<u>Area Chiefs</u> (Sub-Regions), <u>Section Chiefs</u> (Operations,
Programmes), <u>Lead Scientists</u>
(Uniformed, Lt. Col.+)
RSF Colonel John Ford (Chicago, US)
IS Lt. Col., Dr. Olen Nadimov (US/Berlin)(TAP, SC)
ICI Colonel Nakka Tomita (Matsumoto, Japan)

<u>Station Chiefs</u>(Field Offices), <u>Unit Chiefs</u> (Cell Leaders), <u>Science</u>
(Uniformed/Plain, Mil/Civ)
RCT Lt. Col. Brigette Olsson (Stockholm,
also DC Cpt. Bridget Owen, US)
ICI Major Fred Waters (California, US)
RSF Major Milona Devon (Amsterdam/Paris)
Managing Scientist, Berlin
Dr. Michelle Lambert (Bruxelles, Belgium)
Managing Scientist, Atlantis (Stations)
Dr. Quon Ling (Beijing, China)

CG Major Takara Akiyama (London UK, US)
RCT Captain Nasir Rohani (Iran)

<u>Technical Officers</u> (Techs), <u>Case Officers</u> (Cells)
(uniformed/plain, Mil/Civ)
RSF 1st Lt. Geoffery Mathis (London, UK)
Physics Student James Perkins (Aberdeen,
Scotland, UK)
DC Sgt. Judy Werner (Lincoln NE, US)

Special Agents (uniformed/plain, Mil/Civ)
Agents (uniformed/plain, Mil/Civ)
Analysts (uniformed/plain, Mil/Civ)

FEATURED JOINT OPERATIONS

Operation Invader

<u>Gen Madsen's Mission</u>
(Defense Command, Reconnaissance Counter-Terrorism)

Deep Mystery
(Haley/Atlantis: Madsen/Ling, Whitney, Frederickson)
Madsen: Investigate distortion cloud (alien ships discovered)

Operation Tempo

<u>OD Zhang's Missions</u>
(Intelligence Operations, Reconnaissance Special Force)

Progenitor
(Devon, Mathis)
Zhang: Investigate, reluctantly execute (XT) Peter Nexin

Rewind
(Devon 1, Devon 2)
Zhang/Devon 1: Prevent XT of Nexin

Cut-Time
(Devon 2, Mathis, Perkins)
Zhang/Devon 2: Allow Devon 1 to stay in past

<u>SD Franklin's Programme Missions</u>
(Intelligence Science, Defense Development)

Research
(Nadimov, Lambert, Ling)
Vehicle for their discoveries

EMBLEMS AND INSIGNIA

no lettering is used, due to multiple languages

Chancellor and Vice Chancellor
figure with books, podium, columns, *and* scales over UN globe

Secretariat, Senate, Treasury, Court
books, podium, columns *or* scales, over UN globe

Intelligence Directorate
signal tower over UN globe

Reconnaissance Corps
weapons array fanned over UN globe

Defense Force
face-on ship fleet over UN globe

Security Corps
walking male/female officers over UN globe

Orbis, Atlantis, Centurion, Mars 5, others
station's likeness over globe

Command Centres
tower, weapons, fleet, *and* officers arranged over globe

Rank Insignia

simplified rank identification for multiple languages,
cultures, divisions, using insignia worn at collar points

Division Officers
gold squares with gold edges, separated and inline
General of Division (5 gold)
General (4 gold)
Lieutenant General (3 gold)
Major General (2 gold)
Brigadier General (1 gold)

Command Officers
brass/white squares with black edges, close together
Colonel (4 brass)
Lieutenant Colonel (3 brass, 1 white)
Major (3 brass)
Captain (2 brass, 1 white)
First Lieutenant (2 brass)
Second Lieutenant (1 brass, 1 white)
Cadet (1 brass)

Staff Officers
charcoal/white half-squares with black edges, close together
Sergeant-Major (4 charcoal)
Master-Sergeant (3 charcoal, 1 white)
Staff-Sergeant (3 charcoal)
Sergeant (2 charcoal, 1 white)
Corporal (2 charcoal)
Specialist (1 charcoal, 1 white)
Private (1 charcoal)

Special Officer Roles
Admiral, Commander, Administrator

SHIPS AND TRANSPORTS

Operations Craft

Carriers
20-deck, wing of 4x12 scout/robot squadrons, 320x120m
Suppliers
XL cargo hold, minimal defenses, 250x30m
Destroyers
10-deck, strongest defenses, 12 robot squadron, 180x70m
Submarines
6-deck, 12 sub-robot squadron, 120x10m
Corvettes
5-deck, multi-use, high-speed, heavy defenses, 90x35m
Commands
4-deck, com/con rooms, detachable scouts, 70x30m
Escorts
3-deck, diplomatic, sky-blue, heavy defenses, 40x25m
Scouts
1-deck, multi-use, high speed, medium defenses, 8x4.5m
Fighters
1 officer, manned/remote, high speed, heavy defenses, 4x1.5m
Walkers
1-4 officers, crowd control and patrol, bipedal-4m, quad-6m tall

Call Signs
WKR, SHL, FGT, SCT, ESC, SUB, COM, CRV, DES, SPL, CAR

Local and Orbit Transports

Shuttles
(UN/Civilian, various designs and colours)
Coupes, Sports, Sedans, Transports, Hoverships

Cars, Trains
Electrucks, Elecoupes, Electrocars, Magnarail, Trams

Dedicated Ships

Diplomat
Chancellor's Escort
polished silver-grey, extra arms/counter-measures

Statesman and Senatorial Escorts
polished sky-blue, extra arms/counter-measures

Sting Ray, Manta Ray, Black Ray 1-4
Chancellery Detail Corvettes
polished silver-red/black/blue/olive *or* flat black, extra speed/arms/
counter-measures

Sharpfin, Blackfin
Chancellery Barracuda Destroyers
polished silver-red/black/blue/olive, extra arms/counter-measures

Ship Colours
Command (silver with stripes, portions, or full hull treatments)
Intel (fire-red) Recon (basic-black)
Defense (navy-blue) Security (olive-drab)
Orbis, Atlantis (powder-blue/white), Traditional UN (sky-blue),
Response & Medical (white)

Space, Air, Sea and Ground Groups
Joint Command Ship, Supplier, Carrier
joint scout squadrons, manned/remote-control squadrons, walkers
IRDS Destroyers (4 per carrier/asset)
Corvettes (4 per carrier/asset)
Submarines (4 per sea group)
Walkers (48 per carrier for ground groups, SP corvettes/destroyers)

Special Scouts
extra speed/arms/counter-measures, custom colours

TIMELINES BY CHAPTER

The Timeless Trilogy takes place around the first week of March in the "present" time, with asynchronous visits to "past" time periods. Each book generally follows a full day (Book I: Day 1, Book II: Day 2, Book III: Day 3). The times below are approximate.

Book I

Part One

1. Devon: Day 1, *Orbis*, 9:30 - 10:00 UTC
2. Nexin: 6-8:00 pm in Columbia (Past), 01:00 UTC
3. Devon: *Orbis*, 10:15 UTC
4. Nexin: 7:30 am Columbia (Past), 12:30 UTC
   Nexin/Devon: 10:00 am in Columbia (Past), 15:00 UTC
5. Devon/Zhang: *Orbis*, 10:30 UTC
6. Devon/Collett: Orbis, 11:20 UTC
   All receiving the Chancellor: 12:00 UTC
7. Nexin/Lenny: 11:00 am in Columbia (Past), 14: 00 UTC
   Nexin/Devon: 11:30 am in Columbia (Past), 14:30 UTC
8. All on *Orbis*: 12:30 - 01:30 UTC
9. Devon: 11:00 am in Columbia, 16:00 UTC
   Devon: 8:00 am in Columbia (Past), 13:00 UTC
10. Devon: 8:00 am in Columbia (Past), 13:00 UTC

Part Two

11. Nadimov: 2-3:00 pm in Berlin, 13-14:00 UTC
12. Devon/Mathis: 1:00 pm in Columbia (Past) 18:00 UTC
13. All at Science Centre: 3-3:30 pm in Berlin, 14-14:30 UTC
14. Devon/Nexin: 2:30 pm in Columbia (Past) 19:30 UTC
15. All on *Orbis*: 14:30-15:30 UTC
16. Devon/Nexin: 7:00pm in Columbia (Past), 00:00 UTC
    Devon/Nexin: 9:00pm in Columbia (Past), 02:00 UTC
17. Nadimov: 11:00 am in Columbia, 16:00 UTC
18. Devon/Mathis: 1:00 am in Columbia (Past), 06:00 UTC
19. All at *Visitor*: 2:30 am in Columbia (Past), 07:30 UTC

20. All at *Calendar*: Day 1 (Alternate), 1:00 pm, 18:00 UTC

Part Three

21. Devon/Zhang on *Orbis*: Day 2 (Alternate), 08:00 UTC
22. All on *Orbis* and at Senate: Day 2 (Alternate), 10:00 UTC
    Devon: Day 2 (Alternate), 10:45 UTC
    Devon/Collett: Day 2 (Alternate), 11:15 UTC
23. Devon: Day 2 (Alt.), 7:00 am in Columbia, 12:00 UTC
    Devon: (Day 1) 12:00 pm in Columbia (Past), 17:00 UTC
24. Nexin/Crowley: 11:00 am in Columbia (Past), 16:00 UTC
25. Devon1/Jeffers: 12:00 pm in Columbia (Past), 17:00 UTC
    Devon1/2: 1:00 pm in Columbia (Past), 18:00 UTC
26. Devon2/Mathis: 12:00 pm in Columbia: 16:30 UTC
    All on *Orbis*: 17:30 UTC
    Devon2 on *Orbis*: 18:30 UTC
27. Devon1: 2:00 pm in Columbia (Past), 19:00 UTC
28. Devon2: 19:00 UTC
    Nadimov: 8:00 pm in Berlin, 19:00 UTC
29. Devon1: 2:30 pm in Columbia (Past), 19:30 UTC
    Devon2 on *Nording*: Day 2, 08:00 UTC
    Devon1/Perkins: 2:45 pm in Columbia (Past), 19:45 UTC
    Mathis/Perkins: 3:00 pm in Columbia (Past), 20:00 UTC
    Devon1/Devon2: 3:15 pm in Columbia (Past), 20:15 UTC
30. Devon1: 3:30 pm in Columbia (Past), 20:30 UTC
    Devon1: 7:00 pm in Columbia (Past), 24:00 UTC
    Devon1/Nexin: 10:00 pm in Columbia (Past), 03:00 UTC

NOTES ON THE TEXTS
AND COVER ART

*

The three texts of the *Timeless Trilogy* included minor formatting, various corrections, and numerous edits, updates, and changes after the 2003 and 2008 releases during the 2008 and 2013 publishing cycles. Initially, this was to expand minor aspects of earlier texts with details from later ones, but also it was to keep the books unified. While the three novels were written together in the beginning stages as much as possible, they were later branched out and completed at very different times in my life. The books captured a decade or more of varied reflections and interests into different parts of the overall story.

For example, the use of detailed technology in *Book II* affected *Book I* edits, and the greatly expanded military operations and faster action in *Book III* affected edits to both previous books. At the same time, *Book I* had always been a structural blueprint for both of the subsequent books, which has always been revealed in a number of treasures hiding in plain sight throughout. For examples, there are the time offsets in chapters 2, 4, and 7, the expression of subplots leading to the next novel and back again in chapters 13 and 27, the grand paradoxes in chapters 20, the self-confrontations in chapters 25, and a number of other structural examples. Crafting these very complex and very rewarding novels was a long-term challenge and joy on a great many levels for me.

However, by 2013, *Book III* was my last published book to date, some twelve years ago (though not the last one I've worked on, as there are others in process). *Book III* was very much a pinnacle of a creative period in my life which was studded with eighteen completed books and many other creative efforts (indeed, re-releasing all the books this Summer has been *quite* an epic undertaking in itself). In 2014, all of the books were converted to a different text format for publishing, but no additional notable changes were made, despite *Book III* needing more attention. As my professional work, relocation, and other projects took a more prominent role for me, I believe I needed a period of relative calm regarding my book projects. I needed to let the fields lie fallow, to release these and other characters out of my head, in a way. If you are a writer, you know exactly what I mean.

For this 2025 release in paperback, all three books have been revisited anew and edited together side-by-side as one expanded set, with updated cover graphics, as well as added reference materials provided for the first time from among the extensive notes and diagrams I'd kept during the writing phases (particularly for *Book III*). Since I've had another decade or more distance from these novels, numerous minor edits, and some not so minor, began to appear as I took a fresh look at each scene and character. So, I removed remaining inconsistencies, corrected errors, expanded scene and character details, and clarified time markers sprinkled throughout (this last part especially led to an updated timeline reference now provided for each novel). As with my other fiction, the *Timeless Trilogy* has never referred to an actual year in the past, present, or future, because that would literally date the stories. Despite the time travel and science-fiction backdrop, these are suspense and thriller novels. Even I do not know what the year is in the future I've constructed. Instead, these stories are meant to be "timeless".

While re-reading and re-editing the three novels together, a great number of more substantial changes and improvements have also been made, including greater detail in *Book I*, better cross-integration in *Book II*, and a clearer pace of action in *Book III*. A number of other changes have also clarified chapter offsets and characters, re-arranged content for better flow, and a key mission from *Book III* was revisited and expanded backwards into *Book I*, which creates a very moving scene, as well as a pleasing "off screen" timeline offset (among many which were already a part of the trilogy). Over an intense period of editing, changes have now been made to every chapter in all three books. I came to view much of this editing work as polishing, honing, and clarifying, as well as expanding. Each book is a few pages longer now due to this work.

All of the elements, characters, and scenes build the trilogy into a story which is so big, and so complex, even I've been at pains to keep it all straight at times, hence the need to create the reference materials I've had all along. Indeed, the speed and complexity of scenes increases throughout the books, and the number of named characters across the trilogy is very large, with another large group of others referred to but unnamed. To me, the complexity provides rewards for re-reading and contemplation, for fictional escape and emotional catharsis. The result is this all new release of the *Timeless Trilogy* of novels available together on paper for the first time.

*

The cover art and design for each novel has not changed in essentials, but the images have been re-mastered for a full-wrap paperback printing. Like the image used for the *Dynamism Series*, the triptych for the *Timeless Trilogy* (*Prism*, 2003), defies explanation. The three images are indeed straight photographs of something real, not computer animations. Given the times, I'll also note they are not any kind of artificial intelligence (AI), either. Around the early 2000s, I'd kept from work a burned out halogen light bulb, set in a small reflective bell housing. I'd changed it out, and while fascinated with it, I'd left the old one in my pocket instead of throwing it away - I still have it. The housing is mesmerizing, with a prism of so very many tiny mirrors to project light, which fits with a metaphor from Leibniz for Subjectivity. Such bulb housings are much more common today, and I use very similar lights for renovation projects in my home.

In 2002-2003, experimenting with my first digital camera, and very close to the housing, I set things up to reflect the Northern light from a nearby window, capturing three images of blurred effects, owing to slight hand movements during exposure.

Once brought into photo-editing software, I simply changed the colour balances of each to create the triptych. I loved how the images evoked time travel in a visual way, perhaps as spinning or streaking fields from a time machine or distortion cloud, but I also wanted them to represent the stories of the books, and another metaphor, of traditional colours of the chakra system lent itself.

The red theme *Lower Chakra* represents the physical passion of both Milona and Peter in *Book I*, and also her objectification by others. The green theme *Middle Chakra* represents the heart and values which Olen and his family exude in the dark and emotional *Book II* story. The blue theme *Upper Chakra* represents the intuitive and mindful leadership by Nishiko and others in the complex *Book III*. As can be found in *Dynamism* and all of my other current books, details like these are now revealed for the first time in this 2025 paperback release.

M.R.M. Parrott
Charleston, August 2025

M.R.M. Parrott's books include the novella *To Lie Within the Moment*, travelogue *Driving Home*, stage play *Ctrl-V*, Philosophy and Science series *Dynamism*, monographs in Philosophy, and chapbooks of poems and short stories.

mrmparrott.com

rimric press

*

www.ingramcontent.com/pod-product-compliance
Lightning Source LLC
Chambersburg PA
CBHW032238010726
47494CB00002B/540